FIREWING

Jennifer R. Povey

ISBN-13: 978-1-7335179-6-6

To the health care workers fighting the COVID-19 pandemic, and to the researchers seeking a solution. All luck to you.

1

It was a no moon night. Neither Seliene nor her daughter lit the night sky, only a myriad of stars. From where Cathren stood, it seemed as if the sky was stars upon stars, a mere lace of black against the light beyond.

Yet, spreading darkness came from the west and she shivered a little. Reason told her it was simply storm clouds, but she had been so on edge lately. As if some internal darkness shaded her.

A storm would only fit her mood. A natural storm, her mage-sight told her. Good. One could never be sure, not here. Not with all the mages in Losana.

There always seemed to be too many and too few, all at the same time. Cathren turned and walked back into the academy.

She felt so confined. So...trapped. She had her shop, she had her journeyman status...but she was not going on any journeying.

That was it. She needed to go somewhere. She needed to move, to keep moving, to fly until the moons set and the sun rose, casting summer's heat across the land. Laran, though...

He had told her exactly what would happen if she left Losana. In as many words. If she ever left Losana.

She would like as not outlive him. He would like as not find somebody else to be her jailer. The one person who truly understood was out of town.

She knew she was fortunate to even have been permitted to live, to be permitted what she had. A livelihood, a lover...that was more than so many had.

Tolerance and acceptance? Too much to ask, and she knew it. Even if she slipped away, followed the trade routes north, she would be no more welcome there than here.

She needed to fly. She dared not. Beria was occupied, so even that substitution was denied her. For what it was worth; they both knew the other was a mere distraction, nothing more.

Once Laran was out of town, she could at least go far enough to fly, without him 'shooting her from the sky'.

It was bad enough that he hated her. Worse that he seemed to have enough power, enough support, to treat her like...a child.

She abruptly knew exactly where she would go. It was the middle of the night, but that would not matter. Pulling on a cloak, she walked out from the academy gates.

The guards did not stop her...curfew was for students and Cathren had graduated. Had the ring, even. She had feared they would deny her that.

It was a warm night, and she regretted the cloak, but it would serve as a stave against recognition. Yet another reason to want to leave Losana. For the largest city on Yirath, it was small indeed.

Along the street, there were more people out than one would expect for the middle of the night. Beggars who had no place to go mingled with drunks returning from the taverns. A man groped a woman in the garb of a prostitute right in the street. She ignored them, even as the woman giggled.

Normal people, ordinary people, going about their lives...although not decent, hardworking folk. Even at this time of year, such would likely be in bed.

She kept walking. Her eyes flicked from side to side, wary of thieves and footpads. Any who tried anything with her would regret it, of course...she firmly held the words of a paralysis spell in her mind, in case she needed it. Normal practice. She was a woman alone, apparently easy prey for those who were neither decent nor hardworking.

Perhaps she should let the ring be visible. It might deter at least some of those inclined to attack. Others might take it as a challenge.

Instead, she shifted her cloak a little, so that the fact that she carried blades was visible. Whether from that or chance, none harassed her on a quick walk through town.

The tavern was closing its doors as she arrived, but the young woman doing so opened them again swiftly when she saw Cat's face.

"Cat!"

"Can I come in?"

The door opened the rest of the way so Cat could step into the common room. The drunks had been expelled, but the place not yet cleaned. It smelled of mead and wine.

The woman who was in the process of pulling a broom out from behind the bar stopped. She dropped it with a clank as she moved to hug Cathren. Not swiftly, for she was not a young woman and had clearly indulged much in her own good cooking.

Cat hugged back, carefully. "Mother."

The most casual of glances could have told that this was not, in truth, her mother, but the affection between them was clear. She released the much shorter form after a moment.

"Something...let me guess. Is Brother Laran being an ass again?"

"Mother!" came the voice of the younger woman, moving to clean mugs.

"Pheh! When you get to my age, you can use whatever language you like."

"There is no again about it. Laran is Laran. He is never going to change."

"He is not your father."

"He might as well be," Cat said, finally, moving to sit on one of the tavern's chairs. "He is my keeper, at any rate."

"He has been threatening you again."

"Yes." If Laran had his way, she would have been slain as an infant. She could not help but hate him, a little.

"Somebody should talk to him." Mother Liesa sat down as well, her eyes on Cat.

"It's been tried. This *is* his compromise." It was as far as Laran would bend. To confine her to Losana, where the academy mages could keep an eye on her.

"He still thinks you're going to wake up one day and summon Arok."

"What if he's right?"

"Cathren!"

"What if there's a geas on me that might cause me to one day do just that? We don't think so, but there are gods involved. We can't be sure." She looked down at her hands. "I suppose the reason I don't outright defy him is because I wouldn't trust me either."

"I trust you."

She looked up at the woman who had been her mother. "You're biased."

"So is Laran."

"Laran is worried about the big picture. Somebody has to be. He's still an..." She tailed off. She was not using the language, even if Liesa was.

"Ass," Liesa supplied, gaining another shocked look from her daughter. "He's a narrow-minded fool. Besides. He should know he can't keep you confined forever."

"Just because I'm miserable..."

Liesa cut her off. "What was it R'vor said?"

"Wanderlust. But there's nothing to be done about it. He'll track me down and kill me if I leave. And while I could take him...he wouldn't come alone."

"No, he wouldn't. Maybe if R'vor was here...no, it wouldn't change his mind. Apparently, he'd rather have you go stir crazy."

"And then when I acted on those feelings, he'd have a reason to take me out." Her shoulders rose then fell. "More likely, he simply does not understand." Did not understand that she needed to fly, to escape, to see something other than the city and the academy and the shop. To travel.

"Most likely. Does any human really understand a demon?"

"If there's anyone capable of understanding both races, it's me." Cat brushed back her dark hair. She looked completely human, but for a moment, it seemed that her eyes shaded to red.

"And even you have problems." Liesa paused. "I have just the medicine for you." She ducked behind the bar, coming out eventually with a small cup. "Here."

Mead. Good mead...expensive, the best Liesa had. Cat sipped it slowly, savoring the flavor. It was too strong for even her to want a tankard of, too strong and too sweet. It was, though, exactly what she needed. "Can I stay here tonight?"

"Always, Cat."

A promise that, for some reason, sent another chill over her, and this one was not the wind coming from the threat of storm.

The next morning, she went to her store. A canik got right under Cat's feet as she headed for the store. "Out of the way," she growled at it. She was almost in a bad enough mood to kick it. Almost.

Kicking a canik would get her bitten for sure. The creature hopped up and ducked out of the way, forelimbs tucked against itself and tail lashing behind it. It was clearly worried somebody would step on said appendage.

At least it had a collar on, like they were supposed to.

She opened the door and then the shutters, but the wanderlust was still with her. A vague dissatisfaction. This was not the life she was supposed to be living. Even if it could make her rich.

She did not care for money. Laran was right...she was more demon than human in mind, if more human in physiology. She felt the summer heat...although not as much as some. She felt the wind, though, could almost see it.

A cage was a cage, no matter how large or gilded. She shook her head, setting up for the day. The worst part was that she would get used to it, that she would become just another citizen of Losana. Just another merchant. Her only chance of freedom was Laran's death, and she was sure he had deputized a successor. Watch the halfbreed. Be sure she never does anything significant or important.

She might have killed him herself had she not had the fear that he was right. Visiting her foster mother had helped a little. A little. She needed R'vor. She needed Beria's arms around her.

She needed the wind. Tonight, she promised herself. He could not completely deny her, they had tried that. She had gotten the worst imaginable case of cabin fever.

Tonight, when the light faded, when people would be less likely to observe her and make the signs of various deities in fear. Not that those same people would not come to her store if they needed to. There were few good alchemists in Losana.

Despite that, her only customer of the morning was a bustling housewife who sought a preparation efficacious against tela fly.

All she could do was mix powder in her mortar and think. Thinking was the last thing she needed to do.

She had no choice, her mind would not quiet. Female demons came into heat. Perhaps what she was feeling was some vestige of that cycle. Yet it could just as easily be Arok trying to influence her. Or simply the first thing that had come into her head.

Demons were wanderers. Demons did not stay in one place. Humans did that, settling in their villages and towns, spreading across a world that had been given them by the gods.

A world the demons claimed the humans had no place in. The worst part was, the demons were right.

* * *

The bell behind the door rang and a tall, thin man came in. She tensed instantly. "Laran. Checking on me."

"It's my job." His voice was always quiet, and there was never any emotion in it other than contempt.

"Be careful." He was dangerously close to one of her displays.

He snorted, but stepped away from it. "Alchemy. Useful, but you wouldn't catch me trying it."

At least he freely admitted some of his failings. His failings of skill, but never of personality or...no. It was not a failing of courage, it was over-caution. The two were different things. "Afraid you might spill something nasty on yourself?"

"Knowing my luck with magic, I'd turn myself into a toad."

Not far to go, she bit back. What she actually said was, "No. That's very advanced magic. You'd just give yourself warts."

He laughed, as if they were friends not enemies. Or...whatever they were. Then he sobered. "You look tired."

"I'm fine." Saying anything about how she actually felt would come over as begging or whining or acting like a child. Maybe she was acting like one, but she could not shake the strong desire to get out of here.

"You shouldn't let yourself get tired. You might mix the wrong things and blow yourself up."

Like he cared. There was nothing, no hint of genuine concern in his voice. Faking it, acting it. Not even for her benefit so much as that of anyone who might walk in.

"Worst thing I'm going to do with this stuff is make an aphrodisiac when I wanted a poison."

He laughed. "So, you'd make more vermin instead of less."

"Good point. You're right, I need to stay sharp." How could she, when the city itself closed in around her? They probably had a tracking spell on her ring. So they would know.

She did not trust herself. Ylsa trusted her...but she suspected there were limits even on that. Limits, that flowed around her, walls of suspicion and hatred. Walls, too, in her own mind.

There were few people with whom she could be herself; Beria was one, but she knew their relationship would not last. She knew that, sensed it. She was not the one, not Cathren's mate. Perhaps she would have none.

She was very human in that regard. Laran watched her with a smirk. "Look. You're out of it and I don't see any customers. Why not take the rest of the day off?"

"Because I don't have anything better to do," she snapped back, regretting it instantly...although not that much. It was, after all, only Laran.

"Cathren..." He studied her for a moment, then he turned and stalked out of the store.

She watched him go. She did have nothing better to do, and if she set the mortar and pestle aside, she would go insane from boredom. Her wings literally itched with the desire, the need to fly.

Get me out of here, she thought, then worried about who might have heard that thought.

"I'm not helping you avoid Laran."

Cathren sighed. "I'm not asking you to. He may not be my father, but he is yours." They had been close as sisters for a while, then hated each other, and now sisters again. Not lovers; Cat had had a number of those, but none of those women touched her heart the way Ylsa did.

Perhaps they would be lovers if Ylsa did not prefer men.

"I wish he wasn't."

"You help."

"Do I?" Ylsa turned to face her.

"As much as anything does. I'm sorry."

"It has occurred to you this could be...him."

The name was not spoken between them. A simple agreement. "It has. I think it's more likely that I am just not meant to stay in one place like this. But I know. I have to be where they can keep an eye on me."

The reason remained unspoken.

"You should go find Beria."

Cat smiled a little. "I should." Sex would make her forget for a while, yet only for a while and then it always, always came rushing back to her. But she had yet to find a woman who could be her partner, her leri...her wife, in all but name.

Tava thought Neir had intervened to make her female. Maybe she had done this, too, so she would be less likely to breed...out of fear that a son of hers could be the vessel Arok needed.

Arok was picky, she thought with amusement. She would have thought the god desperate enough to take the form of a woman, but apparently not.

She shook her head, feeling tears prick in her eyes.

"You are going to leave. Maybe not now, but in the future." Ylsa's words, breaking through her thoughts.

"I..."

"I know you even if you do not know yourself. Same as Beria does. We all know. Why do you think Beria won't commit to you?"

"I know why Beria won't commit to me. She wants a husband. Children. I can't give her that."

Ylsa shook her head. She brushed back her curly hair. "Children could be adopted. She knows you'll leave. And I know you'll leave, and I'll miss you, but children grow up. I have. You have."

"I can't leave. I'm trapped here."

"R'Vor will come back." Firm notes, a reminder.

"Laran will not let me leave. The only thing that will free me from his vigilance is his death, and I don't wish him ill. Well, not that level of ill." Cat had to admit she was tempted to spike his drink with something interesting on occasion.

"You'd very much like to turn his hair pink, though."

Cat tilted her head. "Purple. He'd look far worse in purple."

Ylsa giggled, the serious moment having passed. "Father is just..."

"Laran is doing what he believes is right. He is a follower of Tyrn, he will always do what he believes is right. The fact that he's causing me pain is unimportant."

"He wants you dead." The source of the old quarrel. Still between them.

"I don't know about that any more. I think part of him would prefer it, but at the same time...sometimes I detect a hint of concern for me." You couldn't watch somebody for twenty years and not become concerned for them. Nobody could. Nobody sane, anyway.

Ylsa shifted away from her, looking at the sky. "Maybe. I don't trust him."

"He's your *father,*" Cathren pointed out.

"That doesn't mean I trust him. I don't think he would help you if you were in the lurch."

"Depends on what help I needed." Cathren stretched her wings as if to catch the last of the evening sun. "Would he stop Arok from getting me, yes. Would he save my life if it needed saving? I doubt it. But that's why I have blades and magic."

"You have fire."

"Which I would rather not use, but I have the right to defend myself." She'd rather use her swords if it came to it, give her enemies a clean death.

It had never come to it, not yet. She had enemies, but they tended to use other weapons. Usually their tongues. Words could hurt, though. Words could do lasting, real damage to a woman.

Words about how she could not be trusted, about how they had to be ready to kill her if they needed to. She had fire. She had magic in her blood.

"Sooner or later, somebody is going to try and solve the problem you present."

"And with R'vor out of town, I'm down an ally." Of course, she hoped her relationship with the demon gem trader was discreet. It would prove too many people right if it became known.

"R'vor might not be much help. He is an odd one. But then, he is a renegade from his own culture."

"He is proof that demons don't have to all be evil followers of Arok who burn everything in sight." Cat knew she sounded defensive for a moment.

"You know that, I know that. Those people, the ordinary ones? They don't. Don't and never will."

Cat wished her friend was wrong. "Don't say never." But it might well be never. It might well be that humans and demons would manage, at best, an uneasy truce...and that would fade with time.

Humans bred so quickly.

"Never. It would take...I don't know what it would take to earn peace. I mean, you can't even find peace with yourself."

She was so accurate that Cat laughed, short and harsh. "No, I can't. But then, people won't let me properly look. Laran expects me to be entirely human, Liesa does not know what she expects and as far as Beria's concerned I'm just a good lay."

Ylsa laughed. "Aren't there worse things to be called than that?"

"Far worse. I should know, I've been called most of them." It had been easier at the academy than as a child at the tavern, when they had whispered behind her back. At least the other kids had insulted her to her face, openly.

"Children are pretty cruel."

"Not just children, but yes." Cat stood. "I need to find Beria." And she spread her wings and launched into the air. Laran was not there to see.

2

The academy's salle was not often used. The majority of human mages elected to learn only basic weapon skills. Most never intended to fight, the rest did not have time. For Cat, with magic in her blood, things were different. It took her a fraction of the time to learn spells...unless, of course, they were ice spells. Those were worse than a headache.

She trained, for now, alone...and she trained with live steel. The demon-forged blades formed a wall around her. She was not as good as a true warrior. But she was good, very good. Her feet were light on the ground. Had she been working outside, she would have used her wings. As it was, there was not space for that in the salle.

She had to train in confined spaces. That was where she would most likely be if called on to defend herself...and she dared not use her skill any other way. Even in tourney, who would face her.

The salle door opened. The man who stepped in, as she turned, was a stranger. Her wings snapped out to their full extent instantly, no magic to conceal them now. She knew everyone who had a right to be in here by sight, if not by name. He was not overly large, shorter than Cathren herself and slight.

He was not a mage, but had some of the strongest protection spells she had seen cast on him, and he was drawing a longsword.

Combat sharp. So were hers. He could be a visitor from another city. He could be a mage's bodyguard, bent on getting some practice while his employer talked shop. That was the most logical explanation.

Except that, without a word, he was closing on her, the blade held expertly. His stance was that of a master swordsman.

He was here to kill her. She knew that with sharp instinct. Demon instinct, and that same instinct wanted to call fire.

The floor of the salle was wooden. The fire would not harm her...even more than were she purebred. Yet, she could not get away with burning down the salle, even in self-defense. Not without any other choice.

The blades crossed, meeting his. He still said nothing. He'd never heard the stories in which the bad guy lost the fight by bantering. Or, more likely, he had.

She forced his blade aside with hers. Lighter they might be, but his was not demon-forged, only of human make. Hers were shorter, but she definitely had reach.

Skill would decide this. Or cunning. She did not ask him why he attacked her. She knew.

Right into the academy. Somebody had let him in, somebody who wished her ill. She wished the list were shorter even as she stepped back, her left blade darting under his as the right spun in a blocking pattern. It did not hit hard enough, skidding off the mail he wore.

And her only in a leather training jerkin. Still, she had not needed armor in the past. She went up, leaping over him...even in the tight quarters, she could manage that much. Now she was the one closest to the door.

An advantage, a small one, and she would take it. She backed towards the door. If she could get him outside, then this would be seen...

...but whose side would the students take? She could not trust them. She could not trust anyone except herself and maybe Ylsa. Maybe not even herself.

She let him drive her back, back into the corridor...which was short. If she could get into the open, she could fly.

He realized his mistake too late, eyes widening, and he pressed the attack. His blade moved faster, but not as fast as hers. It was simply too heavy.

Then...it happened. Her blade struck his at an angle...and his sword shattered into pieces.

His eyes widened, the expression of somebody who knew he was a dead man. She stepped forward, pressed a point to his throat.

"Yield."

The eyes widened further. Clearly, he had not expected to survive.

"Who hired you?" She pulled the point back enough that he could talk, but kept it there, her eyes on him.

"I serve the true gods."

A religious fanatic, then. Pheh. Arok was as much a true god as any of the others. He was a bastard, but that did not make him less of a god. An odd thought, that. "As do I. I understand your fears. I even share them."

He stepped back, lifting his hands, then...lowering them, his face changing. "You do not trust yourself?"

"I don't trust Arok." She regarded him. "Go."

"You're letting me go?" His eyes showed a slight smile. "Perhaps you *should* trust Him."

"If I kill you, then what do I prove? Go. Before security finds you."

He picked up what was left of his weapon. Then he fled towards the academy gates as if an entire horde of demons pursued him, not merely one halfbreed.

She sheathed her blades as he ran. Not even a worthy opponent, part of her thought. No, he had been. It had been the blade that failed, not the man.

She would have to keep her eyes open. He might try again. He or whoever he was working for. She had no doubt but that there was an organization behind him.

A moment, then she stepped out into the air. A moment later, with a sweep of her wings, she was airborne. She knew who to check on first.

Beria's home was outside the city. Cathren did not often approach by air, but the thought of the organization, the thought of an assassin bold enough to enter the academy and who knew her schedule...

R'Vor was out of town. Laran could look after himself. Ylsa could...look after herself most of the time. Most of the time. She did not have nearly the competence of the older man. None of his experience. The weak link....

So, why was she worried? Because it was in her nature, she supposed, dipping a wing to spiral downwards. Magic flowed around her, buoying her up. For a moment, she allowed herself to be demon in truth. She could not afford to stay that way.

She touched down outside Beria's cottage.

"Beria?" she called softly.

Her lover stepped outside, and for a moment she wanted to rush to her, wrap her wings around her. It must have showed in her eyes.

"Cat..."

Cathren shook her head. "Somebody just tried to kill me. I wanted to make sure they hadn't targeted you."

A slow nod. "I'm fine."

"No, you're not. Something is wrong."

"Cat..." Beria took a deep breath. "Garon's back."

Cat let out a breath. "And now you have to choose. And I know how you *will* choose."

Never her leri, but a man's wife. Somebody who would give her the children she desired.

"Cat..."

"No. If you choose me it will always be this, furtive, never quite the future we want. If you choose Garon, then I will gladly attend the naming of any children you raise."

Beria let out a breath. "I love both of you."

"And I would be as happy with that. But Garon won't."

She had known this was coming. She had sensed something wrong. She looked at the other woman. At her lover. Wishing Beria would share. Knowing she wouldn't. "I'm sorry, Beria," she added.

"Don't wait for me," Beria said, quietly.

"I won't. But I won't stop loving you either." Which she knew was true. "Stay safe. Get Garon here, he's good with a blade. I'm going to deal with this."

A promise to herself, that. If anything happened to Beria, she would not forgive herself. But she also had the feeling, strong within her, that she would never see the darker-skinned woman again.

Never wrap her wings around her.

Never love her.

It was over, but it could have been so much worse. Then a horrible thought hit her. She had come to Beria first, but *Beria* was not the one in the most danger.

"Mother Liesa!" she called as she leapt upwards once again, feeling a burn in the muscles that attached her wings. She might fly, in part, by magic, but it was still work.

The tavern was below her. The windows had been smashed, furniture spilled out into the street. Anger and fear rose within her, burning like the brilliance of fire, threatening to burst from her.

It took all the will she had, all the strength within her to quench the flames before she stepped into the tavern...and nearly tripped over a body.

It was not a man she knew. "Liesa?" Now her voice was querulous, hesitant, the fear of what she might not hear audible within it.

There was a second body. This one was face down. She turned it over, and the floodgates almost broke, very human tears flowing to the surface. It was Laran.

How had she defeated her opponent so easily and the better fighters fallen? The answer was obvious. They had not intended to slay her. And the second body, her hair a poof around her, her blade on the ground next to her, she didn't even need to turn over. She knew. *Ylsa.*

They had intended to hurt her, and she moved into the back room, blades drawn. They glowed a little, channeling the heat of her rage through them, as demon-forged swords were wont to do.

Liesa was there, curled with her daughter Mari. Alive, thank Seliene. Alive.

Laran had sacrificed himself to save them. He had never been the target. Perhaps Ylsa had been. They were both gone.

Liesa stood up, releasing Mari, who tearfully launched herself at Cathren.

Her blood still felt like it was on fire. She had come so close to losing it, so close to surrendering to the magic. She still was.

When and if she found them, they would die, all of them. For Laran, for all that she hated him. For all that he drove her crazy. Crazy. She might be crazy, but she was...

A servant of the true gods. He had not meant everyone except Arok and Birrur. He had meant Arok and Birrur.

Liesa moved over to retrieve the child. "I am not harmed."

A reminder, that, "No, but they killed Laran. They attacked me, in the salle."

"Gods. Who are these people?"

"Dead people."

"Cathren..."

At some point, she had grabbed a heavy tankard. She detached her hand from it, lifted it with fingers spread. "I am not out of control, Mother. I am angry, I am upset and I am not going to take this lying down. But neither will I let them turn me into some kind of servant of Arok. I promise."

"Yet, you commit to no god."

She stared at the tankard. It had mead in it. She did not drink any. "I feel no need to. I know it might make me safer, but..."

But it felt wrong. Which was part of why she feared her own self almost more than any other entity.

"Cathren. Do not lose yourself."

"I won't. That's what they wanted. That does not mean I am going to pretend this did not happen. You don't have to be me to need some payback." She should have killed him. She should have. She had thought him to be some fool, trying to take down the half-demon.

A distraction, to present a threat to her. To ensure she could not save Liesa and Mari. They had not gone after Beria.

Because they had known. *She* might have missed Garon's return, but her enemies had not. They already knew she was going to lose Beria. Had she known, perhaps she would have predicted this. She might have come here in time to save Laran and Ylsa, and guilt flowed through her. Along with rage.

"No, but you don't have to be you to poison yourself with vengeance either."

"They'll come back. For you."

"That's an excuse." Liesa's tone was flat, but she pulled Mari into her arms.

"Liesa. I have to do this."

"And if Arok himself is behind it, and he uses this to claim you?"

"Do you trust me?" A stupid question, even as she said it she knew the answer.

Liesa did trust her, Ylsa had trusted her. Laran had not, but it had... Something broke, and she dropped onto a surviving bench, dropped her head into her hands and wept.

She could feel a hand on her shoulder, she knew it was Liesa's, but it barely existed for her. If she did not let the grief out, now, then it would turn back into anger. Anger that would get her killed or worse.

Anger that would let the beast out. She would become what they feared if she let it rule her. Laran was dead. Ylsa was gone.

There was a hole within her now, one that might never be filled. Or which might be partially filled, allowing her to move forward. She had loved, she had lost. She had known she would lose Bera, though. She had always known. She had let herself love too much, had given Beria far too much power over her. Had let herself dream and imagine, with Beria tucked under her wing, that their love could freeze in this moment. Would never fade.

Yet, it would also never grow. Laran. She would never make up with him, not this time. Their last words between each other had been the same words so often spoken, the painful ones. The anger. The mistrust. The love that had twisted into something else.

"Better?"

"Somewhat. We need to get these bodies out of here."

Neir's temple was swathed in black. It was not birth they honored, after all, but death. Cathren could not leave...out of some respect...before Laran was given to the goddess.

As she turned to walk out, though, she knew it was all meaningless. He was already gone. Funerals were for the living. The goddess had already taken him by the hand and led him to her realm, to rest.

Too soon. She was calmer, though. The fire was locked away, where it belonged, stored deep within her. She might not be above using it on the murderers...those who lived. Laran had killed his opponent, both falling together. It was oddly typical of him.

Gods, she would miss him...even if there had been days when she wanted to kill him herself. His acerbic voice echoed in her mind for a moment, reminding her of Liesa's words, 'Don't lose yourself'.

She *was* losing herself, and she exerted all of her will to force the heat down, the flames back to that little core within her.

She would not, of course, risk damage in Neir's temple. She owed the goddess too much, perhaps her very existence. Had she been born male...

She thrust the thought to one side. She was who she was, and there was never a sense in might have beens. She thought of too many of those, it was time to deal with what was.

What did she need to take with her? A caba might be a good idea...she could fly all day, but it might be best to travel with greater discretion. No, two cabas...one for herself, one as a spare. She knew where she could purchase them.

Her blades, a portable alchemy kit, the two most useful of her spellbooks. Tava would go with her, but Tava was out of town.

The question was where did she go? Then she knew. East. If Arok had sent those men, then they had come, ultimately, from Arok-Kor. She would corner the demons and cultists in their own den...but then, what would that achieve? Her death? That would be a good thing for the world, if Laran had been right.

Her capture? That would be a bad thing. They might force her...rape her, or try to turn her. What was she doing?

She had to go. She had to get vengeance, but that would not bring anyone back. Don't lose yourself.

Yet, she had to go somewhere. Laran was dead, and nobody had approached her, nobody had warned her to stay in Losana. He had not had the chance to find a new watcher to take over. She had to go somewhere.

The wanderlust would not leave her alone now. She had no escape from it.

The decision was made. She would follow her feelings where they led her. She would not seek revenge for Laran and Ylsa, but if it happened to cross her path...she would not let any of the cultists live.

Balance. It was important to find herself again, and she had lost it. A little. Not a lot, not as much as Liesa feared. But a little.

Two cabas, then. although she feared her own motivation in doing so. Arok-Kor was east...many days ride east and then more north. Yet, it lay in this direction. If she went there, she put herself in their hands.

She could not go to Arok-Kor. She should have gone west, not east, but she did not seem able to make that choice.

She rode slowly. She had never gone more than a day's ride out of Losana, but she knew enough to know she should spare the cabas. There was no sense tiring them...and herself...out.

She knew about saddle sores too. At least, once she was out of the city, she would only be an unusually tall woman. She could hide her wings. Nobody would know what she was, as long as she did not fly.

Hoof falls on the road were silence. She had never been alone this long. She had never been permitted to be. She was alert to the sound of a galloping caba, coming up behind her, then ahead, stopping. Forcing her back.

Back into her gilded cage. A human woman would have been content within those bounds, most of them anyway. A half-demon?

A magical being, who should never have been conceived. The world would have been better off, but she wondered. Would the soul that occupied this body have been demon or human? What life would she have had? The possibility that she would never have existed also occurred to her.

She kept one hand on the reins, the other on the reins of the second caba. She wished R'vor had been in town. That she could have left him more than a note with Liesa.

He would understand the wanderlust...but perhaps not the depth of her grief.

She would have been better off one thing or the other. Her caba picked up its head and its pace without urging, the spare hanging back for a moment. Something ahead had their interest.

She had nothing else to do but investigate. She might as well go where the cabas led her, even though she knew in her heart. She was going to Arok-Kor.

3

What had attracted the cabas' attention was another traveler.

A priestess of Neir, to be precise. She rode a rather bedraggled looking mount, but Cat also noticed that it seemed a quiet and well behaved animal. Looks were not everything.

The priestess was an older woman, and she slowed as Cat approached.

"Company for the road?" Cat offered. She was, of course, well-armed. The priestess was not...but then, even demons hesitated to mess with Neir's priesthood. For one thing, it was entirely probable she had a poisoned blade hidden under her robes.

The woman took in the cloaked and leather clad form of Cat...her wings, of course, were hidden by glamor. "I do not need company. But then, perhaps you do?"

"I would appreciate it," Cat admitted, shifting so that the spare caba would not be between her and the priestess. It snorted a bit.

They were, of course, both females. Male cabas were far harder to handle...and a lot, sadly, ended up as food.

The priestess shifted her hand on her reins. "So. Adventuring?"

"In a sense," Cat admits. "There is not much left for me in Losana." Only a foster mother who was better off with her gone. The trouble would, hopefully, follow her east.

"Ah. And besides, in Losana, there are many mages. Like as not you will make more money elsewhere, eh?"

"I'm not a mercenary!" Then she caught the teasing note in the woman's voice, too late.

"There is nothing wrong with being a little bit mercenary, providing it is not your primary...shall we say...motivation."

"Right now, I don't know that I have motivation." Revenge, but that was piss-poor. Money? She would not turn it down, but if she wanted to become rich, she could easily enough. It was certainly not the only thing on her mind. Freedom?

She had never had that, and she never truly would. "Mostly, I needed to get out of town for a while."

The priestess nodded. "My name is Mari."

"Cat," Cathren introduced. Which could be a short form for a number of names. She did not want to risk Mari having heard of Cathren the Black. Mari, on the other hand? The same name as Liesa's daughter. A ridiculously common name.

If she realized who she was, she gave no sign of it. She did, however, notice something, a slight narrowing of her eyes. "Those are demon-forged blades."

"Acquired from a renegade," Cat admitted, truthfully. She didn't say 'graduation present'.

"Even the renegades do not part with those lightly. You must have made an impression on him."

Cat made a great show of fiddling with her reins. The cabas both slowed a little. "Perhaps I did."

She had wondered. R'vor had taken such an interest in her. Could it be sexual? Hardly. He had known her when she was so young, he still called her his 'hatchling'.

There was, of course, some small chance that they were related, distantly, but she felt that, too, unlikely. Not for the first time, she wondered what he really wanted.

"You should be careful. Weapons like that in the right hands...or the wrong ones..."

"I'm not sure which I am, yet."

Mari laughed. "Good. Most, at your age, think they are the right hands for anything that they touch."

"I suppose I'm not that naive. However, I would rather have the blades in my hand than in anyone else's."

"For now."

Cat looked at her, askance. "You think I may have to give them up?"

"Do not go to Arok-Kor yet," she said, after a moment. "You will find some answers...and many questions...in Merico."

Cat nodded. "Is that a message from the goddess?" Neir had taken an interest in her before.

But she did not want to give up the blades. "And you did not answer my question," Cat added, after a moment.

"In a sense yes. But when you do, you will no longer need them."

Which could mean any number of things from death to deciding to devote the rest of her life to alchemy to... "Thank you," was all she said. Even cryptic messages from the goddess were better than silence.

Then she saw the head of a snake in the woman's robes. She blinked.

When she opened her eyes, the road was empty.

The encounter rattled Cathren hard. For the rest of the day, she kept glancing over her shoulder.

Mari, of course, was an extraordinarily common name. If she was a goddess, she would use a name that common as part of her disguise.

Mari. Neir. That it had been the goddess herself had been obvious. And she had also possibly prophesied Cathren's death.

No more need of them. The blades were, in many ways, more important to her than her spellbooks and alchemist's kit. They meant something deep and dark.

They were an outlet for her demon side, and maybe that was what she would no longer need. If she was given the chance to become entirely human, would she take it?

She surprised herself with her own answer. No. She glanced down at the blades.

Do not go to Arok-Kor yet. That yet was telling. Did it mean she was supposed to go there? Neir was not always a force for good, she reminded herself. Yet, she was a force for life.

All life. Human and demon. And all death. Perhaps Cat's first instinct was right. Perhaps she would die in Arok-Kor.

The question was whether such a death would be worth it. She did not know her own natural life span, there being no other being like her. She did not know what she had to lose. She did not want to die.

She most definitely did not want to die. Could she be sure Arok would not, somehow, lay claim to her soul? The obvious answer was no. She could not be sure, now or ever. Neir, though.

Neir wanted something, and what a god wanted, she got. Cat closed her eyes for a moment, letting the caba find its own way along the road. Neir wanted something, but she was not clear what.

Surely not for her to serve Neir...she had no talent for healing. And certainly none for midwifery...and there was only one other path. Not a path she was willing to take, for Neir or for anyone.

She would sooner place herself at the mercy of Tyrn. Who, she suspected, wanted her never to have existed. The god of justice and revenge.

Then again, she wanted revenge right now. She opened her eyes and realized she was approaching some fishing village, feeling the caba slow as it descended into the inlet it was set in.

Given the time, this would be a good place to spend the night. It seemed large enough to possess an inn, which was the most important concern.

The second caba balked a little, then followed, splayed feet gripping the cobbles easily, the scales on the top clinking against them. An inn, a stable, and she had plenty of gold for now. If she ran out, then her academy ring would be a passport to earning more. For right now, though, she turned it inwards. Why, she was not sure...but it was not uncommon for a traveling mage to do so. At the very least, she had no desire to be besieged by people looking for cures for what ailed them and love spells.

She had no talent for healing. Other talents she had in plenty, however. And aphrodisiacs were something she was quite skilled at. She had a few bottles in her pack, even, to sell on the road. She braced herself against the saddle, as she entered the narrow street. Her head was almost high enough to see into the second storey windows of the two or three buildings that had them.

Content, but not prosperous, was her read of the place. Most of the windows had shutters, but no glass, but the houses were clean and in good repair. The smell of fish drifted up towards her, making her hungry and nauseous at the same time.

She liked eating fish, but cared little for preparing it. What she smelled was the fish being cleaned and gutted.

Fish stew, no doubt, for her tonight. A child moved up the street. She leaned down. "Is there an inn in this town?"

"By the harbor. You can't miss it," the kid called out, and then ducked out of the way. He seemed a little worried that the cabas might trample him. Then again, they were rather large.

The road, thankfully, opened out just before the harbor. She realized she was riding into the fish market. Somewhat sturdier buildings surrounded it, and docks extended into the inlet. It was evening, however, and there were few boats in.

Only the fishwives, likely, would be ashore. Possibly not all of those...if there was no man, then the woman would have little choice but to take the boat out.

There seemed to be few people around. The inn was as obvious as promised...made so by the sign of a dancing fish and the smell of mead.

Her nose told her it was not as good as Liesa's mead. Her heart wanted, for a moment, to run right back to Losana at that thought.

Was Liesa safe without her? She had arranged for protection, but would it be enough? They had killed Laran.

Then again, perhaps Laran had lost his edge. He had not done anything major in a number of years, after all. He might not have been as good as she thought, as she remembered.

She dismounted, and a girl of about ten emerged from the stable yard as if by magic. No doubt, any boys that age were already out on the boats.

She handed her a copper penny and the reins, and then stepped into the common room. It smelled of mead, sweat, and a little of perfume...that last scent coming from a well-dressed woman with skin almost as dark as Cat's black hair, who sat at a corner table with a younger woman who had 'maid' written all over her.

She wondered what a minor noblewoman, for such she obviously was, was doing in a place like this, then shook her head.

The barkeep looked up at her. "A room?"

She nodded. "A room, breakfast and whatever the common meal is tonight." From the smell, her initial guess was accurate.

Fish stew. "And a glass of mead."

The barkeep nodded, naming a price even as he turned to pour her mead. She glanced around again.

The only people in here were the lady and her servant and two fishwives. The two parties sat as far apart as they could and still be in the same room.

The barkeep eyed her weapons. "I hope there are not more skirmishes than normal."

"Protection for the road." He, at least, did not seem to have the knowledge to recognize the origins of the blades.

"There have been rumors of bandits east of here, but they have only been attacking the unwary and unarmed, if they even exist."

"Thank you anyway." She took her mead and her bowl...yes, fish stew, with tubers...and claimed the third corner of the room.

Neither the lady nor the fishwives struck her as good company for the evening. The former, perhaps. Either would start begging spells if they realized they were in the company of a mage. Being mistaken for a mercenary was probably better on that front. Maybe.

She suddenly felt very alone, the weight of Laran's death and Beria's departure coming down on her. She might not have had much in the way of friends, but now she had nobody. She had to keep away from Liesa, had to be estranged from her.

She could not afford friends. And the only person she had spoken to all day... Her thoughts tailed off. She became very interested in her stew.

Which, at least, was good.

The next day dawned wet. A summer storm of the kind that would likely last all day.

With no destination and no deadline, Cat elected not to travel in this weather. Of course, that left her with but little to do. Little except stare out the inn windows. She could study, but her mind did not seem to want to settle to the task.

She was not the only one rained in. The lady came over to her, moving in a rustle of fine clothing...clothing too fine for travel. No doubt she was the owner of the carriage Cat had seen coming in.

"Are you a mercenary?"

Cat turned. "Not exactly."

"Would you be above taking payment to accompany me tomorrow? I hear there are bandits."

Cat considered that. "I suspect we are going the same way in any case." Above it? No...although she was still unsure of this lady as company. "I am Cat."

"I am Teola." The lady smiled at her. "I do not see many woman fighters on the road."

"Where are you going? Ultimately?"

"Merico."

The same place Neir had told Cat to head for. South of Arok-Kor. She knew little of the city. Judging by this lady's age, she might well be going towards an arranged marriage with a man she did not know.

At least that could not happen to Cat. And at least she would be riding outside the carriage. Inside...she realized something else might happen. She did not look much like Beria, but she was far from unattractive.

Those thoughts she chased away. "Merico happens to be my own destination."

"I hope there will not be another war between there and Arok-Kor."

"So do I." That would...would that fit what Neir had said? Cat giving up her blades...no, it made no sense.

She still thought, feared, that it was her death that was being predicted. She was not ready to die...but on the other hand, what purpose could there be to her life?

The only thing she could do was mix darn good love potions. Ironic. Well, and other stuff. She was particularly good at the clinging fire...but there was only one use for that.

War. War between Merico and Arok-Kor happened with regularity. The two cities were each other's obvious targets, separated from the rest of the continent by the Great Mountains.

"Especially as I am supposed to be living there." Teola suddenly seemed distinctly young and frail. Unsure of herself.

"I can make sure you get there safely." It would be no inconvenience for Cat. She would not be expected to talk to the woman, after all...except maybe in the evenings. And then she could always plead off. Claim the need to practice.

"I would appreciate that. I thought this road was safer than it, apparently, is."

"Can you fight, at all, in a pinch?" Cat inquired.

"I carry a dagger. I could use it if I had to."

"Good. Every woman should be able to defend herself in this world."

"Do you not like men?"

Cat shook her head. "Men are not what I worry about, although some do deserve a dagger in the back. I was thinking of all the several dangers of the road. Your maid?"

"I am not sure. I did not hire her for her ability to fight." The lady actually flickered a smile. "I hired her for her fashion sense."

Cathren laughed at that. "A highly useful skill, in a maid. Not one I possess."

Teola looked her up and down. "Fashion sense is presumably of little use to..." And her eyes flicked to the ring. "You are a mage as well?"

Resigned, Cat turned the ring back out. "Yes."

"Few mages learn the blade."

"The kind of magic I am good at is not all that useful in self-defense." Which was not true, but she truly preferred not to use fire against the living. That was the kind of course of action that caused lynch mobs. "I'm an alchemist."

"Oh, handy. Do you know some of the more mundane stuff, like, say, dyes?"

"I can make dye, yes, although I seldom do." It would not be a productive use of her time...

"I might bear that in mind. I have a dress that I love except for the color."

"Easier to wait until Merico and find the dyer's guild there."

"True."

Cat studied her for a moment. "Unless you have some good reason to have nobody know you are dyeing this dress."

"If it got back to my father, he would probably be offended. He thinks everything he does is perfect."

"Some men are that way." A simple, mundane explanation. But then, this Teola radiated the mundane. Not the best traveling companion, there could be no true meeting of minds between them and the woman would certainly be a temptation to her. However, she would also pay. And Cat would have felt guilty leaving her to journey alone. Especially if there really were bandits. There likely were, if not here, then some point on the road to Merico. It was a long road, a long ride along the coast. If they followed the coast road, it would take maybe three weeks. Assuming they did not lose any more days to storms, which was not an assumption she could make.

She had studied the map extensively. It was a route traders took regularly. Some people in Merico presumably traded with Arok-Kor. Not openly, of course. But smuggling always happened.

She did not want to think what coin they paid in.

"Perhaps we can talk more on the road. I need to get some rest."

Cathren watched her go, doing her level best not to admire the view. She hoped Teola would either not realize how she was or not be worried by it. It was more often men who feared such things, but those women who did tended to be worse about it. Well, what was the worst she could do? Order her to leave? There was no emotional connection, and Cat would happily travel alone.

4

There was little chance to talk on the road. Teola rode inside the carriage. Her maid drove the caba, quite competently. It was a lumbering beast, clearly bred to pull. If all else failed, though, she suspected it would be fast enough to escape an ambush.

Cat tied her own spare mount to the back of the carriage. That left her hands free for a fight if she needed one. The maid should learn the bow, she thought. Or even carry one of the new weapons, the ones that fired projectiles with great force.

She tended to avoid those. There was something about guns that made her a little uncomfortable, never mind that they were made by alchemists.

Maybe that was it. The fact was, they were made without magic, and that was what disturbed her. Magic was her life's blood, and legend had it that in the world on the other side of the gate humans had driven magic away. Had forced it into the small corners, the tiny bits of remaining wilderness.

That was a legend. She was not sure there even was such a place, leaning towards the theory that humanity had, rather, been created by Solus.

Still, the fact that of all the beasts that walked the earth, only humans suckled their young...had to mean something.

There might be a point to Arok and his followers' assertions that humanity did not belong on Yirath. That they were alien and should be removed.

Cat was half human. She would not allow that to happen. On the other hand, she would not allow humanity to become some kind of plague either.

Perhaps that was why Neir had permitted her to live. Perhaps she had seen value in a being that could see both sides of the question.

Then again, she was only one woman...magically gifted or not, she had no great abilities that could bring peace between human and demon. Even if she could see the reasonableness of it.

So could others. R'vor, for one. Ylsa for another. Not Laran...Laran was terrified of demons. And many humans were simply jealous.

They did not have wings. They would never, could never, know what it was to feel the wind. The thought made Cat wish she had chosen to fly after all.

She could not have carried all of her stuff that way, of course, but she might have felt...a sense of freedom.

With a traveling companion, she was groundbound and trapped within her lies. Within the world's lies. She felt warm for a moment.

She shook her head. The money would help, and those who hunted her would not expect to find her playing caravan guard. If things got unbearable, she could ditch Teola on some pretext, in some larger town where she could hire a more suitable escort.

Of course, most of the potential escorts were men. Her fiancé would not, at least, consider Cat a threat to the woman's virginity.

Days on the road, though. She began to regret that she had not instead gone north, along the trade route, in search of R'vor.

She was supposed to go to Merico. Or was she? Nobody would dare, she thought, impersonate Neir. However, the goddess had given her a false name. Had it been only a priestess after all? One that tamed a snake in order to be closer to her deity? Snakes were highly sacred...and not, it was rumored, easy to tame. Not easy, no, but quite affectionate should one succeed. Mari could have been merely mortal, had she not vanished.

Even that could have been an invisibility spell. But impersonating a priestess of the goddess of birth and death? She found it hard to believe the cult would dare. It was possible that even Teola was part of the goddess' desire to make sure Cat went where she was supposed to go.

Which, for a moment, tempted her to perversely head in the opposite direction. It was not as if she had a reason, and a possible threat to her life. She was too used to obedience. Just like Teola, cheerfully heading to a union with a man she had likely never met.

Unless Teola was a cultist. Okay. Now she was just being paranoid. To break out of her thoughts, she pushed the caba ahead of the carriage. It broke into a plodding trot. She was no caba expert, and it was not as fast an animal as she had hoped. Well, speed was not as important as endurance, and it had that in spades. She could learn about cabas. And saddle sores, but those, she was reliably assured, would go away in a couple of days. The coast road climbed upwards, along a crumbling cliff. Several seabirds circled overhead, one of them screamed mournfully. Seabirds always sounded sad.

Smart creatures, birds. Smarter than the cabas, likely, if not close to as smart as human or demon. Still, they did not need magic to get aloft. That said something, although she was not entirely sure what it said.

At the top of the cliff, she hesitated. The road dipped again, and dipped steeply. She turned, calling to the maid. "You're going to need the brakes for this next stretch." The carriage running away would be worse than just bad. Through that stretch, she suspected there had been some bad wrecks.

The maid nodded, reining in the caba.

Of course, that was where the bandits were hiding.

Cat was not caught entirely off guard. Her blades were halfway from their sheaths before the carriage had completely halted.

She was no fool, and this would be the perfect place for an ambush. Demon-forged steel might well give them pause.

If it did, they saw it too late. One of them drew paired blades of his own, although he was on foot. Unfortunately, the caba was not trained for combat. It snorted and leapt backwards, putting her on the far side of the wagon.

She dismounted, moving swiftly towards her opponent, wishing she was better at protection spells. She certainly could not use fire here even if she desired to.

Now two of them were closing on her. The maid was doing the sensible thing and bailing from the wagon on the far side, using it as cover. To her credit, she did not scream.

Cat's blades became a whirling wall, and one of the men hesitated. He had clearly not expected actual competence. "Go," she said as the other closed on her. "Leave now and I will spare your lives."

She would not normally have resorted to such drama, but it felt right, the blades in her hands, and she did not truly wish to kill today.

The one who had not hesitated, though, was on her. He was the one with two blades, and he was not bad, feinting with one, attacking with the other. Not demon steel, but good quality nonetheless. Better quality than she had seen recently. Maybe he had stolen them from a caravan guard.

Not bad, but not good either. She hooked one blade under his left one, and it went spinning away. "Yield."

He shook his head. "I..."

"I can see how desperate you are. I would not kill you for it. Yield." His clothes were barely more than rags, his eyes...they were, after all, just bandits. "Yield and leave."

He glanced around, then did a double take. One of the other bandits was down, a throwing knife in his chest. Lady Teola could defend herself well enough. The rest were either fleeing or fled.

He picked up his second blade and ran.

"Anticlimactic," Cat grumbled. "Lady, are you alright?"

"Did I kill him?"

"Apparently."

Cat folded the man's hands across his chest, then took his sword. It was not of great quality, but she could probably sell it.

"You're just going to leave him here?"

"His friends will be back as soon as we're out of sight." They would, too. They might be cowards and thieves, but Cat knew nobody would leave a friend for the scavengers. That annoyed the gods, and men like that were even less likely than most to risk annoying the gods.

The maid was putting the brake on. "Let's go."

It was the first words Cat had heard her speak. The young woman was presumably horribly shy. She returned to the seat.

"Why did you let them go?"

"Because if there are any more bandits, they will now know that we are not to be messed with."

"They will only attack somebody else."

Cat considered that. "I could have killed all of them. However, they were scarcely worth the effort, and then what would we have done?"

Teola frowned, her brow furrowing. Then, without a further word, she got back into her carriage.

Cat rode behind, not wanting to get in front of it if it did run away. The second caba behind should help prevent that. It was a nasty stretch of road. Somebody should put a sign up.

Maybe somebody had and the bandits had removed it, hoping to cause a wreck. That would be far easier than having to fight guards, of course.

At the bottom, a narrow stream ran into the ocean. A small waterfall tossed it down the cliffs, set into them.

A beautiful spot, but why had the road not gone around? It might, of course, be a shrine. Or it might be that the road had at one point, and the stream had cut it. The waterfall burbled, and sea birds flew overhead again.

She was almost glad she was not talking to Teola. She wanted to go her own pace, not be stuck with the carriage. She wanted to join the birds, and her hidden wings twitched a little.

She was still in a cage. A cage of pretense. She could not be herself...and perhaps there was a small temptation to go to Arok-Kor.

To change sides. Except that she knew what they would do with her. She would be a slave at best, a sacrifice at worst. She could not find her path there, but she was heading there.

Was Arok calling her? She frowned, watching the rear of the carriage and the caba, then cutting ahead as it started to climb again. The maid was descending to remove the brake.

She smiled at Cat, and Cat felt herself relax a little. As herself she would never get a smile.

The only thing she could do as herself was wander the desert.

Those morose thoughts carried her through the rest of that day and well into the next. There were no other problems with bandits. Teola recovered her mood enough to be something of a conversationalist over her evening meal.

Which was fish again. Taking the coast route, Cat thought, was going to make her heartily tired of fish. Well, there was no help for it. At least these people knew how to cook fish...in many and varied ways.

Still, she could not escape her thoughts. Her sense of incredible loneliness. It would be better if there was one person who fully understood. She was not sure even the gods did.

Only the birds, crying overhead. They ate fish too. She did not belong here, not in this quiet, oh-so-human land of farmers and fishermen.

Humans tamed everything. That was what they did. And there was nothing wrong with that, but some wild places had to be left, surely.

Balance. For a moment, she thought she saw it, sensed it, knew it.

Then the moment passed and she was just a lost woman riding ahead of a carriage through peaceful countryside. The only sounds were the footfalls of her cabas and the cries of the seabirds. There would be sea serpents in the water, she knew. A wild canik ran ahead of them, chirring something. She reined in a little, avoiding the animal's path. Wild caniks were smart enough not to attack caba, but she still did not entirely trust them. She had never much cared for caniks anyway. They fawned too much, pitifully grateful to anyone who would rub the back of their head and feed them. For such relatively smart animals, it was far too weak an attitude for her.

She would rather have a rapa, if she was going to have a pet. They at least still acted like normal animals, small relatives of dragons and, for that matter, of demons, trainable and tamable but never, never domesticated.

Damn. She was in a bad mood. For a moment, she saw the humans as livestock themselves, saw them entirely from the demon point of view. She knew better. It was this countryside getting to her. Too regimented. Too...and then there was a wagon on the road ahead.

They were not going to get past, and it was moving at slower than walking pace. That did not improve her mood, not when she wanted to ditch the cabas and the gear and fly.

That was her problem. She wasn't getting enough sky time. Laran had never understood that it was a need for her, almost an addiction. She supposed she was lucky he had never thought to try and literally clip her wings.

She thought she might die that way. She had heard that crippled demons, those who could not fly, commonly committed ritual suicide.

Perhaps, then, it was a need, written into their minds by Arok. Why? To set them literally above the humans? Few of the other reptiles flew, after all. Birds flew. Reptiles mostly remained on the ground.

She did not have feathers. She had magic...and then she wondered if it was not a way of controlling the energy. Of using just enough that the demon did not become overwhelmed by his or her own magic. That was why she needed to fly.

Well, she thought she could find an excuse, a time to slip away. When they were near people, of course, so she was not abandoning Teola to danger...although with that accuracy with a knife, she was a lot less worried about the noblewoman than she had been.

It was good that she had some defenses. Less good that she seemed entirely willing to use them. She pushed any suspicion aside. Like as not she had been trained not to hesitate, because somebody who was not as skilled often had less of an opportunity to avoid killing. Laran had talked to her about that before.

Laran had...and grief rolled over her again, albeit with a wry tinge to it. She was the only person allowed to kill Laran. Some foreign cultist was not supposed to take that away from her.

Not that she would have, in the end. Despite everything, there was a bond between them. A bond that had kept her in place as much as any fear of him. She wished he had not chosen to use that fear. She wished he had allowed himself to love her.

He had probably thought doing so would taint his precious soul. Gods, she missed the arrogant asshole. She shook her head, forcing it to clear, and rode on.

The city of Rios was, even from a distance, visibly not Losana. Not Losana to the point where Cat almost felt a pang. The maid, she could see, seemed a little stricken.

She was probably thinking that if Rios was this different, then what was Merico like? Losana sprawled, it spread out around the edges of the delta. It guarded itself with levees.

Rios clung to the hills on either side of the mouth of the Tor. Said mouth was narrower and deeper than the Los, and formed an inlet that made a nice natural harbor.

Needless to say, it was full of ships. That would have been her other alternative for travel, except she did not like the sea.

Okay, to be blunt. She got seasick. Terribly, horribly, unbearably sea sick. Demons often did, but then, so did many humans. The smaller boats also meant fish for supper again.

Maybe. In a city, it would probably be possible to find other fare. The houses seemed smaller than most in Losana, but she also could not tell where the slums were. Rios was definitely smaller, although still holding many households.

It was also defended differently. The ridges on either side held a wall, and a gate guard let them through...for a toll. They looked in the carriage, to Teola's disgust. Making sure she was not a trader.

Traders, she guessed, paid more. When they saw Cat's alchemy gear, they cheerfully stung her for another half piece.

She did not curse it. Alchemists could be reasonably assumed to be rich. Besides, she might well ditch Teola here, where the woman could hire other guards, and spend a few days acquiring funds.

5

The road was steep enough to need the brake, as they descended into the city. Its noise and smell assaulted her. A couple of ragged children followed them for a few yards, no doubt hoping for a handout. They should go to Kiran's temple, she thought. But then, maybe they or their families were too proud, preferring to go it alone. There were a couple of stores on the road, clothing and perfumes. Wealthy stuff, stuff that she had no interest in. Stuff for ladies. Teola might want to stop.

But no, a murmur from within and the maid drove on. It was late, they would be closing soon, and perhaps Teola wanted to find a good inn. She probably missed good inns. The last one they had stayed at had not even had private rooms...the three of them had had to share.

A good inn. Could she afford a good inn? With what Teola was paying her, most definitely. A shadow passed overhead.

She glanced up...a bird close or a demon far away? Whatever it was was out of sight now. And surely no demon would fly over Rios. Losana or Merico, maybe, but they had no reason to be here.

Her own shoulders twitched. What reason did she have to be here?

The inn Teola chose looked like a good one. Certainly the stables were better, roomy stalls for the cabas and plenty of hay. She left them munching as she walked into the common room. Eyes were on her for a moment, but only that. They saw only her unusual height, nothing else sinister. She had thought of a glamor, but no. No need for that, not here, where nobody knew her. Where they would see and remember only a somewhat unusual adventurer-mage.

Of course, if anyone was looking for her... She dismissed the thought. They would...maybe they could force her to return, but she would only escape again. The heat in her blood lifted her as if she was flying.

"Ma'am."

The barkeep was speaking to her. "A room for the night...and do you by chance have anything other than fish?"

He laughed. "I think we can handle that. Traveling the coast road, are we?"

"Yes. Although I may stay here a few days."

"Get the road grime thoroughly off, eh? Mead?"

She hesitated, "A weaker one. I am not quite ready to retire yet." It was only late afternoon.

He nodded, pouring her a glass. "Any trouble on the road?"

"Bandits just east of Losana, nothing since then." Too quiet, she thought. Or was that normal? Was the world really that civilized, that one had to go halfway to S'rak to get a good fight? Maybe so...but then, why did she feel uncomfortable, not trust the quiet?

"Too quiet of late," the barkeep mused. "Maybe that's a good thing, though."

"It depends on what kind of quiet it is. The quiet of peace or the quiet of the eye of the storm."

He nodded. "Indeed."

She took her glass, slipping across payment for all of the required services...a hole in her wallet indeed, but Teola had promised to pay her tonight.

Even if the lady skipped out on that obligation, she was solid financially. She moved to sit at a corner table, alone.

Now to observe. The quiet of true peace or the eye of the storm. The travelers here might tell her something.

Not everyone in here was a traveler. Some were too clean and well fed to have come any distance. That was a good omen, of course, for the quality of the food. If locals ate here, it had to be reasonably decent.

Or people in Rios had no taste, which was a possibility. They dressed differently from those of Losana. No, she realized. They dressed the way people in Losana had dressed five years ago. Fashion lag, she thought, with amusement. Several had no ability to coordinate colors; another man was so well dressed she suspected him of being a designer. Two female warriors, clearly companions if not leri, sat at another table. One had her arm around the other, and they were whispering to each other. A merchant nearby was glaring at them in vague disapproval.

Not everyone well tolerated that kind of thing. But at least it seemed that unlike some small towns, Rios would not run people out on a rail. It was good, in some ways, to be back in a city.

There was no sign of Teola or her maid. Cat relaxed. She had been surprised not to be assaulted on the road. Unless they were leaving her alone as long as she headed towards Arok-Kor.

They might well think they had her, one way or the other. For now, she settled back into her seat.

"Mage." The voice disturbed her from a slight semi-doze.

Maybe she was ready to retire after all. Her eyes opened. It was a somewhat large man, a local by his dress.

"What do you need?"

"Do you have a means to tell whether an enchanted item is genuine?"

He thought he had been ripped off. She relaxed. "I can certainly attempt it. You have reason to believe it might not be?"

He glanced around. "I think the lousy seducer of caba ripped me off."

Well, at least he hadn't given the fully crude version of that oath. "I can take a look."

"How much?" He had his purse out already.

She thought back through her mind for a fair price, named something slightly higher. If he wasn't willing to pay it, he could haggle.

For the moment, he did not. What he handed her was a ring. "It's supposed to glow a little bit if somebody's trying to pull a fast one on me. Either everyone's dishonest or it's not working."

She couldn't help but grin wryly. "Maybe everyone's dishonest. And even if it's not working, it doesn't necessarily mean he ripped you off. He could have made it too sensitive...it could be picking up any dishonesty. And given everyone lies about something..."

The merchant looked a bit chastened, but only for a moment, "Well if he got it wrong, he can fardling well redo the spell."

Cat was inclined to agree. "Let me take a look, though." A few heads turned...perhaps people who thought they were about to see something neat.

They were not. She murmured the spell, being careful to use the human version. Some of the spells she cast, she cast in the demon tongue. Bad idea in public. A few things in the room started to glow.

She made note that both of the female warriors had enchanted daggers...possibly unable to afford swords. Jewelry with minor spells on it seemed common.

Then she narrowed her eyes towards the ring. "As I thought. He has the spell far too sensitive. He needs to back it off a bit, render it more specific. I am willing to vouch for that."

Which would force the hapless mage to redo his work for no payment, but then, he should have been more careful. She had little sympathy for somebody who screwed up a client's order.

"Thank you. I figured if I asked somebody from out of town, who did not know who it was, I was more likely to get an honest response. Even if the ring insists you're lying about something."

"I probably am. Everyone has secrets. The next completely honest man I meet will be the first."

He flushed a little. "Thank you. Could you...can you give me something in writing?"

"Of course." She wrote a careful note, affixing the seal of her own ring to it for authenticity.

As he left, she glanced around the room, making note of who showed interest. And, of course, who showed fear.

Rios' harbor was a busy place, and Cat stood at the edge of it. She had separated from Teola. She needed to take stock, and staying here a couple of extra days would help.

She felt as if she was on a headlong rush towards something. Some danger, some threat. Yet at the same time, she felt as if it was the right thing to do. That conflict within her needed to be resolved before she went slightly crazy.

Or maybe it could not be and Laran had been right to be worried, albeit for the wrong reasons. Maybe she was destined to be, always, a little insane. She shook her head, looking out at the ship that was coming in, under the guidance of the harbor pilot. She could see the small figures on the deck. Supposedly, ships had sailed outward from the land for days and never come across other land. There was nothing but Tirus and ocean on Yirath; that was the common wisdom. No sense risking lives and treasure searching further.

She shook her head at that. The sea did not attract or repel her, it simply was, flowing into the estuary as the tide rose. Flowing through and around the boats, the three naked children who were swimming off one of the piers.

Cat could swim. She had forced herself to learn. She would much prefer never to have to. From them, she turned away, walking back into the city.

The harbor was the center of Rios. There was no demon city far inland with whom to trade here, and no regular contact with the renegades.

Some were presumably spies. Many assumed all demon traders were spies for their God. Cat shook her head. R'vor had not been.

R'vor served all the gods. He claimed that was the only true path to balance.

She knew he included Arok, but refused to let that bother her. She loved R'vor. Not sexually, of course. But in all the ways that truly mattered, she loved the stubborn old demon.

Maybe he would find her. She shook her head. The note she had left had told him to keep watch on Liesa and her daughters. He would understand.

She realized that her feet had taken her towards Rios' temple district. Not a place she had intended to go, but she had nowhere better. Right now, it was relatively quiet. People worked, apprentices learned. Most of the young children were likely in Kiran's temple or some other school. Only the beggars were free, and they were enjoying their time off, as it were.

A couple of stray caniks, no collars on them, ran across the road in front of her, chasing each other's tails. She stopped, not wanting to get too close to them, especially as she recognized the steps of their dance. There would be more stray caniks soon.

From within Kiran's temple she did, indeed, hear children's voices, raised in reciting an old rhyme. She walked past it. A feeling, she had, that she needed to go somewhere. When such feelings even brushed against the gods, they were best listened to. Else, one could get into trouble. She did not need trouble with the gods. It was not Tyrn's temple she was being drawn towards. It was not even Neir's.

The temple to which her feet took her, unbidden, was that of Seliene.

Seliene. The goddess of magic, and thus the patron of most mages. Cathren had never sworn herself to her, unlike most of her classmates. It had not felt right, and did not feel right now.

The temple was white marble, high and airy. Its roof was painted with pictures of the moons, chasing one another around the sky. Stars, too, spangled it. The sense of space made her want to lift into the air. Seliene's temple always had that effect on her.

Yet it had not been Seliene who came to her on the road. Death. Death stalked her, but then, Ylsa was dead, Laran was dead. It might have been their deaths, not hers.

She needed guidance, and perhaps it was only her desire for such that had brought her here. She walked so far from any human or demon she trusted. There was only the gods. And the gods, she was not certain she trusted either. Not entirely.

Did they have plans for her? Did Fate have her path mapped out? She shook her head.

The temple was completely empty, and she dropped the glamor she habitually kept up, wings visible, eyes shading from brown to red. Her body remained that of a lovely woman, but she stood there as she was. "What do you wish of me?" she asked.

The temple remained silent, almost as if it were a grave. As if the goddess was dead. Or sleeping.

Or simply not deigning to make note of the halfbreed creature who stood before her altar. After a moment, Cat restored the glamor. The goddess could see her anyway, and she did not wish any mortal to perceive her true self.

A moment after she did, a young priestess stepped out of one of the side doors. She could not have been more than a novice, maybe fifteen years old. She seemed surprised to see anyone here at such an hour, much less somebody carrying paired swords.

"Lady?"

Cat smiled. "It is alright."

"Do you need to speak with a priest?"

She hesitated for a long moment. "I am not sure."

"Then perhaps you should," the novice said, fairly cheerfully as she wandered over towards Cathren. "We do not see many warriors here."

"The swords are for self-defense. And intimidation. I would not call myself a true warrior."

Which was true. Yet, Laran had fallen and she had survived. She did wonder, once more, if they had let her live. If they had intended to break her.

No, she was sure of it. She tilted her hand so the light caught her ring.

"Oh!" The novice relaxed a fair bit. Magic, she presumably understood and trusted better.

"But I am not sure if I need to talk to anyone so much as just...think about some things."

"I have not seen you before. Where are you from?"

"Losana." No doubt a common point of origin, with trade along the coast. Probably, she would be assumed...and then it hit her.

Why was Teola traveling by road not sea? For the same reason as Cat or because she hoped to bump into a certain half-demon?

There was no real reason to assume anything sinister, but the skill with a knife, the travel without guards. Teola had clearly not been what she seemed from day one.

But then, Cat had watched her back around her and just because she was not what she seemed did not make her evil. She could have been a friend of Laran's. That was almost more likely.

The fact that she might still be being watched angered her, but there was nothing she could do about it.

"How has the weather been?"

"Well enough." Cat smiled at the novice. "You don't need to make small talk." The girl was still a bit nervous of her. "Or be afraid of...here." She unhooked her sheaths, set the swords down. "Better?"

"I am not used to people coming in here armed," the girl admitted. "At least not so obviously."

Cat doubted many people here went far without a knife. And the girl was obviously not a full priestess yet, or she would have known Cat's nature instantly, glamor or no glamor. "I don't bite. But I find obvious weapons lessen the need to use them."

"I suppose you have a point, and magic has to be used to be intimidating."

"Exactly, and besides, I'm an alchemist, not a war mage." Not that she could not *be* a war mage, any time she chose, but this girl was alarmed enough.

The girl made a face. "Rather you than me. I tried to learn some of that stuff...and all I did was singe off my own eyebrows."

Cat laughed. "Occupational hazard. But not everyone has the right mind for it. You need to be extremely meticulous. The slightest mistake can turn an aphrodisiac into exactly the opposite."

At that, the girl giggled.

"Besides, I would imagine you are training as a priest not a mage for a reason." The goddess gave her priests odd gifts, sometimes. What did this girl possess? Cat shook her head. She realized what the unpleasant feeling within her was. It was envy.

This young woman would not only never starve, nobody would ever dare ill-treat her in any way. She would be respected, she would be listened to. She would be envied and admired.

"The goddess has her eye on me, yes. And perhaps on you."

Cat shook her head. "I have not sworn myself to any god."

The girl looked at her quizzically for a moment, then nodded. "You haven't decided yet."

Maybe that was it. Or maybe it was not Seliene who wished her service...but Neir. *You will have no more need of them.*

She glanced down at the swords. "I think I am waiting for some kind of sign. Perhaps I will never get one, but then, I know people who go through their entire lives without choosing a patron. Or being chosen."

"So do I. It just seems strange."

"If we were all the same, it would be boring." She was not in this temple for her. She was in this temple for this girl, who might well have been raised within its walls. Who needed to be reminded there were other paths. "Serving Seliene might be right for you, but it's not right for everyone. I have a friend who believes the only true balance is to honor all of the gods equally."

"Even Arok?"

Cat nodded. "Even Arok." She did not mention her friend was a demon. "Honor does not necessarily mean serve, of course."

But then again, would Arok change his mind? There was always that possibility. Now, Birrur, that was another matter. Birrur was opposite to Neir, she was nothing but plague and death. Or was she?

"That is hugely strange. And there are no temples to Arok."

"Of course, one could go to Arok-Kor, but that is generally a bad idea for one not sworn to him."

"I hear that they do not treat women well there."

Cathren perked up a little. That did not seem right. Arok loved Birrur, and she was perhaps more powerful than him. Of course, she had apologized and been forgiven, perhaps he felt betrayed?

For him to...but then, Arok may not be fully in power in Arok-Kor. He did not have the power to force his priests to do as he said, to put a leash on them. If they decided he wanted women beaten down. "Not well in what sense?"

"Women are property of their husbands, not educated well, often kept in their homes most of the time. I hear it is revenge for Birrur changing sides."

She had not changed sides, Cat thought. Unless there was more to the goddess of plague than any mortal knew, she remained as evil as ever. Simply more equal opportunity about it. Everyone got sick.

But she was subservient to Neir. Only Neir could decide who died. "That would make a certain amount of sense...even if it is a foolish idea in general."

It was, in her mind, very stupid to oppress anyone. They would, eventually, get mad and get even. She knew she would. She wondered if the renegades ever would. They were outcast from demon society, after all.

The idea of Arok waking up one morning with no followers amused her for a moment. "Women are stronger than those kinds of men realize, and sooner or later they will all wake up missing certain parts."

The girl giggled again. "Good plan. It's a shame we can't just go in there and liberate them."

Cat shook her head. "They have to liberate themselves. It's the only way to be sure they'll stay liberated. Some may not want to be. Some people are only happy if somebody is telling them what to do."

"Oh, I know what you mean. There's this boy who's a novice of Kiran, and he can't make any decisions without somebody telling him what Kiran would do. He can't even work out what Kiran would do for himself."

Cat laughed. "He'll either learn or he'll never make anything of himself. One or the other." Or possibly both, but she wasn't going to go there now. Some people never made anything of themselves, no matter what, even if they were given the best of opportunities.

At least she was not a complete loser. No, just a freak. She took a breath in, let it out.

"I think the latter, but you never know."

"He may just need to grow up." But she had intel. Or rumors. She had rumors, and they might mean nothing. What people observed was not always anywhere close to the reality.

"Maybe."

"But I think I have what I needed...thank you."

She smiled. "You just needed company?"

Cat said nothing to disillusion her. She smiled, nodded, then picked up her swords and left. She was not about to tell the girl she was seeking intelligence about Arok-Kor. Except she had not been. It had sought her.

6

Teola had disappeared. It was likely she had already left town. Cat would have been more suspicious of her but she had, at least, left payment with the barkeep. Everything she had said and done had rational explanations as well as paranoid ones.

Cat thought she was entitled to a little bit of paranoia. There were at least two groups of people likely to be after her, and the fact that she had encountered neither on the road might have spoken to all kinds of things, most of them not good.

It was quite likely that the real enemy had assumed she would be traveling by boat, which was faster. She sensed no hurry...no hurry worth dealing with seasickness, anyway.

Or perhaps they had assumed she would go by air, travel light. The most sinister possibility, of course, and the most likely, was that they would not bother her as long as she was heading towards Arok-Kor. They might well think her actions equated to walking right into their trap.

She thought she knew better. Did she? She would probably find out more when she got to Merico. For now, she set Teola to one side and rode out of town alone, switching cabas. At least they did not seem to care about her ancestry, and they surely did not know where they were heading. It was a brilliant, beautiful morning, the sun promising to heat the land past the tolerance of even cabas and half-demons. She would no doubt have to stop early, but she had started early. The only other travelers she saw on the road were the pair of warrior women she had seen in the inn, and they ignored her. They were in love, wrapped up in one another. She did not want to interfere, and besides, seeing them made her own loss so much more poignant.

Ylsa, she thought. At least they could not have touched her sister's soul. At least they could not have that. Hers might be in danger, Ylsa's was beyond their reach. Already in Neir's gentle arms.

But it had not been about hurting Ylsa. It had been about hurting her. Breaking her, destroying her, taking away her human connections.

She feared for R'vor for a moment. The renegade was a connection too. Cat shook her head and the reins, picking up the caba's pace. The dull green beast plodded forward a little faster.

She was not in a hurry, but it would be good to get as far as she could before the true heat of the sun hit. She wished for winter...even she longed for it at times. Her human blood. Her human weakness, R'vor had joked. Yet then he had told her she had more potential for magic than any he had ever met.

If she did, she could not access most of it. Perhaps she simply needed time. Demons lived longer. Demon mages could, it was rumored, be effectively immortal. Heck, some human mages managed several centuries.

She might live a long time indeed, if she was careful. *You will have no more need of them.*

Maybe Neir meant that she would not need blades, because she had more powerful magic. She was clutching at straws. It was obvious that if that had truly been Neir, what she meant. It was nothing to be feared, if so.

But then, if the gods did not need her to be alive, why had she been saved as an infant? Tactically, Laran was right. They should have slain her. Even Kiran would likely have agreed. It had been, she had been told, Neir herself who had stepped in. Which meant that she had to do something. Some task.

Some task that would take her to Arok-Kor. She knew it, felt it. For now, the task took her to...the mountains.

At first, she thought what she saw ahead of her were clouds. Then she realized it was the tips of the mountains, so high they brushed the stars. The wall of the world.

It was rumored that demons could not fly over the highest peaks, for there was no air for them to breathe. Many humans had died in crazy attempts to scale them. The road would take her through a pass, but it would still not be an easy journey. She almost, for a moment, thought of turning back, of getting passage on a ship.

No. She was committed to this course.

She would need her blades at her side if even a quarter of the things they said were true. There was a tension within her, it flowed upwards and outwards, inescapable.

She had to stop fearing the mountains. Had the gods built that wall for a reason, or had it been an inescapable, unavoidable part of how things had to be? On the far side, was desert. On the near side...the beautiful day was already clouding over. It rained more in the lee of the mountains. She had been told that. And less on the far side, far less. So much less that it was a different world.

The lee of the mountains. On their tips, their very tips, was something that she did not recognize, a white substance. For some reason, though, it made her shiver. For a moment, she saw the world covered in white, she felt a chill such as she had never felt. Then it passed.

Her imagination. She was not prone to visions. Or a message from Seliene, but she was not particularly prone to those, either.

Her imagination, because the ground was not supposed to be white. Maybe it was true that there was no air up there. That she could fly only through the passes. The large circling shape, though. That was not a demon. Or a bird.

That was a dragon, but the sight did not concern her. Dragons only attacked people who got too close to their nests and their eggs. They might steal livestock, though. She watched it for a moment, letting it take her mind off the white.

Then, she rode on, but the chill stayed with her, within her. It was not death, suddenly, that she feared.

The small village where she stopped was another fishing village, and it was too warm to ride on. The threat of rain would not have bothered her, but the heat did. A little. Less, she thought, than it normally would. It was as if the cold of the vision had affected her, or perhaps the sight of the mountains. She sighed a bit as she handed the cabas to the stable boy.

It felt as if everything had descended into a routine of travel for a moment. Surely, she had been to this inn before. The fish stew would be the same, the quality of the mead, the...

"Tava?"

The woman looked up. She did that, and her hair fell away from her face. It was her.

"Cathren Black. What in the name of the gods are you doing here?"

"It's not for discussion in a common room." Cat knew she had to be firm on that.

"Private room!" Tava called. Then, to Cat, "I'll pay."

Cat was surprised the inn even had a private dining room, unsurprised by the fact that it was small and the table was crooked. She sat down in one of the chairs as Tava locked the door.

Once the door was locked, she sighed and let her glamor fall. "What am I doing here? Looking for the people who murdered Laran."

"What?" Tava's eyes widened for a moment, then narrowed. "Somebody tried to murder me."

"They attacked me, and while I was distracted tried to murder Liesa and Mari. Laran and Ylsa got in their way." Cathren sighed. "I think they were cultists of Arok, although the one I cornered had a different story. I was stupid enough to let him go."

Tava slumped. "Laran is really dead?"

Tava and Laran had been lovers in the past, Cat recalled. Might have been again. "He died protecting Liesa. Took one of them with him."

"Okay. What more do you know?"

Cat frowned. "Neir is intervening again. Maybe. I met her on the road. Assuming it was not some fool impersonating her and as they did not get bitten by a snake..."

Tava made a wry face. "Neir would not take kindly to somebody faking things, either."

"She told me to go to Merico. The rest was personal."

Tava nodded a little bit. "Neir has always had an interest in you. I rather suspect that if you were not so thoroughly lousy at healing magic..."

"Oh, don't remind me. Just don't remind me." Cat's face twisted. "Gods damn it, Tava. I feel as if I'm being led around by the nose. And don't tell me I should have stayed in Losana."

"Maybe you should have." Tava lifted a hand. "You are getting very close to the cult, even here."

"I'm not sure I care. I won't let them recruit me...and if they try to control me, the blades will find another purpose." She would definitely prefer death to ending up Arok's whore.

"I'm coming with you, in that case. If you will not turn back, then you at least need somebody with half a brain watching your back."

"Be careful. You're getting kind of old for this."

Tava laughed a bit at that. "I don't intend to retire. And yes, I know the implications of that."

"I can't imagine you settling down with a bit of land or a tavern, no." If Tava came with her, then there was a very real risk that she would lose another friend. However, Cat knew better than to think she could even try to lose such an experienced tracker.

"Besides. You have not traveled through the mountains. I have."

"What is the white stuff on their peaks?" Cat asked.

"It's called snow. Don't try to get up there, though. The air is too thin."

"I saw a dragon, when I was riding into the village." Cat kept her tone reasonably unconcerned.

"It shouldn't bother us. They're smart enough not to nest close to a pass used by humans."

People raided dragon nests for all kinds of reasons, not least among which was dragonshell...the brightly colored shards of the eggs, which faded within days of the hatching if not specially treated. There had also been attempts to tame the beasts, which were possibly large enough to carry a rider aloft. Every one had ended with the hopeful dragonrider either being eaten or, more likely, standing there watching the beast fly off in search of a mate. Dragons were not cabas. "I'd hope so. But they also don't know we're not egg raiders."

"We'll just give them a wide berth. Like I said, they are not going to nest close to the pass."

They would, Cat knew, cheerfully kill and eat the cabas given the chance, but they also knew that humans tended to have arrows and spells. Being quite sensible creatures, they should give the two a wide berth. "I'm a little more worried about wild caniks."

"Those are a problem in this area, yes. But I think we can handle those."

"As long as they don't steal all of our supplies while we sleep." Caniks were notorious for getting into things. Tame ones could be taught manners. Wild ones were little thieves.

"I know exactly how to stop that from happening. Besides, there may be others on the road." Tava frowned. "The men who attacked me fled, although I marked them. One of them mentioned the true gods...which means a fanatic of Arok-Kor *or* a fanatic of Solus."

Cat had not considered the latter possibility. She turned it over in her mind, but true gods plural surely meant Arok and Birrur, not Solus alone. Unless she had misheard. Unless they both had. She took a deep breath. "We should get some rest, then."

Tackling the mountains seemed like something to be done on a good night's sleep.

They started early, with the mountains shadowing their path. For now, Cat rode first, her considerably better night vision combining with the caba's to guide the way. Tava was behind, watching her back. Right now, however, the road was flat. There was another village before the pass, Tava thought they could make it before the day became too hot.

It was cooler once one got into the mountains. That white stuff was snow. Whatever snow was. A few drops of rain started to fall. Cat frowned, but rode on. If they waited for a dry day here, they might wait forever.

She would appreciate rain once they rode into the desert. Awkward silence followed them. The kind of silence that showed up when two people had plenty to say to one another, but neither could work out exactly how to say it.

Cat elected not to break it, but rather to focus on the road. The sun should have risen an hour ago, and they moved in a disconcerting twilight. Streaks of dawn flowed across the mountains, as if they were a wall that could hold back Solus himself.

Then she realized. "Of course. Shadows."

Tava, behind her, "Yes, we are in the shadows of the mountains. The sun should break the peaks any moment."

She set aside her initial, oddly superstitious thought. She knew about shadows, she cast one herself. They were a normal, natural phenomenon.

Then the sun crested the peaks and the world was transformed in a moment. Cat drew in her breath sharply. Streamers of pink dawnlight flowed down across the mountains. Their peaks glittered purest white, and below that the grey of bare rock, and below that deep green. Forests, she knew, crawling their way up, but it seemed that the trees could not cover the peaks.

Not enough...something. Or maybe it had something to do with the white stuff. Every shade of green, though, covered those lower slopes, the pale of meadows amongst the trees. Far greener than the lands around Losana. "Dang."

"Beautiful, isn't it? But dangerous. I doubt humans will ever truly conquer the mountains, or demons. Not unless the gods reshape the world."

Cat shuddered. "Why would they do that?"

"It is said they do it all the time, in little ways."

But that was not what came to Cat's mind. What came to her mind was the mountains falling. Reshaping the world.

Would Arok do that if he was released, in order to destroy the human interlopers and restore the world to the demons? She shivered again, the caba under her stirring. It glanced around, trying to work out what its rider was afraid of. She ran a hand down the crest of its neck, and it calmed.

Reshaping the world. Why was she suddenly feeling as if she was on a precipice?

"Cat?" Tava's voice, concerned.

"Sorry. I think I have too much on my mind." She nudged the caba forward. The terrain was a little different here, and they were already climbing steadily upwards. Something canik-like but smaller ran across their path, vanishing into the brush. Small dragonlets flitted upwards from where it had vanished. Dull brown in hue, they fluttered into the trees. Their alarm calls echoed for a moment longer.

There was nobody else on the road. "Maybe we should have gone by sea."

"The cultists probably have the docks watched."

"I don't know if they care as long as I'm heading towards Arok-Kor."

Tava nudged her caba forward, so it was alongside Cat's. "It could be that they want to push you into a trap, to blind you with revenge."

"From that kind of twisted viewpoint, I suppose that makes sense. It's all speculation, though. We don't know, short of catching one of them and twisting his thumbs for a while." She wished it didn't. But Tava was alive. Liesa was hopefully still alive. R'vor...she might never know. If she was really destined to die on this journey.

Neir could have been warning her off, but Neir had told her to go to Merico. Neir would not seek the end of the world.

Or would she? What reason did Neir have to care about individuals? Neir cared about the cycle of life and death, about the world as a whole. Neir did not care about her. She was sure of that. Only as a tool, a means to an end.

Or did she? Confusion flowed over her. She was following the common wisdom. The gods only cared about their priests...some of them not even that. Why, then, had Neir met her on the road? Rather than talking through a priestess or some other messenger? Why not an angel...or had it been an angel? She was not sure. She could not talk to Tava about it, not more. She already regretted having mentioned it, the thoughtful look on her old mentor's face. Tava had held her as a baby.

Tava had told her only that they had brought her out of the temple at Arok-Kor. That Laran had wanted to slay her, but Tava had won the argument. "Tava, why did you speak for me? Why, really?"

Tava did not respond for a long time. Then, "First, what I always told you was part of it. I did not wish to anger Kiran by harming an innocent child."

"What if Laran had been right and I hadn't been innocent?"

"Second, Neir asked me to."

"Neir...it always seems to come back to her. What would she want with me?"

"Neir is neither what we call good nor what we call evil. She is not connected, not closely, with the other gods. I do not think anyone could possibly even pretend to understand her motivation," Tava said, carefully.

"That isn't important. I fear she may have let me live for one purpose and only one, and that once I have fulfilled it...curtains." Cat frowned. "Then again, perhaps the world is better off without me."

"We don't know that."

"R'vor said I had a lot of potential. Potential I cannot access. I might become dangerous." Cat spoke honestly. She glanced at her demonsteel blades for a moment.

"Some would say any mage is dangerous."

"Depends on the mage. You've met Kital."

"Yes, I have. That man is as dangerous as a blancmange." Tava laughed a bit. "Well, he is occasionally dangerous to himself."

"Not since he got banned from the alchemy workshops."

"Again? What did he blow up this time?"

"Himself, as usual. You'd think that somebody who can cook that well would be good at alchemy."

Tava laughed again. "I don't know why they keep him."

"He *is* very good at certain hearth magics...which would be better if he was a woman."

"Maybe he can marry a woman who is absolutely lousy at such things."

"Maybe he can." Cat smiled a bit. "I can think of a couple who would find him a godsend."

"See. There's a place for everyone." Tava looked towards the mountains. "Even you, Cat."

"I wish I could be more certain of that. I'm not. A task, a purpose, maybe, but not a place." Again, she saw the mountains falling. What did this mean? "I keep feeling this sense of dread. Especially when you talked about the gods reshaping the world."

"I didn't mean it that literally, Cat. It's your imagination...I hope."

Tava could not quite hide uncertainty. Cat glanced across at her. "It probably is. But we'll see what Neir wants me to do in Merico. Or whether it was a trap."

"I think that if anyone impersonated Neir..."

"She called herself Mari."

"The most common female name in the world," Tava said wryly. "Of course, she could actually have been possessing one of her priests, and used the actual name."

That made more sense, except... "She vanished. Of course, that could have been an invisibility spell, too." Cat wished she was better at those. It sometimes seemed that her magic wanted to be loud and spectacular.

"It could. But if it was Her, then you know...."

"She could be capable of pretty much anything." Cat frowned. "But there are limits."

"Only because the gods choose to work within certain rules. Even Arok did not break them."

"Arok..." Cat tailed off. Arok had made the demons and then got Birrur to attempt to destroy humanity. He had wanted this world the way it should be. But wasn't the way it should be with neither humans brought from elsewhere, nor demons created by magic? Cat shook her head. The world was the way it was. It should stay that way.

Reshaping the world. Neir was reshaping the world. Or was she seeking to prevent it? Cat did not know, but part of her felt a strong aversion to the idea. As disturbing as these mountains were, they had been there forever. Would be there...forever?

She did not know. By the timescale of the gods, perhaps, they were as temporary as mortal lives.

7

The road into the mountains was not as well used or cared for. Nobody hauled goods through the mountains, nothing heavy. Egg hunters, no doubt, came up here, and hunters of other kinds. Cat rode first once more, and she rode with one hand on a sword pommel and one on the reins. She did not like this place.

It was the shadows. Reason told her that was all they were, but it felt as if the mountains were leaning on her. They seemed to move towards her, lean inwards. Look down on her with the eyes of the gods.

Shadows. Just shadows, and illusion. The mountains were not moving. She made that her mantra. That they were not moving. Of course, a landslide might happen, but those peaks had stood for longer than either human or demon had walked the world. They would not, could not fall upon her. No cataclysm was going to happen, at least not today.

Something screamed. After a moment, she realized it was an animal, not a human, but not before the caba had skittered across the trail, and she had grabbed the saddle horn.

Tava laughed at her. She glanced over her shoulder. "Well..."

"I know, it does sound like somebody being raped, doesn't it?" Tava flickered a grin. "I think they make that sound to try and scare larger animals off the cliffs."

"They nearly scared me. Not that falling would be a big deal." Cat did not have to worry about that. It was being buried she feared, it was rocks and snow falling from those high peaks.

"Not for you. We need the cabas, though."

Cat flickered a faint smile at her. "Good point." She nudged the beast onwards, well aware it would not have spooked had she not herself been so startled. Startled was the right word for it, at least in her mind. She was on edge, she was even paranoid. She could not afford to be this way.

The road led up through a valley. A stream ran next to it, clear and bright, with small birds flitting in and out of it. Water dripped from their feathers.

It felt very real, the air was different from what she knew. She wanted to fly more than ever, and perhaps, up here, she could. There were dragons, anyone who saw her, with little perspective, would mistake her for one. Her wings twitched. They wanted to spread, with no conscious thought on her part.

Tava, from behind, "You're tense."

"I have been for a long time." Cat frowned. "Blame Laran. He didn't understand. And you know that's not me de-aging to teenaged."

"Laran never did understand anyone except Laran."

"He just wanted to keep everyone safe from me. I get that. I do understand his fears. Some days I share them." Cat glanced down at her caba's neck, at her hand on the reins. It looked like a very ordinary hand.

"Some days, so do I. However..."

"I was going stir crazy. But I didn't want him dead."

"I believe you. Others might not."

"I thought about that. Perhaps I shouldn't have left, but I had to. I couldn't stand it anymore." She lifted her head, looked up towards the peaks. "He had me so trapped, and I couldn't explain it to him."

Tava nodded. "I wish I had been there. He would probably have let you leave with me."

"And he was making threats again. He did not know how to...I honestly think he never knew how to deal with me."

"He was afraid to love you," Tava said, suddenly. "He was afraid that if he did, you would destroy him. Laran could not handle betrayal, and he had experienced far too much of it."

Cat considered that. "I wish I could say I would never have betrayed him. How can I be sure? How can I be sure there is not something within me, some geas that will cause me to switch sides?"

"You have the same free will we do."

"Do I?" Demons did, or there would not be R'vor. But she had been conceived in fire and magic, created to serve a purpose. Intended to be an empty vessel. Neir had intervened. Rendered her unsuitable for his occupation.

Yet, she was not as much a woman as she might have been. Had Neir done it on purpose, or had this been the best she could do, Cat's sexuality a result of her struggle with Arok? The thought had crossed her mind before.

"Why would you not?"

"Because they planted something. You know as well as I that controlling another's mind and actions is possible."

"Possible, yes. Likely and easy, no. I think that the academy would have found such a geas. It is, of course, possible that the cult is manipulating you."

"I know, and if they are, I'm riding right into it, but...they killed Laran and Ylsa. I can't..."

"Hence why I'm coming with you. If it's a trap, they won't be expecting me."

A cloud passed across the sun. Cat shivered. "And what if you die?"

"Cat..."

"I have lost enough." She breathed in, then out. "But you're right. I can't go alone." Which trapped her in this limbo, this fear that she would lose Tava as well. Would have to watch her die.

The cultists wanted her alive. The...and a shadow passed overhead.

She looked up. It was the dragon.

The beast circled lazily as they rode. Cat kept one eye on it. She did not want to get too close to the nest.

She did wonder. If demons supposedly flew by magic, then how did the dragon stay aloft? Perhaps because it was all wing, or seemed to be from here. It barely moved those wings, either, gliding as it circled. "How do they fly?"

"I am told they live in the mountains because they can't take off from the ground," Tava supplied. "They fly because almost all of their body size is wing." A pause. "They may also have some magic of their own, being kin to demons."

"I was wondering."

"You want to go join it, don't you."

"My wings are getting very restless," Cat admitted. "Another thing Laran never understood."

"No, I think he thought that you just happened to have wings." She hesitated. "I could hold the cabas." It was a serious offer.

Cat's eyes widened. Then she relaxed, slowing her beast and moving to dismount. "I won't be long."

"I trust you."

Those words meant so much. She felt the magic flow through her, turned into the wind and leapt. This was why she would not choose to be entirely human even if she could, the feel of the air under her as it lifted her upwards.

The dragon, startled to be joined, squawked an alarm.

"It's alright. I'm not after your eggs. Or your young." It was summer. They would be eggs, heating in their nest, hatching only when the temperature cooled and food became more plentiful. Demon eggs would hatch too.

She had not come from an egg. And her birthing had killed her mother, slave or volunteer, she would never know. The thoughts were thrust to one side, though, as she flew higher. The peaks were too high to crest, so she had been told. She did not attempt to do so, but circled to face west.

She could see most of Tirus. Or so it seemed. She could see so far, the air perfectly clear, with just the right amount of moisture. In that moment, all of her life seemed to condense into only the experience of flight.

Laran could never understand. Only a handful of mages, who had practiced flight spells, could possibly grasp it. And the demons. She had been given two things of her heritage...this and her gift for magic. Everything else about her was human.

Chance or design? She neither knew nor cared. But she had promised she would not stay up long. While she was, though, she angled her course, gliding upwards, scouting out the road ahead of them.

This was the only decent pass through the mountains without going far north into demon territory. It was an obvious ambush point.

Had those who had been there been human, it would have been easy recon. There were three of them, and they exploded into the air after her.

Demons! Her blades were drawn. There was a reason she used no shield. In the air, one was less than effective. Three on one...she had to lure them into the range of Tava's bow. The joy of flight was forgotten in the adrenalin rush.

They might or might not want her alive. She could not count on it. Her blades caught fire, although that would not intimidate demons.

It might remind them, though, that this was no weak human they faced. The flames licked along them, around her, singing her clothing but not damaging her skin. Instinctive, this magic, more so than the flight.

They retaliated in kind. Good. It was hard for them to harm her that way, and Tava, further down the path, would see all of this as if it were a flare. The sky was brilliant.

"Come with us," one of the demons snarled.

"I don't think so."

"Then you will have to die. You can be on their side or ours." He hovered, his wingbeats twisting in time with the air. He wore nothing except a loin cloth, like most demons.

"I'm on my own side," Cat said, crossing her blades in front of her in readiness. As crazy as this was, she might be able to talk her way out of it before Tava shot anyone. She could almost sense her friend down there, arrow nocked.

No arrow flew, though. Of course, without a fireproofing spell, the amount of flame up here would incinerate the wood before it could strike. Cat had fireproofed and marked some of Tava's arrows, but she had not had time to do all of them.

She might be searching for one.

"You cannot stay on your own side. If you do not, then your father's kind will be destroyed."

"So, what, you intend to kill me?"

"Only to warn you. And your friend down there with the arrows."

Cat did not have a purebred's vision. She could not, quite, see Tava. "She is protecting me." The blades still crossed.

"You have three days to come to us, or we will hunt you down." He veered off. An arrow narrowly missed him as he did so.

"You might as well deal with things now." But they were leaving, angling away. She did not follow, but rather let herself fall back towards Taya, let the wind catch her. "Assholes ruined my flight," was all she said.

"What did they want?"

"The usual crap about leaving the human world and hanging out with them. I get that every so often. Except this group added an 'or die' to the end."

Tava nodded. "So, they will be back."

"Most likely. None wore Arok's symbol, but that doesn't mean anything." They might be renegades who thought they had a plan, they might be under cover, they might...Cat sighed. She restored her glamor, looking once more like nothing more special or different than an unusually tall woman, and walked over to her caba, mounting without a further word.

She knew she should not take it out on Tava, but her day had been ruined, and she also knew she was the poorest of poor company right now. Even the caba sensed it, its head drooping as it climbed further. Finally, she spoke, "They said three days."

Three days set them well into the pass. By silent consensus, they had refused to turn back.

It was possible it was a bluff. Even likely, for these people wanted Cat alive, not dead. Nonetheless, she rode with her hand on her sword hilt again, and a spell on the tip of her tongue. She could not use fire around the cabas, being quite sensible beasts, they feared it.

There were other things than fire. Fog was what she had decided on. Flying in fog was just plain annoying. No attack came, however, and she began to relax. A bluff after all, then. Or perhaps they had not really expected her to continue into the mountains. Perhaps they were following her.

She was not paranoid, and she trusted Tava to check the trail behind, even as her caba set one foot after the other. It was not a happy beast. Each day had become harder, and it missed its warm stable. She missed her bed. A brazier. Access to a library. Liesa's mead.

It was cold. It was like winter up here, and perhaps those peaks were cold. Perhaps the real reason nobody could fly over them was because their wings would freeze. Hers already felt like they were going to.

Tava did not seem to be suffering as badly, but humans did not feel the cold as much as demons did. They could share the world, Cat thought. If they were willing to. If they were... But the thought was chased away by a wind down from the peaks, colder than anything she had ever felt.

Perhaps the demons had not realized that in three days the human and the halfbreed would be higher than they truly wanted to go.

She knew she would see them again. She knew it with a clear certainty. People like that did not give up easily, even if they might delay their attack on her.

"No sign of our friends."

"I'm betting they'll show up. It's cold for flying."

"We might be very glad demons don't like the cold. Are you handling it alright?"

"No, but I can deal." She was honest. "My wings are cold."

"You're not designed for up here. Dragons have sort of proto-feathers, you don't."

"I wish I had actual feathers right now." There was an amusing image, a demon with feathers. "They'd be useful."

"You'll be fine. We don't get that much higher than this on this road."

Cat glanced over her shoulder. Tava was smiling, and that bothered her for a moment. How could she be so cheerful about this? Perhaps because she had, after all, been in worse scrapes. And had ridden this pass before. Cat could not allow herself to forget that. This was new to her, it was not new to the older woman.

The path led upwards. The pass itself showed sheer cliffs and bare rock. Across the rock, lizards scuttled, small ones. Nothing as large as a canik, certainly. Above, more birds circled. Carrion feeders, Cat noted with something between concern and amusement. They weren't dead. Yet. She wished she could chase away that yet, set it aside.

It hovered in her mind nonetheless. She shook her head. If she was going to die, then it would not be the pass that killed her, not the mountains. She was fairly sure whatever forces guided her life would not permit that.

She frowned a bit at the thought. She did not want to be guided by forces, she wanted to have the same freedom as anyone else. Not to be human, no... Did she, then, want to be demon?

She would not be who she was if she was either. She had to be both, that was the only way. That realization both stung and strengthened her.

Night was starting to fall in the west. At this altitude they had been able to push through the heat of the day, but darkness was another matter. She did not want to risk the cabas. "We should stop soon."

"Agreed," came Tava's voice from behind her. "There's a cave around this next corner."

"Hopefully not occupied."

It was, but only by another of the canik-like creatures, which vacated the premises when it saw humans and cabas. Some droppings indicated that, likely, some birds had roosted here, but they either had not returned for the night or were no longer around.

Cat tethered the cabas, then walked to the other side of the road. The ground dropped away. She considered flying, but wondered if that would not expose her too much. They were still out there. She was sure of it, as she was sure of her own name and her own nature.

So she simply stood there, wings spread, feeling the cooling air as day passed to night.

The pass reached its highest point without much fanfare. Few trees grew here, and those that did were stunted. A small lake rested at the highest point, a stream running over its lip, forming small falls, and then away. Cat was colder than she had ever been, even in the middle of winter. She most certainly would not have attempted to fly...and the only thing, she was sure, keeping her wings from freezing solid was the heat spell she was keeping up around all four of them.

Tava said nothing, but a slight smile had shown her appreciation when Cat set it up. The cabas certainly seemed far happier. The ground beneath their feet was rocky, with odd, low plants flowing up the cliffs.

"This is not like any place I've ever been."

"I'm told the passes further north are very interesting. Some are almost lifeless, but others have kinds of beast unique to them."

"It seems like everything here is unique." Cat wondered other things, too. Like why the gods had only built mountains here and at no other place. Were the mountains an experiment? If that was the case, should there not be a god of...

...and her thought was interrupted. Somehow, the demons had got ahead of them. They were not trying to fly in this, but they stood across the trail. The caba spooked, throwing its head up.

Cat drew her blades, although she could not use fire. She could not, they could. At least this part of the pass had cliffs up on either side. There was no cliff for a panicked caba to fall from...and no place for one to go. "It's been more than three days," she said, evenly.

"We got held up. Your choice."

"I thought about it. I am not taking sides. I don't know what's going on, and I need to go to Merico to find out."

"Not good enough." That came from one. The second, though... The second murmured something to the first in the demon tongue.

Cat caught maybe one word in three. And 'Merico' repeated. Tava, from her face, understood little more of it.

Then they were turning and moving further up the pass, as fast as they could. They were not running, but they were retreating.

"They don't want to fight you."

"I noticed. I'm glad. I don't want to fight them either." Her lips quirked a little bit at that. "And not just because I'd probably lose."

Tava nodded. "I admit, I definitely don't want them dead. I want to know what they are on about, and whether it might or might not be something we need to be concerned with."

"I've had recruitment attempts before, but they're usually less direct. More 'Are you happy with the humans' kind of stuff."

"Are you?"

"No. But I don't think I'd be happy with them either. So...I just deal with things as best I can."

"The cultists would try to say that you could be both with them."

Cat laughed. "They lost any chance of gaining my affection or loyalty when they killed Laran."

"They made you."

"No. To be honest, they didn't. Laran made me." Was that a good thing or a bad thing.

"Or Liesa did."

"No child is made by any one individual. I mean, who made you?"

"Touche. Now, what say we work on getting down off this mountain?"

Cat was not going to argue.

The desert lay out in front of them. It was red and gold, spangled with the green of oases.

"Dang."

"It's beautiful. Until you're on the third day of riding through it and can't breathe any more from the heat and dust. The road is clear to Merico. If we go further, we will need to trade in these beasts."

Cat nodded. "Desert cabas are different?"

"Much different. You'll see. But Merico, we can do, there are provisions. You may still want to cover your head, however."

Cat thought about that for a moment. But then, she definitely did not want sand in her eyes. Or even in her hair. She pulled a scarf out of her bags and wound it around her head. It felt heavy.

She did not feel, for a moment, as if she was the same person who had chafed at being stuck in Losana...yet never known any kind of privation. She had felt cold now, she had never truly been cold. Now she was protecting herself from wind and dust.

Not one single cloud marred the sky, and it seemed she could see to the ocean. Could see Merico. Or was it a mirage? Tava had warned her about mirages.

She felt very high. The mountains seemed steeper on this side, the descent rough and rocky. The caba stumbled once, and she shifted her position, helping the beast compensate. She could not afford it to be lamed. Besides, she had developed some rough affection for the beast. As much as one could for a caba. Caniks gave affection. Cabas only ever tolerated their riders, at best. They were not the smartest of beasts.

Some humans made the mistake of thinking demons were stupid too. Or other reptiles...especially people who had never kept a canik.

They thought humans were somehow special in their differences, utterly superior. Cat knew better, could feel it in the blood that flowed through her veins. Before they descended further, her gaze was drawn to the northeast.

Somewhere, in the heart of the desert, lay Arok-Kor, where humans and demons alike served the dark god and sought to bring him forth.

Why would any human seek to restore one who had tried to destroy their race? Cat was human enough to rebel against that thought. Yet, she could not stand the thought of seeing the demons, with the beauty they possessed and made, destroyed.

Where was the middle path? She thought that as she found the trail down the mountain. Not well traveled, no. "You said..."

"There are wells at intervals and inns along the road. It is not well traveled through the mountains themselves, but there are dragon hunter camps and there is mining for gems and metals only a little further north. You will see when we hit the road proper."

They did before too long, a wide if dusty road, enough for two carts to go abreast. Cat felt small. The mountains behind her, the desert in front of her, the rays of Solus falling down upon them. Beating down, even. There would be no traveling all day soon. Even if Cat and the cabas could take it, Tava certainly could not. She had changed into loose robes, offering Cat a set. The fabric was surprisingly cool, although it could not cover her wings. It was still warm, she could feel that through herself, in her blood.

She had been born in Arok-Kor. Now she rode along the mountain road to Merico. What would the people here be like? Very different, the rumors had it. Very alien. A culture isolated by the mountains. Or perhaps they chose to be different.

Perhaps the desert simply changed people. As they descended, the vastness of it seemed to narrow down, fold inward until only her immediate surroundings mattered. There was only the road and the caba's footfalls. She wanted to fly and dared not.

The sky continued to oppress them, and so did their traveling companions. Unwanted, of course. Two miners on scraggly cabas had come onto the road from a side path, equipment tied to their beasts. Neither seemed sober and neither seemed to have either a volume control or a content control on their voices.

Cat studiously ignored them as best she could, focusing on the road, but there was really no escape. Despite the appearance of their mounts, they were having no difficulty keeping up with her and Tava's finer beasts.

On and on the loud talk went, most of it bragging. Cat ignored it until it began to shift in tone.

They were bragging, now, about what they could offer Cat and Tava in bed. Cat exchanged a look with Tava. Telling them they were together could fend off this line of conversation, although Tava was, of course, way too old for her. Still, it might shock them into leaving, even.

Tava's lips were a thin line and she looked like it was taking all she had to restrain from slapping them. Or perhaps knocking their heads together. Cat was, herself, tempted to bend academy ethics just a little. Perhaps a cantrip to loosen their saddle girths.

For some reason, though, Tava shook her head when Cat caught her eye. No, she did not want anything done about them. Maybe she was hoping to use them as a shield if they were attacked.

Cat just reminded herself that she was undoubtedly a better fighter than these prospectors if they tried anything. Or she could just scare them off with a well-chosen glamor. She wasn't the best illusionist, but she was well-practiced at personal disguise. She was pretty sure she could come up with something that would dampen the ardor of any man.

She focused back on her caba's neck plating. The beast plodded on, as oblivious as any of its kind to the doings of sentients. If it had a mind, it was one that cared only about the next mouthful of hay.

They reached the inn at about the right time, and Cat loudly declared that they would lock their doors. Tava gave her a wry look.

The two men glanced at each other, but it did not seem to much slow them down. One of them actually put a hand on Cat's arm.

She shook him off. The innkeeper, who had been nearby, frowned. "Felo, leave the lady alone."

"She ain't no lady."

"Leave her alone. One of these days you're going to pick the wrong woman and lose a finger. Or something more vital."

spells should not be hard. It was a relief to be out of the sun. Tava was still talking to the stable hand.

The few people in here were all men, she noticed, and all dressed the same, except that they had set aside hoods and face wrappings. They seemed a little darker than those who lived further west.

One of them made a sound the intent of which was clear. She glared at him. Even in robes, she could not quite hide that she was an attractive woman, and a woman alone. Some men would take advantage of that.

"Are you alone, lady?" the innkeeper asked as she reached the counter.

"My traveling companion is outside." She studied the man.

"Good. A woman should not travel alone."

She pointedly glanced down at her blades.

"Even an armed one."

"Then neither should a man."

There was laughter from nearby. "She has you there, Armin."

The innkeeper lifted his hands. "Women are more likely to be attacked."

"Not always. And the kind of attacks I've experienced have been the kind fended off with the tongue, not the sword. Some men are crude." She made sure that was loud enough to be heard by whoever had whistled at her. "Now. I need a room for myself and my companion, probably for several days. Stabling for two caba. Board. And...do you have any halfway decent mead?"

"Not decent, no. I have raksha."

"I will try it. It might not be to my taste."

"Some westerners hate it, some love it."

He seemed a nice man, genuinely concerned. "I can't find out without trying." She supposed that there were fewer flowers for bees here, and thus it was harder to make good mead. And elected not to ask what raksha was made out of.

Tava walked in at that point, coming over. The man did not whistle at her...either he had learned his lesson or the weatherbeaten old warrior was not his type. "Tava, raksha?"

"Of course. Be warned, you might not like it."

"I'll find out." If Tava liked it, the stuff could not be that bad, surely. She had always trusted her old friend's taste before.

The barkeep slid two glasses of a red liquid across the bar. Cat took hers, sniffed it, then took a sip.

It was possibly the most vile substance that had ever passed her lips, and that counted the deliberately hideous healing potions the academy dished out to keep students from malingering. Somehow, she managed to swallow it, but the look on her face had to say it all.

The innkeeper laughed. "Love or hate, one or the other."

Cat made a face. "Do you have any wine?"

He laughed again and slid her a glass.

Wine, he did have. It was not the best wine she had had, but it took the horrible taste away. "How can you drink that stuff?" she asked Tava.

"I grew up here, remember."

Cat had...not quite forgotten. "Acquired taste, I guess." She was not sure she would ever acquire it.

Yet, she wondered if she would ever again go west of the mountains. The innkeeper was talking to somebody in the kitchens. "Go, find a table. It's a little early for dinner..."

"We're in no hurry," Tava said, with a slight grin for him. As they headed for the table. "Nice guy. Especially for Merico."

"People seem..."

"People are a little different here. It's the desert. It scares them. It..." Tava tails off. "It is always out there, it is empty and it is beautiful. And most believe it is full of demons."

"And bandits, no doubt."

"Oh, definitely. And nomads. And the sand drakes, which are genuinely dangerous and good reason to keep a close watch on your livestock."

Cat nodded. "It is dangerous, but there is more to it than that, isn't there?" She could sense it, could feel it. The desert drew her. It enwrapped her. It wanted her.

"Remember you were born in Arok-Kor. You have no conscious memory, no, but the desert is a part of you."

Cat looked towards the door. "It calls to me and repels me, all at the same time." Yet was that not only her normal level of conflict. The way she had always been...her own nature repelling her.

"Me too," Tava admitted. "That's the desert. There are entire communities that believe by living in the desert they can commune with the gods. Maybe they are right."

Hence Arok-Kor, Cat thought. Or perhaps not. It was supposed to be the site he himself had chosen, but could she believe that? Likely not, she thought. Gods tended to say things convenient to their worshippers, and they stepped in directly only when people got it very wrong.

She suspected sometimes they laughed at their own followers. She would, if she was a god, and they decided that some silly thing was required for worship. And probably not correct the matter...at least not right away.

Of course, the god of the sea supposedly demanded human sacrifice every now and then. She shuddered. So did Arok, but Arok was a demon god, it was to be expected.

Or was it? Her mother had died. Her mother had been sacrificed to the cause of His return. Why now?

She shook her head. "I'm not comfortable here."

"I suggest tomorrow you try to find out why you are here." Tava did not say it more explicitly than that.

Cat, however, understood what she meant. "Or later tonight. I will see how tired I feel."

"One word of warning. The people here are very afraid of the desert and all that is in it."

Cryptic, still, but Cat caught her meaning on that too. She strengthened her glamor again...and resolved to spend some time trying to understand Merico.

A brief sleep, and she was restless, walking out into the evening. People were coming out now, although she still saw little color. Street vendors sold food and cheap raksha. She ignored both, her stomach already comfortably full...and she was not trying raksha again anytime soon. Instead, she got lost.

Obviously, that was not her intent, and she had thought she was clear on where the temple quarter was, but Merico was a maze. All of the buildings looked the same...rows of white houses interrupted by store fronts. Even the awnings were white. If she stayed here too long, she would forget what color looked like. No, there was a hint of it, a blue glass necklace at a woman's throat.

It was a relief, it flowed through her. Her blades were mostly hidden under her robes, although she could reach them if she so chose. Tava's comment made her keep them that way. Demon steel might not make her welcome here. Demon wings certainly would not.

Finally she sighed and approached a group of children playing at the side of the street. The oldest was almost apprenticing age. "I'm looking for the temple of Neir."

"You're going the wrong way, then," the boy quipped.

"Well, obviously, or I'd have found it by now, right?" It seemed that this good humor was natural to the people here. A way of compensating for the desert.

"Turn around. At the next junction, turn right. Keep going, even if it looks like it's narrowing into an alleyway...you'll end up on the south side of temple square. Should be able to find it from there."

She tossed him a copper, which he pocketed with a grin. She could like it here. Why had Tava left? Heck, why had she not been put into the academy here, not in Losana? Yet, why did she continue to feel such unease?

Temple Square opened out in front of her. The kid's directions had been good...but then, what reason did he have to mislead her? Seliene's temple and Solus' stood next to each other. The layout should be exactly the same as the other cities. The gods were jealous of their privileges. Everything looked as it should.

So, what was wrong? In front of Tyrn's temple was a gallows. That too was normal. On the rare occasions when a criminal was punished with death...these looked to see a little more use than Losana's. Bandits, perhaps. Perhaps they hung them here then put their bodies outside the city as a warning.

There was no reason to be concerned about it. And yes, right where it should be, was Neir's temple and the Houses of Healing and Death. She walked towards the temple itself. She wondered if the child had assumed she came to pray for fertility, not answers. She kept her hood up, her face partially masked. Even anyone who knew her would hopefully not recognize her...including any cultists or renegade demons that were not renegades at all.

The temple door swung lightly at her touch and she stepped inside. "Well," she said to the air, "I'm here."

She got the answer she expected; total silence. A slight frown crossed her features, then she shook her head.

Gods were never obvious. Well, except maybe Tyrn, who was blunt and attracted followers who were much the same way. Neir, certainly, would not speak in a booming voice, or walk out of the priest's door with a snake around her neck.

No, she would expect Cat to work out what she had to do at least in part on her own. Especially as that way she would likely be halfway through doing it before she realized what it was she had to do. That was typical of any God. And it was not like she was actually a follower of Neir.

She walked towards the altar, carved with serpents. Medicine and poison, and the line between the two very slim. Healing potions were amongst the trickiest, for that very reason. It was far easier to kill. Most said that made the healer Neir's strongest aspect.

Yet, sometimes... Cat's thoughts tailed off. There was nobody here. No priest came scurrying out to greet her, not even an acolyte. Maybe they were all busy in the house of healing. That was the most likely explanation.

Busy. Too busy to keep the temple, quite, as clean as it should be. Perhaps there was a message here after all. She strode all the way up to the altar. There should have been a bowl of clean water on it.

There was a bowl, alright, but nobody had refilled it lately, the water had evaporated to leave only a thin sludge.

Did nobody here give Neir proper honor? Or was it simply that hot, even in the building, that the water evaporated the day it was put out. She knew that to be quite possible. It was relatively cool in here, but it was not the kind of cool that she would have liked to be.

Abruptly, with a slight bow to the altar, Cat turned and walked out of the temple. She headed for the temple of Seliene. There she found the same thing. No priests and a vague sense that the place was not being kept up as it should be.

The only temple in good condition was that of Solus.

Pondering what all of that meant took Cat all the way back to the inn. There was not necessarily anything sinister. It could be summer neglect, with people more worried about staying cool and healthy than even honoring the gods. It was not like she had not seen that before. Priests were not immune, although generally somewhat resistant.

Which did not explain the one exception. She did not, right away, share her thoughts with Tava. Yet, she slept ill that night and rose early, making her way back to temple square. This time, she took water.

The bowl was empty, either still or again. She filled it. The air in the temple seemed to shift a little. She sensed the deity's appreciation. And the strong sensation that something was very wrong in Merico.

Yet the kid had directed her to Neir's temple without hesitation. Which contradicted the vague feeling that the only God being worshipped here was Solus.

She needed information. This time, she left the temple rather more slowly, almost reluctantly, moving towards that of Solus.

Not a deity she had ever had that much to do with. He was the sun god, of course, and extremely powerful, but, although patron-less, she had always leaned towards Seliene and Neir.

Solus' temple was one of the two largest, the other being Seliene's...and Seliene's, she thought, had the edge. Yet, within, all was opulence. Offerings of gold, teased out of the mountains, rested on the altar. Although nobody was praying right now, the place had that feeling one only gets in a temple. As if the building itself remembered and echoed the prayers that had been said there. Cat hesitated before walking towards the altar. She felt uncomfortable, as if the place itself was hostile towards her. She had never had that sensation, not even in the temple of Tyrn. She knew Tyrn disliked her, if not as a person, then as an idea. Her existence was not something the God desired. Yet, he was too honorable to smite her. This was outright hostility, outright dislike. She stood her ground.

The priest who came out was greying and a little overweight. The look he gave her spoke of equal hostility. "You."

She did not ask how he knew who she was.

"You are not welcome here. Not in this temple, not in this city. Leave before I call the watch."

She stood her ground. "I have done nothing and caused no trouble. I do not know if the authorities will cooperate."

"Here, we are the authorities." She could sense other figures. "I am being generous. Leave."

Here, we are the authorities. "There are other authorities, Priest of Solus." She did not want to fight them, but... "I am here under direct orders."

"From Arok, no doubt."

"From Neir." She could not help but drop the name into the silence. Why did the priest flinch? Perhaps he was one of those who particularly feared death.

"Neir is as false as Arok. There is only one true God."

She'd heard that argument made before. Or that there were no gods at all, that the gods had been invented as an explanation for how humans, warm-blooded and giving birth, existed on a world where everything else laid eggs.

Of course, the fact that there was no explanation tended to get those people shouted down. "I have heard that line before. In general, Solus appreciates it no more than the rest."

She was in real, physical danger and she knew it. There were enough of the priests now...all men, she noticed...to potentially take her. "But I will not fight in His temple." She turned to walk towards the door.

They blocked her path. "Unless you agree to an escort out of Merico, then you will have to be our prisoner."

This was ridiculous. Why the heck did Solus not smite these idiots? Perhaps he was enjoying the attention.

She did not wish to call on Neir, not in somebody else's temple. That was rude. "Out of my way." What if she rushed them?

No, there was a better way. A much better way. With a murmured spell, Cat vanished from their sight.

Invisible, she darted for a side door and made it through. What she felt was anger, not fear. How dare they? She forced it down. They dared because they knew what she was. Knew it, feared it. She should be used to that by now, she told herself wryly.

She would always be a pariah. Amongst humans or demons, for all that the latter offered her welcome.

How did she fulfil whatever Neir wanted if the priests of Solus wanted her out of town? She changed her glamor, something she rarely did. She made herself look shorter, darker skinned, a little plump. That would not, clearly, fool the priests. It would fool the guard. It would fool any mob they sent after her.

Slowly, she stopped trembling from anger. They were only...doing their jobs. Doing what they felt they must. They could have simply tried to kill her, instead they had just asked her to leave. She supposed invoking Neir's name had not helped.

The question was, had Merico really been taken over by this crazy cult, or...not.

Cat was almost afraid to go back to the inn. But then, the innkeeper had not recognized her. Warily, she dropped the glamor and walked back in, about in time for noonmeal.

Tava was not there. That fact bothered Cat for a moment, although there was no real reason for it to.

Okay. The most sensible plan would seem to be to ostentatiously leave Merico and then sneak back in under another guise, avoiding the temples and the academy. She might still be spotted, but she had to find out what was going on.

Everyone seemed so happy. That was what bothered her. Good humor flowed between the people. Well, she thought, if the entire populace of Merico chose to worship Solus, what business was that of hers?

It was not her business. It might, of course, be Neir's. The goddess no doubt wanted her temple back. Perhaps her worshippers, too. And it was her business if the entire populace of Merico was being forced to worship Solus.

The average person, she knew, would not care. The average person might not care if they were asked to worship Arok and Birrur...as long as it did not directly affect their lives. But the mages, the physicians.

The physicians. It would have to wait until the evening, but perhaps, before she 'left', she could don another disguise and talk to the healers and midwives. She needed to talk to Tava.

And there she was, coming into the common room. She looked exhausted and drained, and hand signaled to Cat before heading straight for their room.

Cat followed. As soon as the door was closed, she spoke, "So, since when has Merico been all about Solus?"

"I don't know," Tava said. "I do know they're killing any demons they see on sight. Mericans have always hated demons, but not like this."

"I was told to get out of town or die. They wanted to escort me to the gates with no caba or supplies."

"In other words, they plan on killing you."

"We need to find out what's going on here. Nobody is even filling the water bowl in Neir's temple and the others look no better."

"No doubt why Neir wanted your help."

"What gets me is everyone seems so happy and content."

"And prosperous. You noticed that? I haven't seen one beggar since I came here."

"If everyone chooses to serve Solus, that's one thing. And you can't blame them for going after demons, when this is the closest city to Arok-Kor. But I can't get it out of my mind that there's something else."

Tava nodded. "Neither can I, but if we don't get out of town, they will kill you. You can't fight the entire watch and the Temple of Solus."

"I'm very good at glamors," Cat said, softly. "But you're right. We need to get out now." A pause. "No, I do. You don't."

Tava nodded. "I need to find out what is going on."

"Go to the House of Healing. They won't have dared close that."

"You never know." Tava frowned. "I've seen villages throw out all of their healers before. The end result is never pretty, but it doesn't stop the next one."

Cat's lips twitched. "But if they have, that will have told us something. Here. Take this." She reached into her pouch, pulled out a coin.

"Communication token?"

Cat nodded. "I'll get out of town. Where would you suggest I go?"

"Back to the first oasis on the western road. There seemed to be no issues there."

She took a deep breath. "Be careful."

"I always am. I am more worried about you."

Cat simply looked at her. "I can manage."

9

The next morning, Cat took a desert caba and rode out of town. She knew that the eastern beast might make her look bad.

She did not care. She had no intention of leaving the desert until she had answers, and she could trade it back.

Or she could take it to Arok-Kor. Solving whatever was going on in Merico, though. Why the monotheism? Why the fear?

Did they suspect that Arok was about to try something else? If that was the case, then why not destroy Cat right away? They had known who she was, right off the bat. However, she had been in Solus' temple. It was probable they had wished to avoid violence there...either afraid of being smote or, more likely, not wanting to clean up the mess.

Her blood felt hot again, demon blood flowing through her veins. The road beneath the caba's feet was, though, not the western road.

She thought they might have been overheard, and had cut around to the north. There was a road to Arok-Kor, although it was not well traveled, but she had gone past it, seeing the eastern road.

She barely reached the oasis before the day became too hot. But nobody would look for her here, not right away. They would check westward, and, not finding her, search.

Eventually, they would come here, but it gave her a couple of days grace. So did the glamor she wore, making her look, more than anything else, rather as if she was Laran's daughter. She doubted he would mind.

And, just to add to the disguise, she was forcing herself to drink raksha. The stuff might grow on her to the point of being tolerable, but she was certain she would never enjoy it. It tasted as if various bitter herbs had been mixed in with it.

Okay, she thought to herself. What do I do now? It was not much in her nature, of course, to simply sit around and wait. She dared not fly. She had to act completely normal, completely human. A mere traveler. An adventurer, of course, although she had glamored her blades to look as if they were human-forged and taken off her ring. There would not be enough female warrior-mages for her not to stand out.

She had contemplated a male disguise, but that would have been hard to maintain.

As she sat there, though, she was approached. A craggy-faced man, clearly an adventurer himself.

"You got magic, girl."

She looked up at him. "I have a friend who's a mage."

"Ah, yes. But not with you?" He looked her up and down. "Just gave you a few protection spells?"

Good. He could tell she had a spell on her, but not what it was. "Hey, what else are friends for?"

"It is one of the things that makes mages useful to know, yes." He tapped a ring. "One of them gave me this. Handy for detecting wards."

She got no vibes from him that were not friendly. "I wonder if Sari could make one of those."

He flickered a grin. "Can only ask her. Worst case, she doesn't know how." He studied her again. "I have a feeling I've seen you somewhere before."

"Coincidence. I haven't ever been this far east."

"Demon hunting."

She shook her head. "Treasure hunting. Hoping to find something worth enough to help out my dad in his old age."

"I hear the mayor of Merico is offering a pretty heavy bounty on demon hides."

"Never was much for hunting bounty. Even demon bounty. I rode through Merico. Is it me or is something weird going on?"

The man frowned. "Yeah. I think the mayor is going crazy and taking the city with him. He started by expelling the renegade demon traders. A few tried to stay. He killed them and several of the humans who traded with them regularly. Then he moved on to the priests."

"Even the healers?"

"Even the healers, except perhaps a few that hid in or near the house. And quite a lot of the mages too."

"Where did they go?"

"How do I know you won't tell him?"

"Because I don't worship Solus, for starters. Well, not as a patron." She did honor Solus, and she did not blame him for the actions of crazy followers. "And certainly not as a fanatic."

"He's been attracting those, too. Some of the priests of Solus left with the healers, though."

"Good. So. How do I find these people?" She might get an answer from the priests of Neir. If she could find them.

"I don't know. I've probably already said more than I should."

Yet the people seemed so happy. Nobody short of a god could place a geas on them such that they did not see. Perhaps it simply spoke to the fact that so many people did not care. As long as their ordinary little lives stayed unaffected.

Until people started dying. "You've said exactly what you should. Without the healers, people are going to die."

And Neir wanted her to do something about it. Well, maybe, maybe not. Most likely, Neir wanted any ally she could find, and Cat did owe her one. "And I owe Neir one."

She did not explain. She did not need to. He would assume that it had to do with women and fertility and leave it alone. Or some near escape from death.

He shook his head. "I can't trust you. My sister is with them."

She nodded. "Then I won't ask you to." She would find them on her own, but she knew only one way to search. She was not sure she trusted an invisibility spell that much. True invisibility was much harder than a disguise glamor. The mind knew something was there. She breathed in, then out. "Trust has to be earned in this world. For all you know, the god I worship is Arok."

He frowned a bit, but did not flinch as much as most would. "And Arok would have more than enough reason to burn Merico if he could. I suppose we should be grateful for his exile."

Cat nodded. "Yes, we should."

Except right now, she was almost angrier with Solus for not getting a leash on the crazy mayor.

10

The desert surrounded her. It seemed empty, but she was no fool. There might be a dozen bandits within fifty yards, clothed to blend in, knowing the terrain in a way she never could.

She dismounted from the caba and ducked behind a rock, apparently to relieve herself. A moment later, she was invisible. A moment after that, she was airborne. She left the caba tied loosely enough that if she never returned, it would eventually break free. She did not wish the poor animal to end up dying of thirst.

She had her swords and water bags. The hot desert air lifted her easily. It was great for flying. Why had she never come here before? The north, the deep desert, those belonged to the demons, where it was too hot for humans, too dusty.

Higher and higher she climbed. To the west, the mountains formed a wall. To the east, she could glimpse the ocean. Half of the continent was laid out before her. Her vision was as acute as any bird's.

She still did not see the new city. She saw the shimmer of the magic protecting it. It was enough, and she dropped like a stone, wings furled, getting out of the sky as swiftly as she could.

She could not trust any glamor. Of course, when she landed, somebody was untying her caba.

She stepped out from behind the rocks. "Ahem. I'm going to be nice and assume you thought the animal abandoned."

The bandit looked startled. Then he studied her. She was still disguised, but her hands were on her sword hilts and her face said it all.

He fled. Her laugher followed him. The poor man was probably desperate. The caba just gave her a look. Needless to say, it was too stupid to care who owned it.

South and east. South and east. She mounted and set off across the trackless desert. There were no great dunes here such as supposedly surrounded Arok-Kor. Instead, there were rocks and cacti, and small lizards that scurried away from her beast's feet.

Some kind of long-legged bird crossed her path, moving at remarkable speed for a bird on the ground, neck stretched out and wings partly spread for balance. It did not look like it would be able to fly well.

Tava had warned her about sand drakes, so she kept her eyes open. Some kind of large carnivore, she supposed. Something large enough to fancy a human, or even a caba, as dinner.

She saw no such creature yet, though. The bird seemed to be the largest thing around. A snake hissed from a rock.

She glanced at it. It could just be a snake, but it could also be a sign or a warning. Neir was very much involved in this, and snakes were her invention. It seemed to be just a snake, bright yellow and black.

Poisonous, and she went no closer to it. Its venom could be medicine if used correctly, but if it bit her, she might die. She was not going to die of something stupid, not here, not now. No bandits approached her. Perhaps they thought she was crazy, perhaps the light glinted from her weapons. Most likely a bit of both. Her mind wandered a little. It visted her childhood in Liesa's kitchen, when she had not known she was different from any other little girl.

Don't take your necklace off, Cathren. She had not known the necklace had a glamor on it, a safeguard until she was old enough to cast her own.

Don't fly, Cathren, Always that. And *Stay away from the traders.*

Liesa had done her best. Liesa had done well, given the circumstances. Cat shook her head. She could see an oasis, but she was no fool. It was a mirage, a heat illusion. The desert caba, at least, needed almost no water.

Tava had said that if you cut open the purplish cacti, you could drink the sap. It was how they stored water. She elected to test the theory the next time she saw one, slipping off the caba and carefully slicing into one of the leaves. She did not want to risk killing the plant. The liquid from within tasted sweet.

She drank, and then refilled her waterskin. The caba munched on one of the other cacti, raiding its stored water in its own way. Sensible beast, she thought, and left it to it, stepping a bit away to take stock.

She had never been this far from any other sentient being. Laran would never have allowed it. Alone, she felt a certain freedom. She wished she dared drop her glamor and ride as she was, but she could not risk it.

Those she sought would not trust her, and the hide from her wings would probably be enough for the bounty the man had mentioned.

A price on demons as if they were vermin. Yet, Tava had always made it clear to her that people in Merico hated demons. She wondered if that was part of why Tava had left, or if she still hated demons, Cat being the rare exception to the rule. She could ask her, but she doubted she would get an honest answer.

She remounted and, ignoring the mirage, continued in the direction in which she had set her course. The heat was starting to get to be too much, and she saw no shelter. A cooling spell, murmured, would help them survive. She was not a good enough conjurer to make water that would quench thirst, as opposed to merely being taste and illusion. She could, though, keep them cool.

The desert here was not flat; she found herself climbing a low ridge. Exposed rock sliced up through the thin soil. Scraggly shrubs grew along the edges, perhaps taking advantage of trapped water. There were no animals visible, burrowing underground, no doubt, against this heat. No birds either, not even scavengers.

Was this what the world had been like before the Gods had placed life upon it? Cat looked around. The legends, though, said something different. That once the world had been an inferno in which nothing could live, then it had cooled and the ocean had covered it.

She did not know whether the legends were true or not. People told all kinds of stories. She had heard both that the Great Mountains were the breasts of the earth goddess and that they were the result of a spat between Solus and Seliene.

The truth was probably closer to the theory that the gods had thought the mountains looked good. That everything in the world existed because one or the other of them simply liked it.

Did any god like her? Maybe Neir. Maybe Neir wanted her as a follower even if she couldn't heal worth beans.

More likely, Neir was collecting the debt, by asking Cat to help these people.

The third day, and she reached the edge of the city. She was exhausted and thirsty, but felt quite triumphant to have found it. A glamor ward blocked it from view, but she could see the magic itself, she rode through it.

Almost immediately, she was surrounded. "Peace. I am not working for the mayor of Merico."

"Dismount."

She did so. There was one obvious way she could prove it, but she dared not. Just because they had been tossed out, did not mean they had any more love for demons. She slid down, making sure her hands were away from her weapons. The rocky ground was hot.

"What is your name?"

"Cathren." She had returned to her own appearance. Her own name. If they recognized her, then so be it.

She could hope that they would see a potential ally.

There was a long pause, a whispered consultation she could not quite hear. "Come in."

She rode through the gates. Such as they were.

It was a tent city, its walls a palisade built out of whatever they could make use of. Mostly dirt. Wood would have been better, but what wood could be found, here?

Tents, mud huts...improvised dwellings of every kind. She guessed there were maybe a thousand people living here, with space for more.

The refugees of Merico.

She slid down from her caba, looking at those here. There were three of them...two men and a woman. The woman, at least, wore Neir's symbol.

"I am here to offer what assistance I can."

"And what assistance would that be?"

She reached into her pouch, tugged on her academy ring. "I am an alchemist, and also have some knack for glamors."

The woman nodded. "That could be useful. But why not return to the west?"

"Because I want to know what's going on. My companion is still in Merico. Hopefully she can find something to help us all." A bit of honesty, Cat thought, would go a very long way in this situation, with these people. If she seemed to have an ulterior motive, even curiosity, they were far more likely to trust her.

"What we would like to know is if this is an argument between the gods or just a few people going crazy," the woman admitted.

One of the men stepped forward to take her caba. "I'll put your beast in the corrals and your saddle bags right outside."

She nodded. If she did not show trust, she could not expect trust. She fell in next to the woman. "I hope that the fanatics change their tune when people start dying."

"So do I. They seem to be doing something to cause people to be less unhappy with what's going on." The woman frowned. "I am Kera, by the way."

"Cathren."

"An unusual name."

"I'm told it's very old. Not used very often any more."

"Your parents had interesting tastes."

Cat flinched. "I'm an orphan." She tried not to snap it out, the reminder not being something she appreciated. It was not this woman's fault. She had no way of knowing.

"I'm sorry."

"You did not know. I was named by the woman who raised me, and I am not sure why she chose the name. I am not sure she was sure herself."

Kera laughed. "One of those 'it felt right' situations." She glanced around. "The mayor is completely insane, but these fanatics he has surrounded himself with, they are far worse."

Far worse. Cathren nodded. "Fanatics usually are. I've encountered monotheists of various stripes before. And Solus is a common target."

"And there are those who believe all the gods are actually the same person, just presenting different faces."

Cat shook her head. "Explain Arok and Birrur."

"I didn't say I believed it. But it is far less dangerous than calling a god, any god, false or fake."

Cat glanced up at the sky. "Fast way to get smited that. But I imagine Neir is..."

"Neir may simply be letting the expulsion of the healers be its own punishment."

She had a very good point. "I believe Neir...encouraged me to come here. Perhaps she thought I could help. I owe her a debt."

Cat did not explain. She did not need to, a look of sympathy crossing Kera's eyes before she nodded. "Perhaps you can," the woman said. "We would certainly not turn down the assistance of a trained mage. Do you serve Seliene?"

"I have not formally entered the service of any God. Procrastinating about it, I suppose." But then, she might go her entire life not doing so, she reminded herself, and nobody would question it. Except those who would wonder if her true allegiance was not to Arok.

She was not sure right now which side was worse.

"You are different," Kera mused. "The magic I sense about you is not like any I have encountered before." She frowned. "Almost like demon magic."

Cat just sighed. "I..."

"You're the one, aren't you? The half-breed. I have heard...that such existed."

"I am. And if you want me to leave, I will." Whether because they feared her or what her presence might draw.

Kera studied her. "Do you serve Arok?"

"No." Cat answered without hesitation. "I cannot guarantee that He will not find a way to use me, however."

"I have a feeling Neir would not allow that."

"Not unless it served Her purposes." A reminder that Neir was death as well as life, loss as well as joy.

"Would the destruction of humanity serve Her?"

"No, but we don't know what She has in mind. Other than the obvious, which is getting the mayor to let you guys back in." Which meant pressure. There was one obvious source, but what else could they do?

"Not just us. He has expelled all priests who are not of Solus and anyone not willing to change patrons."

Cat shuddered. "Changing patrons is a bad idea."

"Exactly. He also expelled a few demons who were trading, and killed others. Some of them are here, also."

"I'd like to talk to them." She might get some answers on what was going on on that side. Assuming those who had cornered her were not Arokian fanatics, which was an obvious explanation. Obvious, but did not quite, in her mind, fit the facts.

"Do you think they would help us?"

"Not all demons are loyal to Arok. And not even all those loyal to Arok agree with everything he wants. There are plenty who would quite willingly live and let live, let the humans have the cooler south."

"And given no sane person wants to live in the tropics, they're welcome to them. I wish more people thought that way, though."

"We could not have many fewer people thinking that way." It was annoying. People had such a black and white view of things. All demons were evil. Or all humans were evil.

She knew the latter was not true and was pretty well convinced of the former. "Maybe two species were not meant to share a world, and that was the true error."

"Maybe so, but we are here now, and I doubt the Gods will send us back where we came from."

After ten thousand years, where they came from did not exist, not in the same form. Society had to have changed, as it had here. And probably in different ways, such that the two worlds would be more and more different. Even humanity had changed. Not just the names they used and the clothes they wore, but there were pictures in the temples that showed humans with light, almost white skin, paler than Cat's deep beige. And pictures that showed ones the color of coal. Everyone these days knew humans were light to medium brown...but perhaps that was what one got when the two bred together for generations.

Or perhaps there was some other reason for it. Cat shook her head. "They can't. Not unless they also manipulate time. Which, I suppose, they could, but there was a reason they brought us here. Has that reason gone away?"

Kera contemplated. "If we were no longer welcome here..."

"I thought we were." Cat tailed off. The image in her mind now was war between human and demon, the kind of all out conflict that had not happened in centuries. The mayor of Merico seemed determined to trigger it, and she doubted he was the only one. Was that what Neir sought to prevent?

Why would Neir care? So, was it what was happening here?

Cat shook her head. "But I suspect what Neir is most worried about is people needing healers." And the other, less often talked about, function of Neir's priesthood. The one Cat hoped not to need for a very long time.

"Likely. I have asked her, but all she has said is that they need to be stopped."

"So, let me talk to those demons. They might say more to me, or nothing at all, but is it not worth a try?"

"Of course."

11

The demons had their own section of the camp. Outside one of the tents, meat was roasting on a spit. It smelled like caba meat, and Cat wrinkled her nose. Caba meat tended to be tough.

Demons, of course, were less fussy about such things, but Cat had been gifted with a human set of teeth. "What ho!"

A female came out of the tent, stepping towards the meat, then regarding her. "The halfbreed. Why am I not surprised?"

"T'la?" Cat's eyes widened. She knew this demoness, albeit from a long time ago.

"In the flesh. Is R'vor with you?"

"I haven't seen him," Cat admitted.

"If you do, tell him he owes me a beating."

Cat laughed. "Did he kick your butt?"

"Of course he did."

"Isn't that what brothers are for? Not that I'd know." Demons did not hug, as much as Cat wanted to hug T'la. This could go nothing but well. "So, what do you know about what the hell is going on?"

"Solusian fanatics. Why is it always Solus?"

"Because he's the obvious choice to be the one real god if there is one?" Cat suggested. "It's fanatics, it doesn't really matter whose fanatics they are."

"They deserve to get smited."

"Solus doesn't seem in any hurry to do that. Are we sure and certain He does not have plans that involve being in charge of a city?"

"No. And there are a lot of things moving, Cat. Things you've been sheltered from." The demoness dropped gracefully to the floor by the spit. Blankets had been laid out.

Cat joined her, furling her wings. "Laran wanted me to lead the most normal life I could. Not so much for my benefit though, as for his own peace of mind."

"Where is he?"

"Dead," Cat admitted. "He died protecting Liesa from assassins apparently sent to kill..." She tailed off.

T'la swore in demon speech. Cat wished she did not understand a word of it. Unfortunately, she did. It was not pleasant.

"And you tracked them here?"

"Frankly, I just needed to get out of town, then..." She paused. "I got a message from Neir to come here. I'm guessing she wants me to help deal with the fanatics."

"That would seem reasonable. The fanatics killed six of us and drove out the rest. I am having difficulty controlling the natural desire to use a few well-placed fire bombs."

Cat laughed bitterly. "Solus' temple is stone. Sadly, I doubt fire would be much use."

"Depends on how hot you get it. But I suspect the humans have...not trained you to your full potential."

Cat thought of Laran. She let her shoulders drop a little. "Nobody knows what my full potential is. Not even me." She should, by the way breeding worked, be weaker than a full demon, but all the indications were that she was stronger.

"Few know that, and fewer still reach it," T'la opined, demon words of wisdom. "Or do you not know those who glide through life."

"Quite a few of them," Cat admitted. "I've never been the type to, but it was clearly what Laran expected of me."

He would have been quite happy had she not striven for anything beyond basic control and then just got on with her life. Of course, he was not that way himself; why would he expect her to be? Because he was afraid of her.

"Laran, from what I saw, was incredibly cautious about certain things. Of course, I saw little of him. I think he would have been very happy had I and R'vor gone away."

"No. He would have been happy had you never existed. He hated demons." Which had not made him a good guardian for Cat, but she could see no other options. Tava had been even less suitable and who else was there?

"A lot of humans do. And many demons give the humans reason."

"Goes both ways." She glanced pointedly north and west, towards Merico. "Aren't you tempted to burn the place?"

"Yes, but I won't. The mayor, maybe, if I can get my hands on him." T'la flexed her hands, the tips of her claws emerging from their sheaths for a moment.

"I don't think I'd get in the way of that...even if it is rather the wrong way to go about it." Cat knew about revenge. "But I have a feeling you might have to get in line."

"I don't know. I think most people here would be content to see him removed from office. Unfortunately, it's not that easy. Merico has no good mechanism for such."

"Then we make one."

"And he seems to have the support of those who glide through life."

Cat frowned. On that, she knew T'la was perfectly correct.

The desert was dark when Cat risked communication with Tava. She stepped outside the wards, walked a good distance, to do so. She was fairly sure her spell could not be tracked, but she could not guarantee it. She did not know what the Mayor had in the way of mages.

"Cat. You're okay."

"Yes. I'd rather not say much, though. He might be able to have us intercepted."

"There are two Mericos," Tava said. "The surface one and the real one."

"So you know why people seem to be so happy?"

"The mayor has lowered taxes...and the old-fashioned bread and circuses. That contents most people."

Those who glide through life, Cat thought. The demon saying fit much better than anything of human speech. "But the religious, those would not be content, even if not all would have the courage to leave their lives."

Tava's voice came clear. "The academy seems to be split, too. Sadly, the Dean is on the mayor's side...no doubt trying to reduce the number of mages being expelled."

"That's unfortunate." But they could still, perhaps, count on some magical support. "What about the Council?"

"I don't know. I'll see what I can find out." And then the soft sense of her presence was gone.

Cat stood, but did not walk back to the camp right away. The desert enwrapped her, gently, the breeze cool against her wings. As she had in the mountains, she felt very alive for a moment. She felt as if she was in the presence of some nameless deity...or perhaps she was simply not sure which God touched with the wind.

Neir, perhaps. Or Seliene, for the moons were still high in the sky, Lara tagging along after her mother as any child would.

Children. Out of the question for Cat. She might not even be capable, Tava had pointed out to her once, when she brought it up.

And she had no interest in lying with a man...human or demon. But Tava was probably right, that she could not breed, and if she did, what would she produce? Best not to risk it.

She shook her head. Always best not to take risks. She sounded, in her own head, like Laran. Too much time with him, too much time talking to him.

T'la was right. He was a cautious man, and that had colored all of their dealings. He was a frightened man.

She missed him painfully. She missed Ylsa's quiet friendship, and Beria's passion; but at least she knew Beria was safe.

Tava was a friend, but not to that depth, and certainly not one who would ever be considered for intimacy. She needed trust. She needed understanding. She needed somebody who would look at her wings with fascination, not fear.

She wanted to fly, but for now, she was not sure it was a good idea. Instead she stood there, watching the moons, for a long moment. A long pause in her life. Sometimes those pauses were needed.

Yet, she could not find her balance. It had always been a fragile, teetering thing, a child walking across a narrow plank. Even with wings, that was hard.

Perhaps she had never had balance, perhaps she had never had anything other than the pretense. What did she need to do? She could not...acknowledge...too much of her origins.

Neir had asked her to come here, and then rubbed her nose in the conflict between human and demon. Had it been for Merico, herself, or, perhaps, both?

Most likely both. In any case, she had committed herself to helping these people, now. She would not abandon them. Would it mean her death? Or something else, perhaps even something worse.

You will have no more need of them. Well, one day, perhaps she would not, but she was in no hurry to die. In no hurry to change her life...except possibly in terms of finding a new lover, and even that had no sense of urgency to it. There was no hurry; it made her wonder if the longer demon lifespan would prove to be one of her gifts. Slowly, she turned, she walked back towards the camp, her wings folded. She felt alone and exposed.

She felt a vague sense of threat and turned. Rather than quickening her pace and potentially leading trouble past the wards, she shifted her hands to her blades, preparing a spell with a mutter. It might be nothing...some creature, more incompetent bandits.

It might be something. The wind suddenly picked up, almost throwing dust into her face. She spat out a counterspell.

A mage. There was a mage out there, and not one whose intentions were peaceful. A shield flared around her. "Who are you?"

No answer, but now she could see the shape in the darkness. Human, not demon, and glowing faintly to magesight.

The figure stepped forward slightly, lifted a hand, and threw lightning at her.

She leapt skywards before it struck, knowing that a lightning spell could do no damage to her when airborne. Fire flared around her, hopefully alerting anyone awake within the walls. "I have done nothing to you!"

"You exist."

She'd heard that before, that response. The voice, though, held no familiarity. "The mayor sent you."

"He is offering a lot of money for your wings, half-breed."

Her shoulders prickled. If there was one thing she feared more than death... "Come and get them."

He did not try, but rather threw a blast of icy air at her. No doubt, he was not good enough at flight spells to trust his life to them.

Good, that gave her the advantage. She dodged the blast, albeit barely. Chill flowed over her wing, and she realized he had intended to freeze her out of the air. Her own fire erased it in a moment, restoring heat and comfort.

"Dammit!" he swore, then did leap upwards. Crookedly.

"You need to practice that." The air was her domain, and she was suddenly not afraid of this man. He sent another ice blast at her, but his flight became rockier. "You're going to hurt yourself."

She could have burned him to a crisp in an instant. She hesitated. If she let him go, there would be more. If she did not, then this was no fair fight.

The decision was taken away from her a moment later. There was a faint sound from below and an arrow struck the mage in the chest. He gasped, and then fell to the desert ground.

Cat landed. "I was just trying to decide whether to kill him or let him go." She did not know the archer, a young man...younger, she suspected, than her.

"He might have led people here..."

"I think killing him would have won." She walked over to the body, checking it quickly, and then casually robbing him of his grimoire, academy ring and a pouch of herbs he was carrying. The archer did nothing to stop her. "But the thought of him going and telling his friends how tough I was had a certain appeal."

"Are you that tough?"

Cat considered her answer, folding her wings tightly. "Only when I have to be."

"I'm not sure he wasn't just that bad."

Cat laughed. "He certainly needed to work on his flight spells." And he was out hunting demons alone. She looked at the ring. "He needed to go back to school." She closed her hand around it.

Technically, it should be returned to a Dean, but she had no easy way to do so. She tucked it into her belt pouch instead. Hopefully, she would get the opportunity. Then he could at least be identified.

The archer moved over to the body, then frowned. "We can't leave him here, we can't bury him in this."

"Go get one of the priests of Neir." She crouched next to the body. He could at least get some rites.

The archer nodded and ran off as quickly as he had appeared. The kid was good, she noted; he vanished remarkably quickly, well before he would cross the wards.

Who was this man? He had not given his name, and while his sigil was on the inside of his ring, it meant nothing to her. He had trained in Merico, not Losana. He had, supposedly, learned the same ethics she had.

Supposedly. But then, many people considered demon hunting perfectly ethical, and perfectly normal. It was not even an argument for them. Demons were not human.

Others felt that some courtesy should be extended, but never the same courtesy. They did not trust demons, was what it boiled down to. Cat did not entirely trust the average demon herself. Then again, she did not trust many humans.

She hid from them as she moved amongst them. She would have to do the same thing in a demon camp. They would not accept her either. Even the gods did not seem to accept her.

"So, you were attacked outside the camp?" Kera asked.

"I was using magic to contact my friend in Merico. Likely he detected it. I didn't want to do it here and risk..."

"You probably did the right thing, but next time, take somebody to watch your back. I'm fairly sure the mayor would double the bounty for *your* hide."

"Rarity value," Cat quipped. "And the entire abomination thing." Did the Gods really think of her that way? She was fairly sure Neir did not...but she was not sure about...meh. What mortal could guess what the Gods thought? Certainly not this one.

"You seem sane, at least. I would have expected you to be far more troubled."

"I've learned not to show it." She turned towards...she had to look down slightly...the young woman. "I've learned that if I look troubled, people fear me more. But it depends on the day. I'm prone to cabin fever."

Kera nodded. "I can understand that. I like to stretch my legs myself." She looked meaningfully at Cat's wings, which she was not hiding right now.

"It's a little bit more than that. Demons don't tend to settle in one place."

"Neither do all humans," Kera pointed out. "And children who are raised on the move..."

"I was raised in a tavern in Losana. It has nothing to do with upbringing." Cat did not miss Losana. Some of the people, yes. But not the place itself. She could just as happily have settled in Merico, had it not been for the insane mayor.

Or live under canvas the rest of her life. She had always supposed that was a demon thing, this lack of attachment to place. Or feared that it meant she had some connection to Arok-Kor, such that she could not feel at home anywhere else.

Kera laughed. "A tavern? Seriously?"

"By a follower of Kiran with two children of her own. I suppose the temple arranged it."

"But still, a tavern." Kera was amused. "The idea of the most unusual person on all of Yirath serving beer..."

"I never did much of that. I was taken by the academy at

apprenticing age. They hardly had the choice on that." She fingered her ring.

"They always say they don't," Kera mused. "But I sometimes wonder..."

"They did a good job. Or the best job they could. They never understood me."

"Who could? No offense."

Cat considered that. "A demon might have a slightly better chance, but...I have a demon's wanderlust, a human's desire for affection *and* I prefer women as lovers."

Kera did not laugh this time, although Cat could see her trying not to. "At least you can find people who understand the last of those...although don't rub it in the face of Petru, if you meet him."

"Petru." She would remember that. Some people found homosexuality very hard to handle. Presumably this Petru was one of them.

"And while you're at it, watch out for Neruk. He follows Lirut."

Cat frowned. "Fanatically?"

"Not totally, but enough that I wouldn't trust him. Fortunately, we're far from any water here."

Lirut's followers had a habit of throwing people they did not like into the ocean and calling it a sacrifice to their God. If they couldn't find somebody they didn't like, they would sometimes jump in themselves.

Cat had never understood why Lirut would expect even the most occasional of deliberate deaths, but they claimed it kept him placated so he was less likely to wreck a ship.

They claimed. Cat was still unsure on the entire matter. She shook her head. "What is he doing this far from the sea?"

"Supposedly he was visiting family in Merico. Or he tried to. All he wants is to get in and say hello to his sister."

Cat nodded a little bit. "Anyone likely to shout 'abomination' at me?"

"On that, I can't be sure. I think your help will be appreciated."

Cat looked up at the desert sky. Where she wanted to be, riding the heat that came from the sands. She seemed to be adapting to it, feeling it less. Or as if the heat inside her was growing to match it.

It was almost as if with Laran dead, she was growing and changing. No, it was likely just age, nothing to do with him or anything he had done or not done.

He was not capable of binding a mage's power anyway, and she shook away that suspicious thought. If anyone was, it was the academy. Or was she out of their range?

If they had bound her in any way, she thought, it was through the training and their attitude towards her. Never get angry. Never let yourself love. She had broken both rules...and what had come of it?

She was alone and her losses had hurt, but they had not destroyed her. She had not let them. And she had let herself be angry, but she had controlled that anger. She had not burned anything down and while her departure might have been viewed as reckless by some, she lived.

She lived and Arok did not have any stronger a grip on her soul than he had ever had. She was not sure how strong that was, but she knew that she was here by her own choice. So, what did their rules mean?

Don't get angry had made sense. Fire magic was so easy for her that losing her temper was, indeed, a bad idea. She could burn something down by accident if she truly lost control. She understood why they had said that. And no doubt they had feared her losing control if she lost somebody she cared for.

They had tried to keep her from caring, but she was too human not to. Too human not to have passions.

Perhaps catching that her attention was no longer on her, Kera smiled faintly. "I have some things to take care of. Please don't go outside alone."

Easy for her to say. "Alright."

Kera walked away, and Cat felt a sudden sense of urgency within her, strong enough that she almost called the priestess back.

12

Cat walked towards the center of camp. They could have no great temples here, but they had shrines to the gods. All of them except Arok...even Solus, despite their attitude towards the fanatics.

It was that shrine she stopped at. Part of her wanted to lecture the deity about leashing his followers.

Maybe she had done some damage with her anger, after all. Lashing out at the gods was always a bad idea. The fact that she was tempted to demand that Solus control his followers and Neir tell her what she wanted indicated...

...that she was still angry. She laughed at herself, looking around at the shrines. She did not have as much control over her anger as she thought, and she was subconsciously channeling it towards people she could not hurt.

She had met Neir. She was now more sure of that. Had she met any of the others, unknowing. Had Tyrn, say, stopped by the tavern for mead? He was rumored to be very fond of mead.

Of course, the form of the gods was not really that of men. She knew that particular piece of philosophy. Neir would appear to demons, if she chose, as a demoness. She had appeared to Cat as a human because Cat would have expected a human, on that road. Nothing more, nothing less. Even the snake was not actually a snake. The gods were light and energy and pure power.

Solus could well be here, right now, watching her, and she would never know. She did not get that sense, though.

She got a quite different sense. That the deity was...paying attention, yes, but definitely not there.

She felt as if she was being watched by all of them, for a moment. "What do you want?" she asked the air.

Some instructions would be good. Some advice, to help guide her path. She got a sense that she had to make her own decisions...and that much hinged on them.

Was she supposed to choose between human and demon after all? She could not. Would not. She was exactly who she was...caught between the two, and she could not change that.

She shook her head. So, she was supposed to go into things blind?

Everyone did, she reminded herself. Who was she to expect special guidance from the Gods? She who should be most forsaken by them?

Because she did not have a guide on her path. Perhaps that was it. The desert sky was open above her.

She longed to fly.

The rider came from the direction of Merico, on a caba so exhausted it collapsed to the ground once he had dismounted. Several people rushed to tend to the fallen beast.

Cat found all of her attention drawn to the rider. She had a feeling she had seen him somewhere before, but could not place him. Perhaps in some tavern in Merico?

Yet the urgency that flowed from him...he was in no better state than his caba. "What is it?"

He looked up, and fear shot through his eyes. She had forgotten to hide her wings.

"It's okay. I don't bite." That was all she could think of to say.

"They've gone too far..."

And she suddenly placed him. He was one of the priests of Solus. One of those who had tried to corner her in the temple, to kill her or to escort her out of town. That was the source of his fear, not the forgotten glamor so much as recognition. "I won't harm you."

"They killed a child. A child."

"Demon or human?" she asked, softly.

"Demon. In the temple itself."

Her blood heated. "Kiran will not be pleased."

She said that a little louder than the prior conversation, hoping to attract the attention of any followers of Kiran that might be listening. They needed to know about this, so that appropriate offerings could be made and promises...oh yes.

She wanted to kill those responsible. When this came out, there would be at least a small war between humans and demons. The child's clan would seek revenge, and they would come clear into the city to do it.

"The people responsible for this have to be found and brought here," Cat said, suddenly, rising to her feet. "Somebody find T'la."

T'la knew demon culture better than Cat herself did. But she knew what the demons would want, what they would demand.

What Merico would not give. The lives of those responsible for this travesty. A child. "And did they pay bounty for this child?"

"Yes," the priest whispered. He was on the edge of passing out. Somebody offered him a skin of water.

He drank more than would normally be polite in the desert. Nobody said anything. The caba seemed to be a loss. Well, it was only a beast and not a particularly affectionate one at that. Cat felt little regret for it. Then, she had never had a pet, or an animal companion. If she survived this, she would fix that. A bird, perhaps.

"Somebody get this man into a tent so he can rest. Put salt in that water." That was Kera, taking charge despite her youth.

She might be high priestess someday, Cat thought, wryly. Or just the high priestess' nightmare. One or the other, for sure.

Cat turned her head towards Merico and sniffed the air. She was supposed to make her own decisions, the same as everyone else. She knew what she wanted to do.

She knew that what she wanted to do was stupid. If she went after them, it would not be alone.

"I wish," came a voice from nearby, "that temple was not made of stone."

A demon voice. T'la. "The building is not the problem."

"No, but I would like them to be *inside* it." T'la's wings were half spread, her entire body language showed extreme agitation.

"Tempting." Cat could not even say it was descending to their level, if they made sure nobody else was. Then she shook her head. "But stupid. They'd shoot us down."

"You're right. And stone does not burn well." The demoness furled her wings somewhat, although one could certainly not call her relaxed.

"We do have to do *something* about them, though." Cat frowned, flexing her hands. "Rushing in, though, is probably what they were trying to provoke."

"You think it was to draw us out." Flat, the words not a question, T'la turned towards her.

"At least as part of their goal. It makes sense, in their terms." Or in any terms, except who involved children? People whose desire was genocide. Cat knew the word, in highly abstract terms.

Human on human genocide was unknown on Yirath. There had never been enough of them. It occurred to her that if there were no demons, that might change.

"Don't give yourself a headache thinking like them," T'la suggested, her tone lighter. Perhaps Cat had got through to her some.

"Somebody has to. I need to try and think enough like them to guess what they're going to do next...maybe we all do."

"Wait for us to attack and then use that as an excuse to start a war," T'la said, after only a moment of hesitation.

"Exactly. The kid was provocation, and we need to respond in a way that gives them no such excuse."

"We can't use diplomacy. They'd kill any emissaries on sight, and then war would be very hard to avoid."

"I'd offer myself as an emissary, if...no. They'd kill any *demon* emissaries."

"Human ones might have a chance."

Cat wished she could have gone with them. She had no feelings about their likely success and failure, but a firm sense that she herself should stay put. In any case, she knew at least some of them could see through her glamor.

So, she stayed in camp. Not that she was idle. War might yet be unavoidable...and thus, she was in an open area, working on something very dangerous.

Firebombs. She hoped they would not have to use them, and hoped more that nobody would use them on civilians. But they had their uses...and if combined with demonfire, they would intimidate the heck out of the opposition. They should, anyway.

They would also encourage opposing mages to waste their energy countering devices and thus... It was a smart tactical move, but still did not sit well with her. There was too strong an undercurrent of vengeance in the camp. Vengeance and fear. It could boil over at any time, and then people would not be thinking about tactics or ethics. For this reason, she made sure nobody was nearby. She would not reveal the existence of the weapons until they were needed.

They were easy enough to make, as long as she had enough small ceramic jars. That, of course, was an absolute limit.

By the time she was done, she had fifteen of them. It would have to do. She cached them carefully and set out through the camp. It was almost to the hottest part of the day, but again, the heat in her blood seemed to match it. Heat. It flowed through her, and she felt more invigorated by it than drained.

She still wanted to fly but dared not. The purebloods had to be feeling worse, she thought, grounded in this place.

She did not consciously realize she was heading for the shrines until she got there.

Then she stood, looking at all of them. She wondered if a shrine to Arok would ever join them...and wondered why she had even thought that. He was the enemy, after all. She had always known that, deep in her bones. Arok was the enemy.

Or was he? She realized it was her anger at the Solusian fanatics coloring her thoughts again, and tried to force them aside. They were not so easily moved.

Okay, think, woman, she told herself. Arok and Birrur tried to destroy humanity. Birrur apologized. Arok did not. Birrur, thus, stood with the other gods, Arok was still in exile. Yet Birrur was disease. Sickness. Be it of the body, the mind, or the soul, she was the darkness that kept men from being well.

So, why was she honored at all? Because she could stay her hand as easily as use it, yet people who were sick were more inclined to pray to Neir.

Because she existed and was a deity, she should be worshipped? It was that shrine towards which Cat walked now. Perhaps she spared her followers...or they thought she would. Not that she had many...more among demons, but still not many.

What benefit was disease? And why did it not simply fall under the sphere of influence of Neir? She shook her head.

Philosophy. Meaningless philosophy. Besides, ultimately, that line of thought led to monotheism. Cat wasn't ready to go there. She was bored, she realized. Bored and restless, and her mind racing ahead of her body.

"What benefit," she mused out loud.

"To what?"

"Disease," she said, simply. She turned to see who the speaker was...and came face to face with one of the oldest humans she had ever seen.

"I have been told that the lack of disease can be as harmful as its presence." The man looked thoughtful. "Questioning the aspect of a deity."

"There's nothing in any of the rules that says we can't question the gods. It's insulting them that tends to get one into trouble." Cat's tone was defensive, she recognized it as such a moment too late. The words were out, hanging in the air.

"Birrur does seem to hold an odd place. Perhaps she exists because we need something to fear."

"I've never been particularly afraid of her...but then...I don't get sick much."

"Then there may be some protection on you."

"Who knows." Maybe Neir did like her after all. Maybe... "I know what it is I find hard to grasp. That sickness is not simply under the jurisdiction of Neir."

"Neir is life and death, the cycle of that. Sickness does not always bring death."

"Birrur's plague would have destroyed humanity."

"Yes, but that was an unusual situation. Most plagues make the race stronger, in the long term, as unpleasant as that is."

Cat frowned a bit. "It still makes very little sense." She knew she was talking to a priest of Birrur. That much was obvious. She was trying to be polite, but finding it distinctly hard.

"Sometimes, a sickness is needed to make somebody well. But I can see that you are struggling with this. Perhaps I should let you alone."

After a moment of hesitation, she nodded, then walked away from Birrur's shrine. To Neir's. Sickness a separate thing from death? Well, true. Most of the time when somebody got sick, they were miserable for a while and then fine. But still, Neir's jurisdiction was also healing. Were Neir and Birrur really the same goddess in different moods? She could make sense of it no other way, but if she mentioned that possibility to priests of either, she would not be popular.

Yet, that made no sense either. Okay. She suddenly laughed at the thought that hit her.

The thought that maybe she should just ask Neir.

Of course, she could not just go and ask a goddess about anything. That was not how things worked, and she knew it. Yet, the thought lingered. The priest of Birrur had tried to explain, but he was caught in a paradigm, unable to see how it did not make sense.

Unless, of course, Birrur was not really the goddess of sickness, but had only gained that association somewhere. Just as she could not blame Solus for the actions of his followers.

So, she went and asked somebody she knew would have a totally different view on the matter. And who probably needed her mind taking off things as much as she did.

T'la handed her a chunk of cooked meat, demon fashion.

"Don't forget. I didn't get the claws." Cat's hands were like those of a human, only the slightest thickening of her nails...which, of course, were not retractable.

T'la laughed and handed her a knife. "Sorry."

"Are you?" Cat asked with distinct amusement.

T'la laughed again. "Mostly."

"Okay. So, something's been bothering me. If Neir's sphere is healing, life, and death, why do we have a separate goddess of sickness?"

T'la tilted her head. "You do ask the deep ones. And why did it never bother you before?"

"I never thought about it. Or rather, I tried not to. Thinking about Birrur is too close to thinking about Arok."

"And I don't know the answer, except that there is...one thing. One strand."

"Was she always the goddess of disease?"

"That's the strand. That Birrur was condemned by the other gods to such a sphere after she betrayed Arok. So that Neir could keep her in line."

"Then what was she before?"

"I do not know. I suspect we are not meant to know."

Cat nodded. "That is a better explanation than the one that first came to my mind." She cut off a piece of meat, popped it in her mouth. A human would have been panting and reaching for a glass of water. "Whewf, T'la, just how much ilor did you use?"

"Enough to drive the average human to jump into the river."

"Tell me about it!" Cat laughed, and to show she was not upset, reached for another bite. She had always been able to eat spicy food...she was not sure why, as Liesa had hardly been adventurous with the heat.

"But I can see that you do, indeed, have demon blood."

"Anyone would think you..."

And a runner was suddenly approaching them. A boy, not much past apprentice age. Cat wondered how he had ended up a refugee.

"Come to the gate. Both of you."

"What's up?"

"I was...just told to tell you to come."

Cat took in the lad's expression. He wore the face of somebody who had just seen something more unpleasant than he had known before.

She did not hesitate...and she did not walk either. She leapt skywards, skimming low over the tents. T'la, somehow, was already ahead of her.

They touched down just inside the gate. The runner could come back or not. Cat suspected he would not. From the air, all they could see was a knot of people around two figures. A strange man was one of them, a tall, lean, man, his face and form hidden under the robes of a desert dweller.

And at his feet lay something green.

The crowd parted, and Cat felt, for a moment, nothing. On the ground, lay R'vor. He was naked, he was scarred in many places.

And somebody had cut off his wings.

T'la caught ablaze...the demonfire licked over her. Everything human leapt back, but Cat stayed with her. She could feel her own blood heating, but years of strong restraint kept it from exploding into the same brilliant aura.

"I'm going to kill them!" T'la exclaimed. She stepped over to her brother's form. Reached down, touched the hollow of his throat.

"Does he live?"

"Yes."

"Then cool. For a moment, cool." Cat turned to the desert dweller. "Where did you find him?"

He had moved back himself. Then, softly, "In the desert, about a mile south of Merico. I did not see what happened."

"But you knew enough to bring him here."

The man was regarding her evenly. "This was the closest place."

How had he seen through the wards? Cat narrowed her eyes, pulling herself together enough to use mage sight. And saw black fire.

The man was a cultist of Arok. But right now, she did not care. The only people she wanted dead right now were those who had crippled R'vor. It was quite likely he would not choose to live. As hard as being maimed was for a human, a demon with no wings had nothing.

They carried him to the tents that served as a house of healing. Kera stood in the doorstep, a question on her lips which died when she saw him.

Instead, she turned into one of the tents and called a name Cat didn't quite catch.

The man who emerged was one of the oldest Cat had ever seen. Like as not, he was the most experienced healer present. "Bring him inside."

Perceptive enough to determine demon gender. Cat glanced at T'la. She was no longer blazing, but her face was absolutely set in lines of control. It was clearly all she could do not to accidentally burn down a tent or two.

Cat was glad of the training she had had in emotional control. It kept her from being in the same state.

"I can save him," the healer said, softly. "But I cannot restore what he has lost..." He tailed off.

It was T'la who cut in. "That has to be his decision, not ours."

The healer did not frown, even for a moment. He nodded, moving for some of his equipment. "I need you to leave. I promise, when and if he wakes up, I will call you."

13

Cat stepped out of the tent. She would be nothing but in the way, and T'la was likely to be worse. In fact, the demoness stepped out a moment later and simply launched skywards. Hopefully she would not betray their location in her anger.

Kera looked up. "Cat..."

"Let her go. If she stays here she's likely to burn out half the camp. That's her clutch brother in there."

"Oh hell. Will he live?"

"I don't know." Cat did not want to explain the very real likelihood of R'vor committing suicide. "He won't fully recover..."

Kera simply nodded. "And not everyone *wants* to live crippled. Who did that to him?"

"I don't know. Particularly cruel..." Then she tailed off. "I'm going to kill them."

"What?"

"The man who attacked me. He said he would be paid well for my wings."

"And that demon male is about the same size you are..." Kera tailed off. "Well, hopefully the Mericans will take out their own trash."

"That won't be good enough for T'la." Cat's own wings twitched. "I'm not sure it's good enough for me. I'll be back." Her anger was such that she could not be around anyone right now, especially people she liked.

She walked straight towards Neir's shrine, head held high. The few people around gave her a wide berth. She must have looked as furious as she felt, the heat in her blood burning through her.

She walked right up to the altar. "I'm tired of this. Am I supposed to stop having friends out of fear of them getting hurt for me?"

Whoever had crippled R'vor had not even known she knew him. He had probably been coming after her, looking for her.

Looking out for her. And Laran had died protecting Liesa and Ylsa had just died, and she could feel the fire burning within her. "I won't let anyone else die for me. You hear that?" Raging at the goddess was probably not smart. It kept her from doing anything else stupid.

The response was what she expected. Utter silence, the desert wind blowing past her, around her, teasing at her hair. It wanted to lift her, and for a moment, she wished she had followed T'la. Got some of this out of her system.

She had filled the water bowl in Neir's temple in Merico, and the image of that came, unbidden. She stepped to the water bowl here. Full, despite how precious the fluid was. Full.

How the heck was it full, when any water left unattended would evaporate swiftly in this heat? Her scalp pricked. "You are here."

No answer, not in words. "Help me protect my friends." She had never expected to be this close to Neir; as a mage, she was supposed to care more for Seliene, who had given magic to humans.

Arok had given it to demons. She was not about to ask *Him*. Or was she? For a moment, it was tempting.

Something came over her, then, and she reached out to touch her fingertip to the water. Cool flowed through her, as if that small bowl could overtake all of the heat in her blood.

Her head cleared. "Thank you." The anger was not gone, but the fire that came with it was suddenly manageable. It no longer threatened to control her. She knew full well that Neir had done that, or her touch, in that moment, would have boiled the water. She had helped her protect her friends by getting her to think straight again.

Now she had to find T'la. She leapt upwards, not bothering to leave the area of the shrine...it was not, after all covered. The desert air caught her wings. Where had the demoness gone?

Not far, Cat knew, not with her brother still lying in the healer's tent. She would not leave him to seek vengeance.

R'vor. Who had told her she had such great potential, told her not to let the humans cripple her. Who had given her her swords. A graduation present.

Now they would be used to avenge him. But there was a coolness to her now. She no longer wanted to burn them alive, slowly. She still wanted them dead, because of what they had done. Because R'vor would likely not survive.

She would not if it was her, for all that her human friends would never understand. And there, circling, a speck as high as any demon ever flew. Cat found a thermal, let it lift her up and up.

The camp dwindled to toy size, then smaller. T'la was pushing her limits...burning the anger out of her system in flight.

She did not greet her, but joined the wheeling circle. The air lifted her with almost no effort. Her wings did not seem to tire...but that cool strength still flowed through her.

Maybe Neir did want her after all, but for what? She was no healer, no midwife and no assassin.

A small voice in her mind seemed to say 'patience'. Yes. Neir wanted her. Finally, T'la began to descend. "Where did you go?" the demoness asked.

"The shrines," Cat admitted.

"The human part of you."

"Not entirely. It's not always that simple." Things crossed between the two, flowed between them. Sometimes, she thought she was not both human and demon, but neither, a being apart.

"I would imagine not. Will you help me hunt them down?"

"He was my friend. Although the Mericans might well have taken care of them for us. I doubt fanatics take well to being tricked."

"I..." T'la tailed off. "You sound almost as if you hope for that."

"I don't want you to do anything stupid. Or to do anything stupid myself." Cool. The air up there had been cool, but now they descended back into stifling heat. They touched down outside the tent.

T'la studied her. "I was all set to find them and burn them to a crisp, but we need R'vor's help..."

Unspoken was the possibility that he might well not remember the attack, or be in any state to speak of it. And unspoken was...

No healer could restore what he had lost. Not even the high priestess of Neir in Losana. The healers might well be led to end things for him gently...although he might not choose that. Cat glanced at her own sword hilt.

More likely, he would ask T'la. His clutch sister. Who would grieve and carry on. She could not imagine that R'vor would want to live.

She was human enough to cry.

* * *

A night and a day passed with R'vor under the healer's care. She wondered how they felt about saving a life that they knew was likely to be ended anyway.

It had to be his choice. The healer had been oblique about the suggestion of euthanasia, but it had been there. Of course, they did not understand demons. Even a renegade would not choose to die in his sleep.

He might choose to live long enough to help them take down those who had maimed him. He might...

Cathren had not slept. Despite Neir's assistance, her mind had not been able to settle down enough. She had spent most of the night sitting just inside the gates, staring out into the desert. Nobody, not even T'la, had joined her.

Nobody knew what to make of her. Some at least did not trust her, and she could hardly blame them for that decision. Trust was something that had to be earned. Her clear wrath over the harming of a demon had probably not helped. They tolerated the demons in camp, but they most definitely did not like them.

Out of them, Cat trusted only T'la. Out of the humans, she was starting to trust only Kera. It went both ways.

The human part of you. T'la and R'vor had never much turned to gods, perhaps because they did not trust them. A demon who did not serve Arok was unwelcome in any other temple with the possible exception of Birrur's. And Birrur...

She shook her head. Neir was the god she was most interested in right now. The deity was up to something, and she was not sure what.

Was there any way to save R'vor? She did not know. No healer could regrow missing limbs or organs; that was the limit. Neir herself presumably had no limits, but why would Neir help a crippled demon?

"Take him to the house of healing in Merico."

Cat jumped. She jumped so high she was technically flying for a moment. Then she looked around. She did not see anyone. "What?"

"Look more closely."

A small yellow snake was curled on one of the rocks. "Okay. I see you now."

The snake hissed laughter. "Take him to Merico."

"That won't be easy. But I'll do my best." She knew better than to promise success to a deity's companion. That was how people got themselves geased.

The snake hissed again. "Good." And then it slithered back under a rock.

She could have been hallucinating. Gods knew she had lost enough sleep to. "I should have asked him what Neir wanted," she said out loud.

She got no answer except the one in her mind. He would not have told her. Of course he would not have. Companions of deities did not betray those deities' secrets. Not if they wanted to stay out of the canik house, anyway.

She stood up and walked back into the camp proper.

R'vor woke about two hours later. The second the healer told him Cathren and T'la were here, he demanded to see both of them.

He seemed very small and diminished...scars crossed his body, but he was alive.

"Brother," T'la said, meaningfully, reaching to take his hand. "Who did this?"

"Mercenaries. I did...did not see their faces. I'm sorry. I..." He tailed off.

"You won't have to..."

Cat cut T'la off, softly, "I have a message." She had not had time to speak it. "Neir asked me to bring him to the house of healing in Merico."

"Easier to go to the one in Losana." R'vor managed a hint of his old humor.

"We can do it. I'm an expert at glamors, I can disguise us all as humans."

"The Solusians saw through your glamor before."

"Point."

"The only way we're going to get R'vor there without being caught and killed is to take back the city."

"Which we were working on anyway." Cathren reached out, placed a hand on R'vor's chest. "I don't know...what she is offering or asking. She wasn't that specific. But stay with us a little while. Please?"

The demon's chest rose and fell. "A little while."

She wanted to hug him, but demons did not hug. That kind of close physical contact outside of mating made them uncomfortable.

If the only way was to take back the city, then take back the city they would.

The question was how. They certainly, Cat thought as she sat on the back of a caba...a means of getting more height to view the camp without actually taking off...did not have enough people for a city siege.

No, this would have to be done from inside. Tava was already in there. She might be able to help, or she might call Cat crazy and refuse to participate.

She could be counted on only to a point. No. They needed a plan. If the people were really content under the mayor's rule, then this would not be easy.

The death of the demon child might be something they could use as leverage, as much as she hated to do so. And most Mericans would not see it as that much of an atrocity. It was only a demon, after all.

She shook her head. Only a demon. Those words echoed in her mind. Only a human. Far too easy to turn them around.

She was not only a human to R'vor. And Neir was using him as bait to get what she wanted. She knew that. She disliked being manipulated, even by a goddess. On the other hand...there was a small shrine to Neir here, but it had not echoed with the goddess' presence for thousands of years. The one in Losana would have been better...but as dangerous as it was to get him into Merico, getting him across the mountains in his current state? They would be likely to end up dragon food. Or just robbed by bandits and left to die in the high passes.

No. Maybe it simply was the best plan...except if Neir could send a messenger out here. Or appear on the road. She was using them.

"You know," she murmured to the air. "You could just have asked."

Of course, in a way, she had. The extra incentive...but then, what Neir offered to R'vor might be nothing more than ease. Or might it?

Cat shook her head. The goddess could, in theory, do whatever she wanted. In practice, there seemed to be limitations on the gods. Rules, perhaps, that they themselves chose to live under. It might be essential to the balance of the world that they did.

It might be that they did not want to risk another situation as had happened with Arok. So, Neir could not retake the city. She had to ask them to do it. Offering a reward made sense, even if it...

Cat got it straight in her mind. Focus, she told herself. Focus on the task at hand.

A small team, go into the city. Assassinate the Mayor and his cronies. That could work, if people really did not care which regime was in charge.

If they actually supported him, though, it could create a monster.

The Solusians could see through glamors, and they had to take R'vor with them. Okay. Think.

It was only in stories that people sneaked into cities through the sewers. Merico's would be narrow and grated, by the nature of a desert city that could afford to waste nothing. Over the walls, with an invisibility spell? Risky, but possible.

The truth was, though, people in Merico were happy. What right did she have to mess with that?

They were happy, but they only had one temple to worship in. Which was more important?

Over the walls. Could they do it without taking back the city?

No, ultimately, the people of Merico had to choose. Whichever way they chose, R'vor's fate would be decided. Or would it? She shook her head. Nobody in Merico would choose to help a demon. Or even the half-breed.

However, they could choose to welcome back in the priests of Neir. She frowned, then she hopped down from the beast and went in search of Kera.

14

She found the woman coming out of the tent that still held R'vor.

"How is he?" Cat asked.

"Depressed. I do not think he wants to live like this. And Neir is not giving me a straight answer."

"Neir wants us to take him to the healers back in Merico. I doubt she cares exactly how we achieve that."

"I would normally suggest waiting until people become desperate..."

"It is very likely somebody in there already is. If that person is significant enough to put pressure on the mayor..." Cat tailed off. "R'vor might not be able to wait that long. He wants to die. I do not blame him."

"I suppose I cannot understand that."

"Would you be depressed if you lost your legs? Now imagine if your culture wrapped up usefulness in the ability to walk." Kera was a healer, but she was also very human. Humans and demons did not understand each other.

Cat could, she realized, be a bridge. An emissary between the races, if they were willing to talk.

"Alright. I will not pretend I understand, but the analogy helps. Do you think Neir will help him?"

"One way or another." If Neir would not, then either Cat or T'la would have to help R'vor die. She did not explain that to Kera, though. Not yet.

"And we both know what the other way is. However...she only encourages us to do what needs to be done. With us expelled, people will start dying soon."

Cat nodded. "The best idea I have is to simply go in and kill the mayor."

"Not enough. We would have to take out the radicals amongst the Solusians too. And..."

"If you do that, it is followers of Neir against followers of Solus. If I do it..." She was sworn to no god. "Then it is revenge for R'vor." Cat could not let revenge rule her, but she could channel it.

"I was actually thinking..."

"I am sworn to no god." None had ever felt right. Had she been steered against that course? Logic suggested that, and she frowned inwardly. On the other hand, it was highly useful now. "I will take the team."

"You will need some expertise."

"I will probably take T'la. Apart from anything else, if I don't, she is going to be a loose cannon." She also had to take R'vor.

"I have a couple of other recommendations. Do you plan on going over the walls?"

"I don't see any other way we're going to get in there. I would not fit through the sewers and I doubt a human would either. I'd wear a glamor and walk right through the gate, but..."

"They detected you before."

Cat nodded. "They will be watching the gates. Do you know..."

"Wait. There is one gate they might not be watching."

One gate indeed. The gate of the dead. The gate used solely to take bodies out to their shallow graves outside the city.

Naturally, it was not intended to be opened from the outside. There were spells that took care of that. Cat frowned as she murmured one, sliding the gate open and slipping within. Five people, three of them demons disguised as humans.

They had had to wait until R'vor was well enough to move, and even now, he was not well. He said nothing...he had barely spoken to her. He was angry with her for asking him to stay alive.

She hoped it would be worth it for him. The gate let out onto a street that ran straight to the temple quarter, but that was not their first destination.

The young man who moved ahead now was the same archer who had helped her against the mage. He knew the way.

It was that part of the night when most slept. The desert and the city were both bitterly cold. Only a warming spell kept R'vor and T'la from going into cold torpor. Cat, thanks to her human half, was doing somewhat better.

If they were caught they would all be killed for sure. Or worse...crippled like R'vor.

She shook her head. If they were caught...this was an act of war they were committing. More than that, it was an act that could legitimately lead to such punishment. They were about to take down a regime.

A regime the people liked. It felt a little sour in her mouth. Somehow, she felt, they should give these people the choice. And how to do it slowly flowed into her. They were not setting out to kill the mayor.

They were setting out to capture him. Softly through the cobbled streets. Here and there a sign swung in the breeze. Merico at night did not give that impression of unmitigated white it did by day. Rather, it was a place of shadows. Shadows. She checked that she had remembered that detail of the glamor. Paranoia.

Nerves.

She had never done anything like this before, and she had offered to do it. She had spoken with such confidence nobody had questioned that she was ready.

It could not be Neir against Solus. The entire coup had to take place without the healers, without those sworn to any god. One of those behind her was even Solusian himself. The dead child might convince these people.

Or she might. What better evidence was there that humans and demons could live together...or at least in an uneasy state of truce. Nothing better had ever been achieved. They did not understand each other, they could not.

She shook her head a little. Worry about the task at hand. The task, first, getting to the palace and taking care of the mayor. Then dealing with the Solusians. The palace was, of course, centrally located.

It looked nothing like Losana's Imperial complex, that being a small city in and of itself, with its own walls. Instead, it was a squat, square building. Small slit windows allowed air in and kept out heat and cold. In short, it looked like any other building in Merico, except for its size. Its size and the heavy doors that blocked all entrances.

"How are we going to get in?" That was R'vor. He spoke for the first time in what felt like an eternity. His voice was so soft.

Her heart strings tugged. She felt horribly guilty for this. "A simple knock spell is not going to do it. Their locks..." She tailed off. She could blast their way in, but that would wake up the immediate area. The front gate was guarded, but...she moved around the side, around to one which might not be. There. No guards, just a door as heavy as the front, if not more so.

"How well protected are the hinges?"

The hinges. She walked up to them. "Aha." She rested a hand on one, murmuring a spell she had only cast once before. Slowly, the metal began to rust. It was a fire spell, but a very slow one.

Rust was iron burning, slowly, she had been told. Then she pushed the door inwards, gently. It swung on the lock.

"Nice," the archer complimented. He slipped ahead of her to take point.

She stepped inside. This was a side entrance, a servants' entrance no doubt. It was narrow and the first door on the right was a store room. It was firmly locked, and she ignored it beyond testing that. They did not need anyone coming up behind them.

There were no torches in the corridor, and after a moment, T'la took over from the archer. Cat cast a gentle light spell, one that was deliberately intended to give only what demon eyes needed.

She suddenly realized what was happening. Two humans, two demons and her. Working together. How often did that occur? Not often enough?

But there was Arok, there was the ancient war, there was conflict so deep that it could not be simply set aside. She shook her head. There might be the slightest hope of peace, but she would not hold her breath for it.

This place was a labyrinth. Kitchens...which she poked her head in. She found it hard to resist stealing food, but anything left out now was hardly going to be fresh. A cook was lying by the stove, on the floor, storing softly. Possibly her way of making sure she was up early enough to start breakfast.

Cat moved on. The cook did not strike her as a threat. Stairs led upwards and the archer bounded up them. He emerged a moment later. "Servants' quarters," he whispered. "Everyone's asleep."

"Let's hope they stay that way, Marrick." She took a deep breath, and then they were in the inner courtyard.

A fountain lay in the center, but it had been turned off. In the desert, a way of demonstrating wealth. There was even some greenery, although in this light it looked dark, black even. Just the shape of leaves. "Okay. So..." She turned to the other human. "Where does he sleep?"

The young woman had been keeping her head down. Now she developed a nervous expression. "He sleeps right up in the tower."

Cat nodded. "Guard room below?"

"His women's quarters are immediately below, then a guard room, yes."

Cat noticed the plural of women and felt a twinge of pity for the man's wife. Nothing spoke of dissatisfaction more than a husband who kept concubines under his own roof. She shook her head. "The women are not to be harmed. The guards...try to avoid killing them, but make sure they don't wake up any time soon." T'la nodded, moving ahead again. The demoness had a metal staff. Cat readied her blades, but did not draw them.

Not yet.

The lowest floor of the tower was simply a room. It had virtually no furniture in it, and stairs led down. Probably to the well, for all that the paranoid part of her whispered dungeon. Stairs led up along the outer wall, vanishing into darkness.

She strengthened the light spell a little and followed T'la upwards, the archer bringing up the rear. R'vor had his own weapon out, she noticed. Her blades slid easily from their sheaths as T'la...simply kicked in the door.

Now the alarm would be raised, but at this point, it did not matter.

There were three guards, and they rolled to their feet, weapons in hand. They had been asleep, but apparently lightly enough for it not to matter. That or they had already been woken by wards, but not moved until they were sure.

T'la's staff became a whirling wall as she came into the room. "Stand down, and you won't be harmed."

"Demons!" one of them snarled. He sounded more angry than surprised.

"We have no quarrel with you," Cat said, softly.

"By all the gods, it does exist," he snarled.

It. Cat did not waste the energy on being offended. "I am here."

Then, there was a soft voice, coming down the stairs. A female voice. "Neir sent you."

"Not exactly." The woman who descended was one of the most lovely Cat had ever seen. Her skin was dark, very dark, a rich color.

Her hair was black and flowed almost to her knees. Every curve was exactly where Cat would have most wanted it to be. She felt a surge of desire.

If this was the mayor's wife, she could not understand the need for concubines. If she was his concubine...that would make more sense.

"Neir should stay out of this. This city belongs to Solus now."

"It has nothing to do with that." The woman held Cat, she realized she was being ensorceled by a magic older than magic itself. It was all she could do not to drop her weapons and approach her.

Then R'vor was between them. "It has to do with the crimes that have been committed. The expulsion of the healers causes death. The death of a child. And this."

"Get that demon out of my sight."

The guards started to step forward. Cat crossed her blades. She glanced at T'la. "We aren't going anywhere until we have talked to the mayor."

"Ah. I give you joy of that," the woman said. "Let them go upstairs. Why not?"

"Hold her."

It was R'vor who moved. The demons were immune to the sexual allure the woman broadcast. Which did not fit Solus. He was not a god who was big into sexuality. No. Something else was going on here, something Cathren did not understand.

She went up the stairs. The guards allowed her, although T'la was clearly in a position to knock them out and Marrick had switched to his short sword. At the top of the stairs was the women's quarters. A woman slept like a log in one of the beds. Cat headed up the next flight, tucked off to one side.

This, then, was the quarters of the mayor of Merico. In a chair, a man rocked, asleep. He stirred as she came in.

"Mayor."

No response.

She repeated the word louder. He might be hard of hearing. Nothing.

Cat stepped around to look at the face of the mayor of Merico. She saw the visage of a drooling idiot.

The young woman had come in behind her. "He was not like this the last time I was here."

"No. I would imagine...he had a brainstorm." All of the symptoms were there. "And his concubine has been hiding his condition and running the city."

"That would explain everything. I thought he had gone mad."

Cat stepped over to the mayor. "Then all we need is to provide evidence of his condition. That woman, however, will not let us leave here alive."

Cat would probably have to kill the woman, but that would be...no. T'la would have to do it. Cat could not trust herself. The only thing she wanted to do with that woman involved a bed.

"No, she will not."

Cat took a deep breath. She turned to the maid. "I want you to try and get the mayor out of here. I realize that is not an easy task. But I want it to be your only focus. Please."

The girl nodded, her face pale and nervous. As it should be. Cat had given her the hardest job, in some ways.

Then Cat walked down the steps. "Clever," she said as she faced the woman again.

Who was facing it off with T'la. The tiniest hint of flames surrounded the demon.

"Not in here, T'la."

"She is..." T'la tailed off, then she spun her staff again.

The air around the woman flared blue. Shield spell. "I think this one is for me to handle, T'la."

As little as she wanted to. The woman's beauty distracted her once more.

"Oh, really? I am well aware of your preferences halfbreed. Tell me, could you truly harm me?"

Cat willed the rest to flee. To get out of there. She sensed this confrontation was for her. "After what your people did to R'vor?" Cat threw a blast of energy at the other mage. It splashed harmlessly off of the shield.

"Ah. Stronger than I suspected. But not strong enough."

Behind the mage, Cat could see the maid guiding the mayor...what remained of him...down the stairs. Keep her attention, she thought.

"I'd rather not burn down the tower. I suspect you share that sentiment." Cat held off on another attack, throwing the energy, instead, into her own shield. Her magesight was focused on her opponent.

She had never dueled for real. For play, of course, for training, with everyone careful not to cause real harm.

This was...not for real. The blast the woman threw back was clearly a fraction of what she was capable of. "You also don't want to kill me."

"Perceptive. Your friends think they can get away. Half of the Solusian cult is outside. You will be alone, Cathren the Black."

Keep control, she told herself. Control. "Don't underestimate them. Besides, they have your puppet with them."

"A pity. He was useful. However, they will not be able to prove his illness did not happen yesterday."

Cat did not attack again. She regarded her. "You can't say this was all to get to me."

"Of course not. Your arrival was simply a pleasant bonus. No, this is all about ensuring human survival until the end of the world."

"Really."

"Really. By the time we are done, halfbreed, there will be no place on this world for demons."

Cat circled the woman, still regarding her. Then she threw the most powerful dispel at her she could.

It hit with a flare of red-gold, and when it cleared, a reasonably handsome young man stood there.

"Wow," Cat complimented. "Not even your natural gender. You might be better at glamors than me."

"Nice dispel. They trained you well. It will avail nothing, of course. Unless you join me."

"Why would I want to do that?"

"To be free of the taint of your blood."

Cathren laughed. The guard room, sadly, had no windows. Instead of going down, she ran upwards, knowing the other would follow.

He did. He followed her up into the mayor's quarters. "To be free of the darkness."

"This is only a taint when people say it is." She spread her wings. "It is something you cannot understand. No human can." And no demon, she wanted to add, but felt somehow it would ruin the effect.

"So, you choose to be one of them?"

"And you put a bounty on my wings." Cat could sense the other readying a spell.

"You would be better off without them."

And Cat leapt. Upwards, as quick as she could, her shield flaring around her and demonfire licking along her wings. The blast that followed her clipped her left wing, tore away part of the membrane, but she was away.

She hissed between her teeth, spiraling downwards. Where were the others? Fleeing seemed the wisest course of action. She could possibly have taken the man, or woman...she was suddenly no longer sure which...but it would have taken everything out of her.

They had to show the mayor's state to the people of Merico. Then they would hold elections, choose somebody else. That was how it worked, that was the system. Working within it...

Her wing hurt. Her wing hurt a lot. She landed near the others and T'la flinched. "She nailed you a good one. I think we need to get you somewhere where I can patch it."

Cat nodded, folding her wings. "She was trying to shoot me down. Damn near succeeded. Or he. I'm no longer sure." The pain faded to a dull throb. "Let's get the mayor to the house of healing. And then we need to get the healers in here."

Her heartrate was returning, slowly, to normal.

"What about the mage?"

"I'll deal with him. Just not right now. I need preparation. And we need to...I know what he's up to."

"What?" T'la asked as they moved quickly away from the palace.

"Starting a war."

15

The Solusians attacked them three seconds later. Cat whirled, drawing her blades, but she was slowed by her injury. For a moment, she was sure and certain she was going to go down, then T'la's staff swung into a jaw and one of those on her went down.

"This is not good."

It was not. They were outnumbered, R'vor could only do so much. "T'la. You can still fly. You should take the mayor somewhere public."

"Not leaving you."

"Do it. I can't get off the ground carrying somebody."

And T'la was gone, and the only thing present was the opponents. She could not hold back from killing. That was a luxury for situations when the fight was equal. One blade thrust through a man's heart. He gasped as he slid off it, surprise more than pain showing on his face.

Her wing was no longer hurting, but she kept both tightly furled. She could still, just about, get off the ground, but to do so was to abandon R'vor and the others.

It seemed as if she had been fighting for hours, but she knew it was only a bare few minutes. All she could think about and focus on was what her blades were doing. She had been wounded, but she barely felt it. There were only her blades, and controlling the fire that threatened to sweep out from her, it flowed along her swords.

She hit another man, he caught fire, screaming, she finished him with the second blade.

Then suddenly there was silence. Just for a moment, then a faint roar.

Her opponent turned, exposing his back. Rather than take advantage, she turned too.

People were coming up the street towards the palace. The Solusian wheeled, trying to put his blade into her heart before they came. She blocked, barely, the tip of his sword sliding along hers. Then, he turned and fled.

Cat did not pursue him. She did not know what had caused the people to awaken and come, but she did not care. Instead, she leapt skywards, awkwardly, and flew to the House of Healing.

There was a crowd there too. She almost fell as she landed...and knew she should not attempt to fly again until her wing had been repaired. It would heal, especially with skilled help, but she was going to be grounded for a little while. She wished she could have brought R'vor with her.

The crowd had T'la and the mayor surrounded.

"Are we sure the demon did not do this?"

Cat shook her head. "There was an illusionist in the palace."

"Halfbreed!" The crowd's mood was uncertain.

"T'la, please, go get R'vor. I can't carry anyone right now."

T'la nodded and then took off. Cat turned to the crowd. She was not sure that the crowd by the palace had intended to harm the Solusians or help them, but their panic had probably saved her life. "I realize that I'm probably not the person you want to be talking to right now." She felt a little faint. How much blood had she lost? "But the truth is the mayor was like that when we found him. We don't know for how long. You should worry about finding a new leader, not us."

"You should worry about finding a healer," said a more sympathetic voice.

"Given the mayor tossed them all out..." Cat's voice sounded weak to her own ears.

"We need healers," said another voice. "A healer might be able to fix the mayor."

Cat doubted that. Unless it suited Neir for him to be well again, the mayor would be like this until he died. He might recover some. She forced her breathing even. "We do need healers. Maybe somebody should go and let them in."

The world began to spin at that point, and she collapsed to the ground.

Her next clear awareness found her lying on her side in a bed. Her wing still ached a little.

Slowly, she sat up, twisting around to feel it. Somebody had quite expertly patched the membrane, and her shoulder was bandaged. Other than that, she felt almost fine. Almost.

Yes, her wing ached. She felt a little light headed and a lot hungry. "Anyone here?"

T'la walked in. With a plate full of meat.

It was all Cat could do not to gorge herself. She took a piece and munched on it. "Thank you."

"You need meat. You lost a fair amount of blood. The wing should be fine, I expect I'll be able to remove the patch in a few days."

"How long was I out?"

"Only a few hours. The healers are returning, but they will not be here for a little while."

"R'vor?"

"He has not left Neir's shrine. Oddly, he is praying for you."

"Once I feel I can stand straight, I think I may go join him." She still felt dizzy.

"Take it easy. And don't fly until you are sure you don't feel dizzy or weak."

That seemed like sound advice to Cat. T'la offered her a glass of water. She drained it. "I don't think I've ever really been hurt before."

"Try not to get used to it," T'la quipped. "The healers might be able to help when they get here...at least get some speed healing on that wing."

"I might as well ask." Of course, how often had any of them healed a demon? But the same magic that could spread skin over a burn should work. Cat did not move until she had eaten the entire plate of meat. It felt heavy in her stomach, but she knew she needed it. Would she have a scar or two? Most likely...but then, she had never cared that much for her looks. Not in the way some women did.

T'la had already departed. Slowly, Cat made her way out of the room and down a corridor that led to the priests' entrance to Neir's temple.

Not a view she had ever expected to have, as she entered to one side of the shrine itself.

R'vor knelt there. He seemed a small, broken figure, and no matter how much she still ached, the image of him praying for her...

She walked over, rested a hand on his shoulder. "R'vor."

Then she turned to the shrine. He was looking up at her, she saw the relief in his eyes. "Lady. Help him." It wasn't much of a prayer, but honestly, was she not owed something?

Her own injuries would heal, his would not. He was her closest remaining friend, and she did not wish to end his life. Or even to watch T'la do so.

There was only silence. Only silence for a long moment, and a breeze from nowhere rippling the surface of what little water was in the bowl.

Cat frowned. R'vor had probably filled it when he came in here, but she found an ewer and topped it up. Almost a mechanical action, and she remembered when she had done it before. Because it was the right thing to do.

Softly, "I will be back shortly." She stepped out into the sun. The temples surrounded her.

Each one, except for that of Solus, was neglected. Even in Solus', though, the sacred light had gone out. She lit it again, and then went from shrine to shrine, in each one repairing that that which was the duty of the priests.

It should not have been hers, but nobody else had thought to do it, and now there was nobody to, as she suspected, knock over bowls or remove food.

The worshippers would return, but in the mean time, the gods would be reminded that people cared. Or that somebody did, anyway.

She hesitated at Birrur's shrine. Stood in front of it for a long moment. Next to it was the shrine of Arok, but that had been abandoned for centuries.

What could she do, in truth, other than acknowledge even them. If she was going to be completely fair about it, she should light the flame in Arok's shrine too, but if she did...

If she did, everyone would assume it had been T'la and castigate the demoness as an Arok worshipper.

"I'm sorry," she whispered, meaning it. Birrur's shrine, she could tend to. Arok's...all she could do was send a small flicker of demonfire towards it.

What was she doing? Arok wanted humankind dead. Did Solus want demonkind dead? The one was as bad as the other.

The war had to end. She walked back to Neir's shrine, thinking about that. Did ending the war mean...

...that the entire prophecy about her would be fulfilled after all? She shook her head. She had agreed she would not be that person.

Yet, she had never promised, never sworn a sacred oath. Never sworn herself to any god.

She stepped into the temple. R'vor still knelt by the altar. Nothing had changed, and she walked up to his side. Maybe...

...maybe Neir had...she had, after all, promised nothing.

"Oh, you of little faith," came a voice.

R'vor's head snapped upwards.

The snake was coiled on the altar.

"Why am I not surprised it's you?"

The little yellow and black head lifted and hissed. "You are starting to learn." Then he slithered down from the altar and over to R'vor.

R'vor looked down at the serpent. "Messenger." He seemed distinctly uncomfortable.

R'vor had always, Cat reminded herself, avoided having anything to do with the gods, any of them. He had expressed the opinion that all they did was cause trouble. They had had arguments about it, fun ones that went back and forth. Yet now, he was face to face with the servant of one.

And at Her mercy.

"You lack trust," the snake informed R'vor. "Are you willing to give it?"

The tension in the air was palpable. Cat, standing behind the demon, could not see the expression on his face. She could see only his scarred back, the stubs that had been wings. She closed her eyes for the briefest of moments.

"Yes." What else did R'vor have after all, but there was sincerity in his tone along with the struggle. Trusting anyone did not come easy to him.

Snakes do not nod, of course. And all this one did, was dart forward and close its fangs onto R'vor's arm. The demon shuddered and then collapsed.

Cat moved to feel for a pulse. Had Neir granted R'vor only the last of blessings. No, for his heartbeat was there, strong and sure. He was simply deeply unconscious.

She lifted her head from him, regarding the snake.

"Oh, and..." The snake moved again, although this time its mouth was closed. It was suddenly *on* Cat, slithering up her to rest on her shoulder for a moment. "I don't think you have time to wait for that wing to heal."

A warmth flowed through her for a moment.

"There we go. Be ready." And then it vanished.

If it could heal her, then why could it not heal R'vor? She spread her wing, and there was no hint of pain.

She moved to scoop up R'vor. He did not have to lie here...and perhaps the deep sleep he had been cast into was healing of a sort. There were proper beds in the house of healing itself, where he could rest.

He did not stir, but he was heavy in her arms. It was hard work getting him back into the room where she had been kept. She laid him down, carefully, on the bed.

Only then did she notice that the stubs of his wings were a little longer, a little larger.

Kera rested one hand on R'vor's sleeping shoulder. "Neir..."

"Her snake. He has been like this since."

"I would imagine that regrowing limbs while awake would be somewhat painful. Yet...why..."

"The snake did imply that he would be helped if he was brought here. I think it's our reward for restoring her shrine."

"Let's take a look at *your* wing." Kera moved to remove the patching enough to see. "Looks fine. Not that I have ever treated a demon before."

"As long as the membrane is solid across the gap, it's fine. I'll probably still have to take it easy for a couple of days." Cat stretched the wing outwards.

Kera was still inspecting it. "A hunter once brought in an entire dragon wing. The structure is quite similar, you know."

"Well, it has to be to be effective, I suppose." She folded her wings again. "I've only ever seen dragons from a distance. Frankly, I'd just as soon leave them alone. Stealing their eggs seems distinctly unfair to me."

"I suppose it would seem very unfair to a demon, although I have no idea whether you would..."

Cat cut in, "I have no interest in trying the experiment, actually. And the theory at the academy is that I am unlikely to be fertile. Of course, given I only exist because of high level magic..."

"Who knows. But I suppose..." Kera looked at R'vor again. "I suspect he will be recovered in about a week. He is more in a trance than asleep. We will have to trust Neir."

"Who is up to something still, I suspect, but then, I think the gods always are. What's going on bothers me."

"It was..." Then Kera frowned. "You are afraid it was not just fanatics."

"I've had a human faction try to kill everyone I cared about, a demon faction give me the join us or die speech...something is going on. What happened here is just a part of it, and I have no clue how to uncover the rest. And Neir told me I did not have time to rest."

"Maybe Neir just wants to recruit *you*."

"Not likely. I'm a lousy healer and I'd make a lousy assassin. I don't know. She's always taken an interest in me, but I've never felt a calling to choose her as a patron. Her or anyone."

"You never have the slightest temptation to worship Arok?"

"I never have the slightest temptation to join him. Honor him, yes."

"He did..."

Cat hesitated as Kera tailed off. "I know what he did. It does not make the people who go after demons as if they were vermin any better."

Kera nodded. "I can't imagine going after you or T'la...but then, I suppose..."

"Like most people, you have never been in a situation to get to know a demon. Even the renegades keep to themselves." Cat considered that. "R'vor was my friend as a child. He taught me about that part of my heritage...much against my guardian's wishes."

"Your guardian was probably afraid you'd jump ship."

"I can't say I didn't consider it. On the other hand, there are parts of me that are far too human to be entirely happy with them."

She rested a hand on R'vor's shoulder. "For now, I need to take a walk. Please keep a watch on him."

"I will."

"And when he wakes up, if T'la isn't around, make sure he gets meat. Doesn't have to be cooked."

Kera laughed uncomfortably. "Doesn't have to be?"

"He'd probably prefer it cooked, but he also probably won't care that much." Cat smiled at Kera. "Thank you."

16

It was day when she stepped outside, but still relatively cool. People were on the streets...she wrapped her glamor around herself and joined them, watching their mood.

They seemed, for the most part, to care little about events. A few seemed unhappy, a few seemed highly relieved. Most were simply going about their business, the way ordinary people did no matter what happened.

They were those who would be most hurt if this turned into a war. Taking back Merico for reasonable people, had they actually done so, might have prevented it.

Cat shook her head. Humans might grow wings and fly. Her shoulder still ached a little. Neir had, for whatever reason, not healed that. Maybe to remind her to dodge better next time. That was a R'vor thought for sure.

R'vor would live. He would fly again. She had been given that...and she had no illusions but that it was a gift for her, not the demon himself.

She still had one friend. She dared not make more. Kera could easily be her friend, but she shied away from the emotional attachment. Heck, she would not mind sleeping with Kera...except that she was pretty sure that she was not the healer's type.

Beria's face floated before her. She knew her lover would want her to move on, but not yet. Not just yet. And the illusionist, and which form had been the true one? Neither, she suspected. Somebody that skilled could easily put up a second glamor the moment after a dispel to fool the attacker. She could quite probably do it herself.

Laran. Ylsa. R'vor. But R'vor was alive, and she was determined to ensure he remained so. She wondered what next.

Wondered it as the sun vanished behind a cloud. Was that normal? She glanced around...and saw the street rapidly empty. "What?"

A man touched her arm. "You're not from around here. Come on...it might only rain here a few times a year, but when it does..."

She followed him into one of the shops. "It doesn't do it by halves, eh?"

He nodded. "You stay out there, and you'll be a dripping mess in no time at all."

The sky was distinctly darkening. "Thank you for rescuing me, then."

The man laughed. "Some people enjoy laughing at those who get caught out. I don't."

And then...the heavens opened. Cat had never seen rain like this in her life. "You could drown out there!"

"Not quite, but if it actually floods...I don't think this one will, though."

Cat nodded, watching the water stream down. "Does the city have a means to capture this water?"

"Yes. There are drainage channels that will direct it into a reservoir under the city. Not all of it, but enough to help. You are from the west?"

Cat nodded again, looking out through the doorway. "It rains more often, but it does not rain like this. I'm not used to the desert."

"You'll either get used to it...or leave." The man moved back behind his counter.

She realized she was in the store of a perfumier. The smell had not really entered into her consciousness immediately. Now it did, as she was no longer distracted by the conversation. A mixture of scents that flowed in and around her. If she stayed in here too long she might end up buying something.

She laughed inwardly. She did not wear perfume. She would buy it for Ylsa, and Ylsa was gone. She would...it was the kind of bitter laughter one uses to stave off pain.

She turned away so the storekeeper could not see it, examining some crystal bottles. Fine workmanship, that she could have made use of herself under other circumstances.

She found herself missing her alchemist's shop in Losana...and wondering if she would ever go back to it.

She doubted it. Could she really go back to such a semblance of normality? It had only ever been pretense, but it had been pleasant pretense.

Pleasant pretense, she thought again. Wasn't that how most people lived? "Where do you source your bottles?"

"My cousin, Tara. She is very talented."

"So I can see. I might be interested in making some purchases from her."

He glanced at her again. Studied her for a long moment. "Purchases of what?"

"Quality plain bottles. For potions."

"You're an alchemist?" He perked up.

There was, after all, a certain similarity between the two crafts. Cat glanced outside. The rain was not going away any time soon. She might as well talk shop. For once, she had nothing better to do.

The rain had washed Merico clean, the buildings even whiter than before. It had also settled the endless dust. It was a pleasant night, but there was tension. The people were starting the long process of choosing a new mayor.

The old one, it seemed, would not recover. That was the diagnosis of the healers. Kera had, an hour before, voiced that she suspected he had been struck down by a spell.

A spell. Cat knew she should not have let that mage get away. She watched with her magesight for anyone sporting a glamor, but none entered the small tavern in which she sat. She was trying, once more, to acquire the taste of raksha. Her level of success was about what it had been previously. She'd rather have that stuff demons called wine.

Which was also pretty vile.

"I know who you are."

She looked up, then pushed out a chair for the owner of the voice. Stranger or no, she detected no threat from him. His tone and expression were both remarkably pleasant. "You may know more than I do, then."

He sat down. "Do you ever work for hire?"

"That depends on what you want to hire me to do. I've done caravan work." Which was technically true. She wondered where the noblewoman was now. Had she made it to Merico? Had she ever intended to come here?

"I'm afraid it's not caravan work. The nomads took my daughter."

She nodded. "Did she go voluntarily?"

He sank a bit. "I don't know. I would have to find her to find that out, and I can't. I was hoping that somebody who was a traveler and a mage could..."

"How long ago?"

"Two days."

"Do you have anything that belonged to her? Or better yet, a lock of her hair?"

He frowned. "Not with me. I can get something, though."

"If you do that, I might be able to track her. However, what if that's where she wants to be?"

"We'll cross that bridge when we come to it. She is young..."

"And thus possibly foolish, although not necessarily so." Cat smiled at him. "I can help you."

She felt no sense that she should not, despite the urgency the snake had imparted. Of course, she would not have been healed enough to do this without him. Possibly, she was meant and intended to go after the girl.

Possibly it was a distraction. On the other hand, she saw no reason not to try it.

"Thank you." He paused. "I would have asked one of the local mages, but..."

"Let me guess. Half won't leave the academy and the other half won't leave their labs."

He laughed. "With a few exceptions. No offense, but most of the mages I know seem to prefer to keep their noses in books over actually doing anything."

"I think it's the way we're trained these days."

"Maybe. Maybe the entire coup thing will shake some people out of their complacency."

"Well, who knows how long that woman would have..." Cat tailed off.

"That woman...nobody knows where she came from, even. Let alone who she was. She just showed up, and apparently..."

"I suspect she had a love spell on him. She is quite a competent mage. I'm not even sure she's a she."

The man winced. "Is that..."

"If you're good enough at personal illusions, quite possible. I could disguise myself as a man if I felt the need." Cat considered that. "I've used similar disguises. But I cannot be sure if I saw her natural form or another layer of illusion."

"Well. She's..."

"She's not gone. She's out there somewhere, looking for more trouble to cause. Let's worry about what we can solve for now. Get me something that belonged to your daughter."

He nodded, slipping out of the tavern. Within an hour he was back with a broken comb. It was obvious that the daughter would not have taken it with her, even if her departure was voluntary. It had quite a number of teeth missing. It also had several strands of red hair.

Red hair. The daughter was a firehead. It was highly unusual and some people thought it ill luck. Cat had only met one...and he had never struck her as unlucky.

However, if somebody was looking for a concubine, then she might well be valued. She said nothing on the matter, although she was certain she had not been able to conceal her surprise. A tracking spell would be simple now, although she would not attempt it here. "I will contact you in the morning with what I find."

Assuming the girl was not dead. That was a distinct possibility. The cult sacrified people every now and then, and a firehead would be desirable to them.

She felt a sudden urgency at the thought, perhaps only a natural concern to ensure that course of events did not happen. Most likely only that.

She locked herself in her room to cast the spell, not because she really needed to, but because the feeling that there could be a life at stake made her take more precautions. The thought of it flowed over and through her.

A scry, first, to establish whether she was alive and where she was. Cat's mind expanded outwards.

North. She felt that the girl was somewhere to the north, but where she was was dark and...rattled.

She was in a wagon. A covered wagon, dark to protect the contents from day's heat and night's cold. It told Cat little, but at least the girl lived. For now, at least.

North. She would have to do an ongoing tracker to find out more, and she felt a sudden pressure.

She withdrew quickly. Somebody had detected her scry and attempted to send a spell along the track of it. Academy trained, she avoided the attack, although she would not call it easy. She would call it...something, but not easy.

"Well. I'm going to need backup for this," she told herself. "Definitely."

The next morning, there was no sign that it had ever rained. She ate a quick breakfast, contemplating who to take with her.

R'vor was far from able to travel and she would not ask T'la to leave him. Which left Marrick, the young archer. And possibly Kera...although taking a healer along?

Wise or not? She was not sure, and then there was Tava. Tava and Marrick for sure, then.

Would three be enough? More than that would attract more attention. Of course, they would need fast cabas. Alone, she could fly after the caravan and easily catch up a three day head start, but alone she could not take on a nomad group that had at least one mage with them.

Fast cabas, then. The best they could get. The girl's father...she would ask him if he wanted to come along. He had the right, after all, although she had some misgivings. Did he have the fighting skills needed not to be a liability?

He had the right. She told herself that firmly. He was an adult, capable of his own risk assessment. And it was still possible the girl had eloped with a nomad.

North. They were heading north, but it was many days ride to Arok-Kor. More likely they were going to some closer oasis.

Unless the entire thing was a trap and the man in on it. In which case, she should show no sign of suspicion until she was ready to break the trap.

So, yes, he would have to come along if he wanted.

First, though, she had to find Tava and Marrick. Tava was easy...she still had the communication stone. Cat asked her to meet her at the tavern, then went in search of the young archer. She already knew he was competent in a fight and not afraid of her.

Those were definitely the two qualities she needed. Marrick knew what she was and had taken her side against a human. She wondered why. Short of asking him, she could find no answer.

Where could he be? She checked temple square first, on a hunch, but found him not in Neir's shrine, nor Solus'.

She found him in Tyrn's. Of course, she had never asked his affiliation. But Tyrn? It had been her experience that followers of Tyrn hated demons more than anyone. Or maybe she was simply biased by

Laran and his fear of her.

Laran. A wave of grief flowed through her at the thought of the name, she hesitated in the door of Tyrn's temple. Then she stepped all the way in, head held high.

Merrick turned. "Hello..." He hesitated.

"I need some help. You would be paid," she added, with a bit of a smile.

"Paid? I could use the money. What is going on?"

She explained the situation to him, quickly, including her suspicion that it might be a trap. She left nothing out...she would not ask anyone to take a risk without knowing its full implications.

The girl was a firehead. The reason some thought them unlucky was because of the association with Arok. Of course, there was the third possibility...that the young woman had voluntarily joined the cult. They might have promised her a high position, given her coloring, and if she had to deal with prejudice each and every day?

Cat would not blame her if she had, and she could have been in a dark wagon solely to protect her. Fireheads were vulnerable to the sun.

17

Eventually, there were three people in the tavern courtyard, soon joined by a fourth.

Cat studied the girl's father again. He definitely had a pleasant face and manner, and she found it hard to believe he was in on any trap.

"Friends of yours?"

"Tava is a long-time traveling companion. Marrick is a competent fighter. It felt wise to bring some extra support."

The man nodded. "So, you know where she is?"

"With a nomad caravan, somewhere to the north. I have a spell that will help guide us closer. There is, however, at least one mage with them."

He frowned, then took a deep breath. "Please find her. I would ask to come with you, but I struggle to remember that the sharp end goes in the other guy."

Cat couldn't help but laugh a little. "I was going to invite you, in case we have to talk to her. If you won't come, then could you please provide some token that proves we sent you?"

A sheepish look crossed his face, then he tugged his signet ring off his finger and tossed it to Cat. "This should do. She knows I would not leave this around where it could be stolen."

It was a merchant's guild ring, Cat noted as she placed it carefully in her pouch. The man was a dealer in silk. She had never enjoyed such frippery. Beria had, and she wished she could get away with sending her a gift; but by now she would have wed Garon. And Cat would not be there for the naming of her children.

She chased the thought away, corralled it back into the corner of her mind where she kept such thoughts in order to stay sane.

Sane. Was she sane? She hoped so. She at least had not harmed anyone who did not deserve to be harmed. She had killed a couple of the Solusians, and she regretted that.

Silk and perfumes. Death. Blood. For a moment all of those things seemed to whirl around in her mind. Then it passed and she was mounting her caba, its green-yellow scales rough under her hands. They had acquired the fastest ones they could find, bred from racing lines. Hopefully it would be enough. "We must go."

And then they were heading through the streets towards the north gate. The comb was in Cat's pocket. She would start the tracking spell once they were outside the city.

White buildings, white people, she would almost take Arok-Kor if it had more color. Yet, this place owed her, and there was a bond there. The sorcerer...or sorceress, whichever it was, was still out there.

Could it be the same mage who had sensed her scrying? It would not be a coincidence if so, and would prove that this was a trap. Could three people spring this trap safely?

She had to try just in case the girl really was a prisoner, a victim. In case her father was, even if she was not. It was not at all impossible.

The man seemed so honest, but she knew better than that. The city seemed to take forever to pass through. They dared not go faster than the cabas' slow lumber, not with children and caniks playing in the streets.

A canik ran across in front of her and she checked her beast. Stupid thing should check for traffic, she thought. They were smart enough to look, surely.

Just taking for granted the fact that people were too nice to hit them, and there were the north gates.

The gateman opened them. No check on people leaving, and she was out in the desert. She wrapped her scarf around her face and nudged the caba to a faster pace.

"They have three days on us."

Tava nodded. "Do not push the pace too hard. A lame caba will leave us even further behind."

Part of Cat resented the reminder. Another part was only too glad not to push it. The desert traks did not have the most comfortable of gaits. Nor was this a particularly good road. Nobody except nomads went north from Merico.

There was nothing to the north except deep desert and Arok-Kor.

Deep desert and Arok-Kor. Was she being drawn, after all, to the place of her birth? It was still dark, and Cat was shaking off dream fragments.

She did not remember the dream, only the profound emotion of disturbance and uncertainty that accompanied it. The vague sensation that Ylsa might have been in it.

Just a dream, she told herself. Had it been something important, some message from the gods, she would have remembered it. A small brazier provided enough heat to warm water for tea. She drank it, slowly.

It cleared her head a little. She could hear Marrick moving amongst the cabas. An early start, so they would not have to travel through the heat of the day.

The tracking spell leading them ever northwards. Arok-Kor.

The girl was going to Arok-Kor. Cat was certain of it, and that meant she was going to Arok-Kor. Either to rescue her or to fail or to find out she had no desire to be rescued.

Cat was not bringing her home, even from that place, against her will, even if it meant she would not be paid.

Well, she had been paid part of the fee. A fair deal. Part on departure, part on return. Money saved to hire somebody else if Cat and her companions failed.

She finished the mug of tart liquid and stood, holding it over the fire to ensure it would be clean. There was no water spare to wash it.

There was barely water spare to drink and after two days in the desert, Cat was only too aware that she smelled. Only the cabas seemed unconcerned, bred to this environment, they snorted as Marrick started to saddle them.

She moved to help him. Tava was packing up their shelters.

"Do you think we'll find her?"

"I think we have a chance of catching up before they reach Arok-Kor."

"And if we don't?" He turned towards her, his face pale with wrappings, only his eyes visible.

"I won't ask you to go into Arok-Kor."

"I'm more worried about you going there. You're their promised messiah or whatever."

Cat breathed in, breathed out, smelled sand and salt on the air. It had an almost pleasant note to it, a homeliness.

You were made here, that wind said. Come home, Cathren. Or was it just the wind? Was it a geas?

All she could do was live, continue. Hope that the end of the road was not her death.

If her death was necessary, then why had she been allowed to live? Perhaps it was its manner. Or perhaps there was something she had to do first.

Most likely that last. It could be as simple as saving the young woman or as complex as prev...

...and her thoughts were rudely interrupted. Fortunately, they had just placed the last piece of their gear on the beasts when she heard the twang of a bowstring.

Whoever it was missed. Marrick had his own bow slung in a second, ducking behind a caba, looking for them.

"I suggest we just vacate the area," Cat noted. "No sense in stupid skirmishes."

Marrick loosed an arrow. "I will cover you."

Tava was already on board, reins in one hand, sword in the other. Cat leapt onto another caba, drawing one of her blades in her left hand, the right on the reins.

Marrick fired again before leaping on board without, as far as she could tell, touching the stirrup. An arrow buried itself in his packs, but fortunately missed his waterskins.

That would have been as much of a disaster as it hitting him. How many were there? Cat lifted her hand, tossed a globe of light into the air. It illuminated the field of battle, such as it was.

Five, maybe six, and at her display, they backed off. Bandits, she decided, nothing more or less, and she turned her caba's nose north and booted it in the ribs.

The beast was only too glad to vacate the area at a fast lope, flat out, neck stretched out in front of it. Cat could barely keep her seat, but any arrows fell behind her.

She did not rein in for a couple of miles. Tava and Marrick were right behind her.

"Normally I'd have voted for taking those guys out."

"We don't have time," Cat said, grimly. "At least they were bandits, not..."

"...kidnappers left behind to slow us down."

She would be very surprised if such were not encountered, but for now, she let the caba walk, let it catch its breath. It snorted, dropping its head.

Marrick, out of breath, "I wasted like three arrows back there."

"Do you have enough?"

"I should. I brought plenty. But we should avoid skirmishes if we can."

In the desert, there was no way for him to replenish shafts. Heads might be possible, but the nearest tree could well be several days away. "What about bone shafts?"

"If we can find suitable materials, I can do that. But I'd rather avoid it."

Cat nodded. "We'll keep our eyes open anyway." She let the reins fall onto the caba's neck, catching on its ridges. It walked with its head down, its sides heaving a little.

"How far behind do you reckon we are now?" Marrick asked.

It was Tava who cut in. "I would say we have likely caught up a day on them, wagons in this are going to be slow."

Slow. The desert seemed infinite now, no sign of Merico behind them, and on this road there were no way stations. Nothing except emptiness. And the rock was turning into sands. "Especially as..."

"We are entering the sand sea. Wagons here are a liability. They must have goods with them that require it. And if they had ditched the vehicle..."

"Or they do not want to risk the girl escaping, which she might if she was mounted." Cat frowned for a moment. Evidence that she was, indeed, a prisoner. Or was it? The heat flowed over her and through her. "I don't like this sand sea thing."

"It would be quicker for you to fly."

"But then I would have no backup." She nudged the caba into a slightly faster pace. "We will just have to deal with it, will we not?"

"I for one am not turning back." Tava moved her caba up next to Cat's, letting Marrick fall behind slightly. "You need me."

"Just don't get killed," Cat murmured. She wished R'vor was with them. Having a demon with them could have helped... "If we cannot catch them before the city..."

"I am fairly sure we can."

Tava's confidence helped. Cat lifted her head. "If we cannot, then I should be able to get in easily."

"You mean by pretending to join them. A dangerous path."

"You are right, but do you really think we'll be able to..."

"I sneaked in. Many years ago. Of course, they were rather busy at the time." Tava's lips quirked. "And it was worth it, but I do not...Cat I don't wish to lose you."

You will have no more need of them. Neir's words echoing in her mind. She knew how likely it was that she would die in Arok-Kor.

However, would she die breaking the cult? Or...saving them? The hot air flowed into her lungs and, for a moment, her vision blurred with something akin to tears. She was afraid.

She was terrified, but she could not let that beat her.

Neir had chosen to restore R'vor instead of killing him. Had given her the life and wings of one of her closest friends. She clung to that sign of the goddess' favor. The caba's pace picked up further.

"They smell water," Tava commented. "Let them take us to it."

Cat nodded, not touching the reins. The caba wandered, nose down. The water it smelled was a spring.

"I hope this is good water." Cat murmured a little bit as she dismounted, inspecting the spring. It could have been poisoned, after all, by those they were following. Surely they would have predicted pursuit.

But the spell she used indicated it was clean.

She let the caba drink. The beast did not need much water, but it needed it more than she did, in some ways. There seemed to be plenty.

Tava nodded approvingly. "Let the beasts drink, then fill the canteens."

The cabas nudged each other as they pushed towards the spring, arguing over their hierarchy. It was not serious, though, and certainly no intentional harm was done. Cat watched them for a moment.

Simple minds, utterly unaware of the problems of the world. She envied them. Yet, at the same time, she was glad to be, in that moment, exactly who and what she was. Even if it meant trouble and war.

War. There would be a war, she could feel it approaching. Could feel it like storm clouds on the horizon. Could anything she did prevent it? She only knew that she had to try. Even though it could not be easy, she had to...

She stepped forward between the cabas, started to fill her canteens. The water was a little muddy. She tasted it. Not very sweet, but it was drinkable, and in the desert, that was all that mattered.

"You can strain it through cloth if the taste bothers you," Tava supplied from the other side of a caba.

Cat nodded, moving to do just that. "I could, oddly enough, get used to all of this."

"People can get used to almost anything, Cat. People can even get used to slavery and rape. It has been known, many times through history. And some people manage to be happy despite all external circumstances."

"Beria was like that." Speaking of her lover brought a pang, but not the deep despair she had once associated with it. Perhaps that meant she was feeling a little better. A little. The pain was still there, and the pain was not going away, not any time soon. Love did that, and loss did that. "She...dammit. I would give much to have her back."

"Be careful what you wish for."

"Neir gave me R'vor. I will be content with that." She meant it, at least for that one moment. She could be content with the fact that R'vor lived and Beria, having left her, was safe. Laran...

She had to. She filled the last canteen, securing it back to her pack. Water. It would be enough, and the delay they had taken to obtain it would save time in the long run. Save time. They had to catch the girl. They had no choice.

18

It was night, and they did not slow. Resting during the heat of the day was better. The caba could not see in total darkness, and as it faded to that, Cat murmured a light spell, showing their way. It would also make them more visible, but she could do nothing about that.

Bandits were unlikely to attack three fast, lightly armed individuals, one of whom was wielding magic. Not unless they could catch them on the ground, as they had tried before. She crouched forward a little, making herself as light as she could on the caba's back. The beast was starting to tire, and she pulled him to a walk.

Neither Tava nor Marrick spoke. There was no wind, and the stars spangled the sky far overhead, pin-pricks in Seliene's cloak.

It was utter silence, and Cat found herself straining for any sound. And overtaken by an unexpectedly strong desire to take wing. Perhaps because she was chafing under the slow pace forced on her by the humans.

They were her allies. She needed them. The caba snorted, and its breath fogged very slightly. Far less than if it had been a western caba, its body preserving water. Far better than hers did. Yet, she did not feel weakened by the privation. Rather, she felt better than she had in a long time.

Perhaps she had simply had it too soft in Losana. That was probably it. That she had let herself get...lax, like the average merchant, and she would have stayed that way. Laran, perhaps, had intended it that way.

She would have outlived him anyway. Yet, by that time, she might have been caught enough in those patterns to even think she was happy.

She was not happy now, nor was she content, but she felt energized. Then...then the star fell.

She caught her breath and heard Tava and Marrick doing the same. Fallen stars did not, generally, land. They simply fell, but the theory was that their substance could not survive on Yirath.

Occasionally, though, they did. And what they were made of was a particularly pure form of iron. People would follow them, hunt them.

Cat's swords were made from steel forged from star-iron. A rare and expensive gift. She reined in the caba.

Had she not been on a mission, she would have looked for where the star might have landed. A life was more important, yet it seemed an omen.

A good omen or a bad one? Did she want to know? She thought not. Instead, she nudged the caba into a jog.

She was unable, however, to get it out of her mind.

"I wonder," Tava commented, riding up next to her.

"If we were not on a mission of mercy, I would go look for it." For the money, if nothing else. "And take it to R'vor."

Tava flickered her a grin. "See what he could make out of it, eh?"

Cat tapped the hilt of one of her swords meaningfully. "It's a temptation, but it's a diversion we don't have time for."

"We might even catch them tonight, if we hurry. We need to discuss what to do then."

"I think it depends on how many there are. They will quite likely have us outnumbered." Which was unfortunate, but almost guaranteed to be true.

"It does," Tava mused. "How are you with a bow?"

"Not great," Cat admitted. "And they will likely be better. Going up is probably a bad idea. We will need surprise."

"More than that," came Marrick's voice from behind. "If I was them, I would kill the girl if I thought I would be overrun."

The thought was distinctly unpleasant, whilst making horrible sense. "So, we need to get her out without attacking, if possible."

"And if she is there willingly?" Tava asked.

"We cross that bridge when we come to it. I am not forcing her...not for pay." That would make *them* the kidnappers, something Cat would not allow. "Try to talk her into coming back, yes. Physically grab her, no."

Cat glanced ahead, along the road.

"So, we are agreed on that much. That possibility means we should probably try not to harm her escorts."

"Is there another oasis between us and Arok-Kor?" Cat frowned a little. An oasis would be the perfect spot, but they would also be aware that it was. Likely on high alert.

"Supposedly, an abandoned one. They will likely make camp there, yes."

"And post highly alert guards, but it still seems better than on the road." Cat glanced over her shoulder at Marrick. He seemed highly troubled. "Marrick?"

"I can't think of a better plan."

Hopefully that was all that was bothering him. Some kind of nocturnal bird flew overhead. The night was reaching its coldest point, and Cat shivered. Yet, the sun would soon rise.

The abandoned oasis was marked by a cessation of the sand. Instead, the ground was rocky with scrubby vegetation. Cat hoped it had been abandoned because of Arok-Kor, not anything wrong with the water.

An odd formation of stone provided a place to hide the cabas before they approached on foot. With a powerful mage on the other side, Cat elected not to use concealment spells, which might only make them stand out more.

Instead, they crept along the ground. A wagon, and two heavier built cabas, plus three lighter ones. That was a reassuring head count only to a point. Several men could ride inside the wagon.

She only saw three figures. The sorcerer, in his male form, had his arm around a woman, talking to her. The third figure was also female. If either was the firehead, Cat could not tell, both of them having their heads thoroughly swathed in fabric. Only the man could be recognized, and that as much by his aura, his specific signature of magic, as his appearance. Neither of the women seemed to be talented or trained.

She heard the sound of a rock turning. Another man, approaching them. She held her breath, ready to take action the second she was aware that she had been seen.

"Who goes..." He did not finish, glancing at his companion as if he knew who was there.

The woman next to the sorcerer was the one who moved, away from his grasp, to grab the second woman and haul her to her feet. "Whoever you are, approach and she dies."

The firehead, Cat noticed, did not seem too upset.

"Oh, we know who it is. You might as well come out, halfbreed." The sorcerer's voice was soft and feminine. He was, perhaps, caught between the genders. Cat knew how that felt.

She stepped out, making sure she had her hand on her bow. If they thought she was the one who had fired, then perhaps they would not notice Marrick or Tava.

"So, why are you here? Daddy dearest hire you to fetch back his little girl?"

Cat shrugged, not answering that. There was really no good answer.

"She is coming with us. So, for that matter, are you."

Cat laughed. "You'll have to catch me first."

"No, I will just have them do it." He signaled to the two demons who had just stepped out around the wagon.

They were lean and fit, and she could easily see that she might well have problems out-flying them.

"Tell me exactly what you want of me. And I might consider it."

"It is Arok who wants you."

"Of course he does." Cat kept her tone even. While she kept them distracted, there was a chance Tava or Marrick could get to the girl. She glanced at her.

She did not seem particularly frightened. Or happy. Or anything. After a moment, Cat realized she had probably been drugged. A good way to keep her quiet, she supposed. "He wants to empty me like a shell."

"Not at all. He wants you to serve him, yes, but he has no interest in being a woman."

Cat laughed a bit. "So I heard before. So, he wants me as...what? A priest? An assassin? A sex slave?"

Any of those seemed entirely possible. For a moment, something seemed to whisper in her mind. She felt a sudden sense of freedom, as if her defiance actually mattered. Perhaps it did.

"In a way, that is up to you. You will not have to be crippled any more, if you come with us. No, don't try to tell me you have been trained to your true potential. Even if they would have allowed it, I doubt they know how."

Insulting her teachers was almost too much. She felt the heat rise in her blood. And then she thought of R'vor. If she switched sides, after all of that. "I serve no god as patron. That is my choice."

"Ah. Then you will have to come anyway, and you...you will be persuaded, but it will not be a pleasant journey. Take her."

As the two demons moved, the other woman placed herself behind the firehead, using the prisoner as a shield.

Cat recognized her as she moved. It was the so-called Lady Teola.

Cat's mind raced. She could outfly few purebreds, her wings were not quite as efficiently designed.

Her magic, however, was stronger than theirs. Yet, not stronger than this man's. Instead of trying an immediate escape, she turned towards Teola. "I am surprised you let me go alone as early as you did."

Teola's eyes flickered with something. "Oh, you seemed to be absolutely under control."

Manipulated. Except... "Then you know nothing. You know nothing of my motivations."

"Revenge." The word dropped between them.

"You really think it's that simple?"

"What else could it be?"

They expected her to think like them, to focus entirely on the destruction of those who had brought so much harm. Part of her was that way. Part of her wanted to draw her blades and do her best to kill these people.

Teola, though, had stepped up behind the firehead. "Of course, if you do not cooperate, this one will suffer first."

Cat noticed that the girl did not even flinch. Did that mean she had courage, or did it mean she knew Teola was bluffing? Or was she drugged? Cat could not take the risk. She lowered her hands. "Very well."

If all else failed, Tava and Marrick could follow and coordinate an escape on the road. "But I refuse to give my word."

"I would not expect it. You will come to understand," the sorceror said, simply.

"I understand that you killed my mentor." She had to say it.

"I did not."

"Not personally." She had meant 'you' in the generic term. But doubt flickered into her mind. There were so many sides, so many factions, that these were not necessarily the same people. She felt that they were, though. For now, she glanced around the campsite.

Teola, the firehead, the sorcerer, two demons. They were certainly not unbeatable, but she had to take care to protect the girl. Even if she was one of them, Cat was not going to harm the woman she had been hired to rescue unless she had no other choice. She reminded herself that she had already decided not to drag her home kicking and screaming. If she wanted to join the crazy cult, then so be it. At that point, it was not Cat's problem.

She was very aware that Tava was out there, that Tava knew the desert. That Tava had a good chance of helping her, but had to wait for the right moment.

She had to deal with the sorcerer, most of all. Teola, although presumably competent in some way, was not a magic user. The firehead had some potential, but not quite enough to warrant training. She might manage something minor. The two demons were average...for demons. That meant they were quite competent and she would, indeed, have to be careful of them. However, in the very dark of the night, they would be weaker than she, her human blood helping her deal with the extreme cold.

Tava was undoubtedly making the same calculation. However, the demons would see in the dark and the sorcerer...was highly competent. Far better than she was. She could see, now, layers of illusion. His real age and even gender were obscured from her view. For all she knew, he too was a demon.

It seemed unlikely...had he been able to fly, she would not have escaped him in Merico. So, a weakness there. Not good at flight and levitation spells. Or not good enough to want to do them in a fight.

"Eat with us?"

Cat stepped over to the fire and sat down. She murmured a spell to detect poison before accepting the food.

"You do not trust us."

"If I were you, I would probably try to drug me too." Not a matter of mistrust. A matter of tactics and sense.

Surprisingly, the sorcerer nodded. "If I did so, I would have no opportunity to persuade you."

She took a bite of the tough desert bread. "We are enemies. And you worked with the Solusians."

"Of course I did. To make absolutely sure they crossed the line. Now the others will not ally with them."

"So, to weaken Solus, not strengthen him."

"There is going to be a war, Cathren the Black. You will have to choose your side."

"Will I?" She fixed her eyes on him, solidly. "I have never felt it necessary to pick sides."

"Then I will lay it in front of you. Solus plans to destroy demonkind."

"Why would he do that?" Gods. Unpredictable, sometimes it seemed as if they were but children and Yirath one of their toys.

"He wishes humanity to be ascendant, the only truly sentient species on the planet. In order to do so, he intends to remake the world."

Cat nodded a little. "I still fail to see why."

"Because demons are more natural to this world. In the long term, they will always have the upper hand. Add to that the magic they possess." The sorcerer glanced at his demon guards. "The only way to ensure that the humans survive..."

"Not the only way. We could also try our hand at peace." She found the words coming out before she even thought about them. "I realize that's the harder route, but..."

"Or we could simply divide the world." The sorcerer smiled. "I never said I agreed with Solus."

"So, that would be your solution? Not to eliminate humanity?"

"I am human. You have been taught that those who choose to worship Arok are traitors to their own race. That is true in some cases, but not all. I do want Arok back in his place, his temples open in every city. I do not want human extinction."

He seemed so reasonable that Cat's head spun for a moment. Then she remembered what he had done to the poor mayor and shook her head. "I find that hard to believe."

"I would not expect you to change your mind overnight."

"Besides. There is the matter of Laran. The matter of what the Solusians did to R'vor." She kept her tone even. "The matter of the people who died while the healers were expelled from Merico. Your hands are far from clean."

"Are yours entirely so?"

Cat contemplated that for a moment, reaching for a mug of bitter tea. "As much as anyone's are."

"Ah yes. Your keepers saw to that. But tell me, what are a few lives against the entire future of the world?"

"Of demons," Cathren pointed out, softly.

"Of the world. If the world is reshaped, then humans will also die. Caba will die. Canik will die. I do not know if anything can or will survive."

"You would think Solus would think that through."

"Like Arok thought through trying to eliminate the humans?"

Cat frowned. "Are they gods or children?" It was such a disrespectful conversation that she could not help but glance up at the sky. No smiting seemed about to occur, though. She idly wondered if it was the fact they were dealing with gods, not goddesses, and could not help a wry thought.

A thought she chased away with an effort.

"Both, I sometimes think. The fact that they allow us to speak and think freely, however, is a point in their favor."

Cat considered that for a long moment. "Perhaps it is. But you do not wish to extend that courtesy to me."

"I dare not. If you choose to walk with the Solusians..."

"Just because I don't want to walk with you, does not mean I am going to do that." No. She had to escape so she could uncover the truth. If Solus himself planned on 'reshaping the world', then there was a way to verify that from the other side. If they thought it was the right thing to do.

She shivered for a moment, the image of the mountains falling. Of the sky broiling with clouds so thick they blocked out the sun. No. If that was true, she would not support it. Jumping into bed with the Arokians, however? That was not the answer, and she felt it in her bones. But what, a small voice asked, if it was the only way?

Would she sacrifice herself to save the world? She was not sure whether she would have the courage, and she knew there were many definitions of sacrifice.

R'vor would hate her. Neir had saved him. Was that a message from Neir to say she should not go that way? Or had it simply been payment for services rendered? Neir had been trying to avoid open conflict between her people and Solus.

This man had been trying to start it. To isolate Solus from the other gods. Arok alone could potentially take the sun god's place. So, these could be lies, a continuation of that. A passage forward from it. She shuddered. "I have no reason to believe you. You change forms, you change sides...I will not trust you."

She was not sure this man...if it was a man...could ever earn either her trust or her respect. Whoever he was, he had lied to her...several times, likely. She could not simply walk in step with him, now or, likely, ever.

"Unfortunate." He stood up, moving over to check on the wagon cabas. Ending the conversation, effectively.

19

Two sets of demon eyes watched her. If she took off, she would be brought down. The sorcerer had tried to kill her in Merico. Now he was trying to recruit her.

His actions and behavior made no sense. She had felt that shot. It had been serious. He had meant to end her life then. Or had he? Had that all been for the benefit of the Solusians?

She felt eyes on her. Eyes from beyond the camp.

Do it, she thought.

Two arrows, suddenly, out of the darkness. Each one lightly found a demon throat. She leapt upwards, wishing she had a bow of her own. It was dark now, the embers of the fire providing the only light.

The sorcerer. "I see you were not alone."

"Of course not. I am not going to trust somebody who tried to kill me."

"You were never in any danger." He did not fire on her.

"Going to come get me?" she challenged, taunting a little. "Or do you not know a simple flight spell?"

He did not take off. "You will come to me, in the end."

"I don't think so." Without the demon guards, it would be easy enough to retrieve the young woman. Cat was not about to risk trying to carry her, though.

A full demon might be able to, she was not as strong. Instead, she called demonfire, hovering above his wagon. "Now, let her go." The threat was obvious.

He was going to be struggling to move three people with two cabas and all his supplies were in the wagon. If she burned it...

Tava was already in the camp, having switched to her staff. She was circling towards the girl. "I suggest you do as she says. She has a fiery temper."

Not entirely true. Cat was under full control. She could analyze the situation later, and establish whether he wanted her dead or alive. Somehow, that was important, although she was not sure why. Why would it be a concern? He was not her friend or her ally and never would be.

Of course, she was starting to wonder if there were any good guys except her small circle of friends. He tossed a mage bolt at her. It missed, crackling past. Stun bolt. He definitely wanted her alive right now, whether as an ally or as a plaything. She formed a fireball between her hands. "You want to push it?"

He slumped. "Fine. Take the girl. But we will meet again, Cathren the Black. That I promise."

"I look forward to it."

The ride south was awkward silence. The firehead girl said nothing. She had come with them willingly, but she seemed tense and unhappy.

Cat finally reined in her caba next to her. "What is wrong?"

"He told me everything he told you, but I didn't know he had anything to do with the Solusians."

"I don't know whose side he is on, or what his agenda is. Or even who he is," Cat admitted. "If you truly wish to choose Arok's path, that's one thing."

"I want to stop the Solusians. If they are really doing that."

Reshape the world. Cat shivered. "Despite the unreliable nature of our witness, I think they might be. I have had...not quite premonitions."

"I have...heard about you. Just vague legends and stories, though."

"Most people know I exist. Many would rather I did not." Cat summed it up quickly, although she knew it to be far more complicated. "And I intend to stop the Solusians if I can." Did that mean taking on the God himself? It likely did, and the thought caught a breath in her throat. She would not just die, if things went badly, she would be utterly destroyed. Or bound to some hideous fate. Turned to stone, perhaps. Solus was quite fond of turning people to stone.

Yet she would go to said fate knowing she had tried. "What will you do now, Sera?"

"I don't know," the girl admitted.

"You could try explaining it all to your father."

"My father barely acknowledges magic. He does not really believe in the gods."

Cat had met people like that. "Then perhaps he will have to be convinced." Whatever happened to Sera...whatever course she walked, it would be alien to her father. That much was obvious. "Or the two of you will become estranged."

"Before today, I would not have cared."

"He loves you. Think about that when deciding what to do. You have some small talent for magic, but..."

"The Academy testers told me that. That I was not worth the full training, but might consider learning a few cantrips. I suppose..."

"It's not hard for a gifted mage to assess the level of talent in another. I can't do it as well as the testers, though." They were, after all, hired for possessing that knack to a high degree. "My specialties are alchemy and fire magic."

"Demonfire." Sera frowned. "I thought that came straight from Arok."

"Yes and no. It's written into who and what demons are."

"So you feel no qualms about using it?"

"Depends on the situation. I feel definite qualms about using it on *people*." She had wracked her conscience on the matter, yet...it was a natural ability, and it heightened her affinity to the more complicated fire magics. She could no more not use it than she could not fly...something her human friends understood very little. Laran not at all. She frowned at the thought of the name.

Laran. Well. She could not bring him back from the dead. She also would not bow to his memory. Honor him, yes...she had loved him in a weird way. Obey him now he was gone? She could not.

"I would too. I suppose..."

Cat turned towards Sera. "I am who I am. Some people would very much like me to suppress it all, hide it underneath. To be purely human. But I can't. I tried it for a while, it just made me sick."

Physically as well as mentally. She had been depressed, hated herself and her life. That was no way for anyone to live. Laran had wanted her to sacrifice her happiness for the fate of the world.

Could she do it if she knew it was the only way? She was not sure. She would rather die than live without her wings.

"And I don't understand that. I've tried to understand demons, but..."

"Maybe I'll introduce you to R'vor. He's good at explaining things to humans." And he might help this young woman find her balance, make her choices, not rush headlong into self-destruction.

Or was it self-destruction? Cat was no longer sure. She was no longer sure of anything, and her mind went around in circles.

"I think I'd like that." Sera did not ask who R'vor was.

Cat wondered to what conclusions she was jumping, but that was not her problem. It was, entirely, Sera's issue if she got things wrong. "And remember, people will want you for what you didn't choose."

"Or fear me. My dad had the Academy test me because even *he* thought it was a sign of magical ability."

"I haven't seen a correlation," Cat admitted. "But people still believe it. It's a scarcity thing, I think. Just like some people don't trust left handed people. Then again..."

"I wouldn't trust a left handed person. I mean, you tend to watch the right hand."

Cat grinned. "That's why warriors train to use both hands."

"I'm not a warrior. Or a mage. Or...anything, really."

Cat realized she had got to the heart of the matter. "You can be something. Just be sure that what you become is what you want to be."

Cat let out a huge sigh of relief as she saw the walls of Merico. Yet, she knew, she was likely to end up at Arok-Kor in the end. On her own terms. She would not be brought there a prisoner.

No, she would walk in with her head held high and demand answers. For right now, she needed answers of a different kind.Tava had offered to take Sera back to her father. Cathren was only too glad to delegate that duty. She felt restless, the desert seemed to have followed her back into the city. She made her way to the temple square on foot, the caba enjoying well-earned rest.

Amongst the crowds, she felt more alone than she ever had. She felt...as if she was in no way a part of anything here. The unrelenting white of walls and robes.

Maybe she should just go back to Losana. Turn her back on all of it, forget what she knew. She could not. She wore white herself, robes cut to give her wings freedom, but her glamor was up. They saw only a tall woman.

Nobody was paying much attention to her. The life and breath of the city continued around her. That was why she felt alone. She was being ignored. Some people hated cities.

Cat shook her head, weaving through the crowd. She almost tripped over a canik, a young one. It hissed its irritation. "Sorry. I didn't see you there."

Somebody laughed, and she turned.

"Talking to caniks?"

It felt good to be acknowledged. "I did almost step on his tail."

"His fault for running out into the crowd." The voice came from an older man who now had a grip on the animal's collar.

"Well, maybe." Cat let out a breath. "He's not very old, is he?"

"No."

Maybe she should get one. No, to take responsibility for any living creature right now would be foolish. She did not even know whether she would live out the year. Summer was drawing to a close, and she did not expect to live until the new year in the spring.

Or if she did, she did not know where she was. "He's cute. When he's not trying to trip people up."

The man laughed, and started to haul his canik away. The creature struggled, clearly trying to run off again.

Then there was that. She had no more clue how to train a canik than...well, how to cook a gourmet meal. That might be Liesa's fault. She had never liked anyone else in her kitchen. Would Cat ever see her foster mother again?

Temple square was...healthy. That was the big contrast with the last time she had been there, when only a few desultory people had headed through it. It was crowded, as it should be.

It was the temple of Solus she headed towards, however, and that seemed to have the least crowds. People were probably still mad. Or, perhaps, they had had difficulty finding a priest clean of the conspiracy.

Inside, it was light and airy, windows and mirrors catching the sun and the sacred flame burning. Last time she had stood here, they had tried to take her by force. Now, the temple was empty as she walked towards the altar.

"I'm asking for answers," she said to the flame.

Of course, she got silence. She got the strong sense that it was pulling away from her. That the God did not want to talk to her.

Well, she could hardly force Him to her bidding. She thought of Neir for a moment. Maybe that was a better source of answers.

"Need something?"

They had found a priest, after all. He was old and partly crippled, he walked leaning on a cane.

"Information," Cat admitted. "I want to know..." A pause. "What those who were involved in throwing out the other priests really intended."

"Well..." He moved to sit on the bench that ran along the wall, patting it nearby.

"I understand if you don't know." She felt that tension still, as if Solus really did not want her in here. Was she about to get smote? She was not sure. She needed this information.

"I am not sure," he admitted. "I thought it was the normal supremacy or monotheism arguments, but I'm...not sure."

"A specific quarrel between the gods, maybe?"

"I did get the distinct impression there was some specific argument going on between Solus and Neir."

Cat nodded. "That might fit what I saw."

"And I also get the impression he is less than happy with you."

"I know," Cat said, evenly. "But I have no quarrel with him, only certain of his followers."

Quarrel with a god? Why did she get the feeling more and more as if...she had no right to quarrel or argue with any deity. She was only...what she was. A mage, yes, for what that was worth in the grand scheme of things. Except her magic probably came from Arok, not Seliene.

Perhaps that had been Laran's error. Perhaps she should not have been permitted to work magic at all.

Better for everyone except her had she been killed, but Neir and Kiran had not allowed that.

"You were involved in exposing what was going on with the mayor." Not a question.

"Solus is probably annoyed I got Neir's followers let back in the city." Just that. Nothing more, surely. "If you can't tell me anything more about the conspiracy..."

"I can't. I'm sorry." He sounded it, although he seemed tense, relaxing only when she rose to leave.

She stepped out of the temple slowly, not willing to rush or run and keeping her head high. She headed straight for that of Neir.

If she was going to be a pawn in the quarrels of the Gods... Well, it was too late for that. She had already, in a sense, chosen sides. Or had she?

She had committed to nothing, and she had helped only to restore access to healers to the people of Merico.

Only for that. Reshaping the world. She had vague premonitions and the word of a man she knew to be a liar. She did not know anything bad was going to happen.

Neir's temple was occupied. An older priestess was talking to a young man in hushed tones. Few men entered Neir's direct service, although physicians traditionally held her as their patron. She was a women's goddess.

But there were always a few. She ignored the priestess and the postulant, for such he clearly was from his manner, and walked to the altar. "I'm not taking any more sides," she said, softly.

"Everyone has a side." The voice came from the carved serpent on the altar. "Even if it's only your own side."

Cat inclined her head. "However, if there is a war, one can stay neutral."

"Not always. Not if you are dragged in."

She let out a breath. "I will not be anyone's tool. I will not be either what I was created to be or what Laran tried to turn me into."

"A good start for deciding what your side is."

"Solus..."

"You are not capable of taking on a god."

Was there something odd about his tone? "Why is Neir so worried about me?"

"She doesn't tell me everything."

Cat laughed. "Maybe she just has a soft spot?" It was possible that Neir just liked her. The gods had all of the personality of people.

They could make irrational decisions based off of personal feelings the same as everyone else.

"Perhaps. It seems, though, that she pities you."

Cat frowned at that. "Many do. I prefer not to be pitied."

You will have no more need of them. "I also prefer to know what people want from me."

"She wants you to be who you are. Nothing more."

The carving fell silent. Cat glanced around. Had anyone seen her having a conversation with the altar? Only the priestess and acolyte. The latter was shooting an odd look in her direction.

After a moment, she walked over towards them, studying their reactions to her. The acolyte was peering at her as if he could not quite work out what she was, but the priestess smiled.

"Did I disturb you?" she inquired.

"Not at all. Perhaps...would you like to join us?"

She had jumped to an incorrect conclusion, Cat thought as she regarded the priestess. "Depends on the topic of conversation."

"There's something really odd about you," the acolyte blurted.

"I know. Don't worry. I don't bite." She did have her blades with her, but kept her hands well away from them.

The snake had given her one key piece of information. It was Solus himself, not his followers, who had plans. How could she oppose a god? She was not up to it...yet, his tone. What had been in that tone.

"So, what would you like the topic to be?"

"The snake."

The priestess indicated a seat nearby. "Neir's messenger."

"Yes."

"He is an archangel," the priestess started. "His name is Myrk."

"Myrk," Cat repeated. "And he brings word from her."

"To a point. There are stories of him acting on his own, to a limited degree. He is also capable of bringing both healing and death."

Cat nodded. "I have...seen the former." She tailed off.

"The restored demon."

"He is my friend." She had to find R'vor. He was still in the city, but she was not sure where. "I need to talk to him."

"I talked to him. I would say a good man, if he was a man. Yet, I am surprised Neir helped him."

"Payment for services rendered." A fair deal, Cat had decided.

The priestess laughed a bit. "Ah yes. It was *you* who exposed the concubine."

"It was."

"You're..." The acolyte's eyes widened.

"The halfbreed. I said, I don't bite."

"You're nicer than I would have thought," he admitted after a moment.

"I suppose I've had to cultivate nice." She started to stand up. "Thanks for the quick lesson. I need to go find R'vor."

She found him and T'la on the docks, studying a shipment.

"Back to the trading?" she asked.

He turned, jumped, and then moved to offer her a hug. She hugged back, knowing how difficult it was for him.

"How are the wings?"

He spread them, stretched them. "Weak, but functional. I'll be as good as new once I've got enough air time in." A pause. "Thank you."

"Thank Neir." Which she realized she had not properly done. Too busy demanding answers. Perhaps that 'not capable' had, in truth, been a reminder that she was still mortal. That she should still bow to the gods.

To a point. "We need to talk, and soon."

"How about now?" A pause. "Let's fly."

"Not from here." As alarming as demons were, Cat scared people more. Perhaps because she was closer to them.

"Come with me, then." He set off along the docks.

She fell in next to him. "I haven't thanked her properly."

"You got her temple restored. I would call that enough."

"I don't know. I've been...lately I've been so restless I've wanted to challenge the gods themselves."

"Most young mature demons are like that. Your human blood probably mitigates it, but..."

Cat nodded. "The wanderlust."

"The desire to leave the parental group and find a mate."

"I *had* a mate. She left." Anger for a moment flowed through her. A mate with whom she could not have children, true, but a mate nonetheless. But she had agreed with Beria's decision.

"And that probably has made things worse. Your feelings are natural, but be careful..."

"I already have Solus mad with me."

"Then who protects you from his wrath?"

"I think Neir. She protected me before."

"Yet you are not sworn to her service."

"I don't think I'd be much use to her." Cat frowned. They stepped around a building, and she knew they would not be observed.

R'vor spread his wings and leapt. His takeoff was a little slow and awkward, clearly affected by the weakness he had spoken of. She followed him up.

"She wants something from you."

"Just for me to be myself." Her wings caught the air and she spiraled higher, trying to rise out of pot shot range.

"Then be yourself."

"Solus...look. If what I have been told is true, and the source was hardly reliable, he wants to reshape the world in a way such as to destroy demonkind."

"Why?"

"Like I said. Not a reliable source. Whatever is going on, I don't know whether it's that or something else. Possibly something worse. There is a quarrel between him and Neir."

"Neir would not allow any species to be deliberately destroyed." A pause. "And now I am speaking for a goddess. We're a right pair."

"Well, when the gods don't tell us what's going on, I think we have the right to speculate." Cat circled away from him, comfortable on the wing. Nobody below seemed to even be looking up at them.

"We have brains and eyes, and we were not given them to fail to use them."

He'd chided her in those exact words as a child, encouraging her to be curious. Encouraging her to think for herself and not to blindly follow her teachers. She felt a deep well of affection. "Probably why the gods don't smite people for talking about them."

"I think they probably get tempted sometimes."

Cat thought she would, if she was a god. Now there was a crazy thought. Kiran had elevated his mortal wife, Neisha, when she died, yet she was only considered an angel, not a god.

That was assuming the story was even true. She put it from her mind. A lot of the stories people told about the gods were parables and metaphors. Yet to say that about the greatest love story of all time?

Maybe she should ask Kiran, she thought wryly. The only god who seemed willing to talk to her was Neir.

But then, Kiran had no reason to be angry with her. Solus, apparently, did. It was that anger that convinced her. "I think Solus is up to something, though."

"And the other gods can't exactly banish *him*."

"No. They can't. Not unless one of them is willing to take his place." Of course, Arok's banishment had not prevented people from using fire. It was, perhaps, not as simple as all of that. At the same time...Solus was also, in theory, the leader of the gods. Their king. Kiran might make a good...

What was she doing? She forced her thoughts into silence. Forced herself not to think as if she had some say in what the gods did and decided, and focused on the wind. Only the wind.

For a while, it worked, but she slept poorly that night. She curled up, miserable with her thoughts. She could not stop herself from going there, could not keep herself respectful. Was R'vor right and this part of her demon heritage, to be understood and expected? A side effect of losing Beria?

Maybe she needed to get laid. It was hard for one such as her to find a suitable lover...most women (and almost all men) were embarrassed and ashamed to be approached by one of the same sex. There were presumably taverns in Merico where such things happened, but she did not know the city well enough.

Restlessness flowed over her again. Although dawn was still an hour away, she dressed and headed out into the dark, chill streets. Maybe if she tired herself out now, she would be able to sleep through the heat of the day later.

20

Few were out. Some merchants were already preparing to open, those who wished to catch housewives and servants early for produce...such as it was here.

An apprentice hurried along the street. They ignored each other. There was nothing going on to draw her attention.

No, there was a place which drew it now. She followed her instincts, curving around the streets, away from temple square. Perhaps that might have been her first destination, but the draw she felt now was somewhere else.

The academy. It was not constructed like the one at Losana. That one was all airy arches and spires. The Merican academy was squat, with the small, high windows favored here. It looked much like the mayor's palace, in fact. Enough that she suspected the same hands in its construction.

She ensured her ring was visible before knocking on the door. It was safe enough. Somebody would be up at all hours, here. Why had she not come here before?

Because she had not felt the need. There was no obligation on her to check in with anyone, after all.

The door opened, and a student of no more than thirteen yawned at her.

"You're up early."

He yawned again. "No, late. Stupid astrology class."

"It's not stupid. You'll find it useful. You might even find that is where your talent lies."

He glanced at her ring. "The dean's asleep, but I guess you can come in."

"Most sane people are. Asleep, that is." She glanced around. "It's not laid out the same. Is there an alumni lounge or club here?"

"Yes." He seemed relieved that she was reasonably normal. By his standards, anyway.

She wondered how he had felt about being pulled away from his family. She, at least, had always known she would have to go. It was different for those who did not. Of course, he could be the child of a mage, born and bred to this life. "What's your name?"

"Jerom," he said, after a long moment.

"Cat." Would he recognize the name? Apparently not...perhaps they had sheltered the students from events. Teenagers might well go off and do something stupid. She had pulled more than her share of pranks and stupid stunts herself.

But his face remained neutral. "It's this way." A pause. "What's Losana like?"

"Wet." That, she thought, would be the impression he would get. It rained every day, after all.

"It will be wet here soon. The rains are coming."

Cat nodded. "And I will have to be careful not to be washed away."

He giggled at that. "We all will. Somebody will. Somebody always does."

She guessed quite a few somebodies. Of course, she was in no danger from a flood unless trapped indoors. Nobody would travel during the rains.

It might give her time to regroup, time to work on stuff. Yet, could she wait it out? She did not know.

She had to go to Arok-Kor, but she had to go ready. Ready to...do what? She was not sure, and until she was, she should stay here.

There. She had actually made a decision. She needed far more information. She needed...

"Who is the best scryer or seer you have?" She paused. "Well, I don't necessarily need the best."

"Professor Kevan is very good," the boy commented. "But likely in bed."

"Well, maybe I can scrounge some breakfast, then?"

Jerom giggled. "I'll find you some."

The lounge was comfortable, but unoccupied right now. She thought she might manage to nap for a few minutes, but her mind remained relentlessly awake.

A seer might be able to help her, she could not be sure. Most certainly, she should talk to one. Why had she not thought of it before? Because she had been too focused in the present, too on the move. Or because...no. She refused to believe she was only Neir's pawn.

Be yourself, Myrk had said. She focused on that. It had been entirely her own distraction, and she knew it. No excuses.

About ten minutes later, Jerom showed up with a tray of food, then winked at her before leaving again. She hoped to go get some sleep; the boy did look tired. Not everyone was well suited to being up all night. She was one of those lucky individuals who could sleep when she had to.

Normally. These days, she seemed to struggle to sleep at all.

Jerom, however, had not gone to sleep. He had gone to find Professor Kevan. An old man made his way into the room. "Ah. Now I understand."

If he was at all a talented seer he could probably see through her glamor. "Professor Kevan?"

"You are not a student. You do not need to call me Professor."

"Why not?" she couldn't resist quipping. There was something about the light in his unusual, blue eyes that set her at ease.

He moved to sit down. "You, I think, need only use those titles you choose."

Cat shook her head. She did not need her desire to rebel against everything reinforced. It was almost like she was a teenager again. "Professor," she said, firmly.

"Very well then. You need my help?"

"I feel as if I'm moving through a fog. I was hoping somebody more talented in such areas could give me a bit of illumination."

"Well, I can try. I at least know who you are. You can probably drop the cloak."

"I don't want to scare the students." She did, however, drop her glamor, feeling a slight sense of relief.

"Keeping that up all the time has to be tiring."

"It's worth it. And I don't keep it up all the time." Cat settled a little more comfortably, rather glad she had finished the food. Eating in front of another was always rather awkward.

"So. What are you hoping to find out?"

She had gone through all kinds of sensible things to say. That was not what came out of her mouth. "Reshaping the world," she blurted.

Kevan tensed. All of the easy going light went out of his eyes. "You saw it too."

"I think I did, and I also have...a source blames Solus and his cult, but that source is not reliable."

Kevan slumped. "Even a liar tells the truth sometimes. The cult claimed that was their intent, to change or reshape the world. Naturally, we pretended to go along."

"A smart thing to do." She knew the mages would have likely pulled the rug out from under the Solusians.

"Thanks to you, we did not have to do it for long. But..."

"The source was the concubine. She...or he...claims he was just using them."

"Unreliable indeed. Or perhaps simply mad."

Cat had not thought of that. Then she thought of Lady Teola. "Everyone in this has an agenda. Including me."

What was her agenda? Other than personal survival? She wished she could be more sure, could understand her own mind.

"Except, I do not think you know what yours is."

"Mind reader," she quipped. Of course, if he was a good seer, he might well be catching her surface thoughts. She resolved to be very careful what she said, even silently.

"Actually, it's in your body language. You are struggling for a sense of purpose even more than most."

She nodded. "More like...I am worried that one I don't desire will be forced on me." *Be yourself.*

"Aren't we all?" He settled back. "So. You saw it. I have seen it. What I have not seen is how to stop it."

"I..."

"And it will destroy all life, not just demonkind."

"I...suspected that." She had to prevent it, but how? You are not capable of taking on a god. Directly. Myrk had been warning her against an open assault on Solus, perhaps even on his followers. So, what did she do? "What else can you tell me?"

"I do not know. I think, perhaps, we need to try and find out more."

Cat nodded. She hated scrying rituals, but...it might give her some answers, so she was willing to tolerate it. "Alright then."

"We might as well get it out of the way. Have you eaten?"

"Yes."

He nodded, and began.

The only thing Cat could think of as she hurried away from the academy was the image that had filled her vision.

She needed to be alone. No, she needed...and, for once not caring who saw, she leapt upwards into the darkening sky. She needed the wind. It lifted her up, it bore her higher.

She had seen it all now. The skies raining fire, and then the sun fading, Solus' eye no longer watching the land. She had seen the white come down from the mountains, a carpet that spread across the fields. The crops withering and dying, caniks lying down, starved, to die in the cold.

Humans and demons dying. She had no word for what she had seen, she who had not even known the word 'snow' until recently could not understand 'ice age'. Yet, it had been more than that.

It had had a cause, and the cause was a star touching the heavens. Bits of it falling to earth, sending up dust and clouds. She did not fully understand.

She did understand that Solus was either causing this or failing to prevent it, and that he was doing it because he was angry with Arok and Neir. That much had come through.

Arok was exiled. Arok was trying to come back. Neir...had saved Cat's life. That was the cause of the pain that had driven her to the sky. She was the cause of it.

The thought of dying filled her. If she was dead, then Arok could not use her in any way, shape or form, and Solus might back down. Why had Neir saved her? Was it Neir's...

Were the gods merely squabbling children? She had thought of going to Neir's temple, but she had elected instead to get somewhere Myrk could perhaps not come.

Perhaps. He was an angel, he might be capable of growing wings or even flying without them. However, there was no voice. She wanted to rage at the heavens, but knew it would do no good.

She knew she had to stop this. The pull to Arok-Kor?

She would die in Arok-Kor. She knew that with sudden clarity, and she had to, because if she did not... Why not let her die as a baby? Why force her to make the choice? Because there was power in it...that was the only answer.

She was being sacrificed, but Myrk had told her to be herself. None of it made sense, and she flew a fierce circle above the city.

Only slowly did she realize she was not alone. "R'vor?"

How had he found her?

"You look like you could use a good fight."

"Maybe I could." She changed her course, fell in next to him. She wanted to be alone, but she did not have the heart to make him go away after he had searched for her. "The world might be coming to an end."

"So, how do we stop it?"

"You don't understand. It might be coming to an end because of me."

"Because Neir saved you?"

They had had conversations about it before. She had questioned before whether her life should have happened. "Yes. And I can only think of one solution."

"Cat..."

"Got a better idea?" She could not read his face, she could barely hear his voice.

"No. But I am going to find one. You are not allowed to die."

"If this happens, we will all die." She realized she was not afraid, or at least not as afraid as she should have been. If she did end her life, she could do it quickly and easily.

Be yourself. She did not want to die. It was not who she was to give up so readily, but what could she do?

"Then think about every possibility first. It's not like you to give up."

His words echoed her thoughts. "I'm not giving up. I'm contemplating my choices."

To take things into her own hands, that was a choice. To not go to Arok-Kor, that was a choice. It would break the pattern if she went back to Losana. Or if she died here.

The sorcerer had needed her to go to Arok-Kor. Every feeling she had was that she should. Maybe she should do it right here, right now, place a knife in her own heart and then revel in the sensation of falling. End it all.

What was she doing? She was not that kind of person. *Be yourself.* "I have to find a way. But I fear that any way I find, R'vor, will end in the same place. Part of me wants to just get it over with."

"What if there's something you have to do first?"

Power. She almost swore out loud, another thought coming into her mind. "I need to be alone, R'vor. I'm sorry."

He simply banked away, accepting that. She would talk to him later, but thanks to him there was a later. She had come so close to destroying herself, but she had a good reason. *Be yourself.*

What was she? A halfbreed, and a mage. A mage who's teachers had been accused of holding her back.

Who could stop Solus? Neir could not. Arok could. Yet, if she brought Arok back, he would probably try to destroy humanity again. She would be a traitor, too, to everything she had been raised to believe and understand.

Which gave only one course of action. She knew now why she had to go to Arok-Kor. Why she had, in the end, no choice, not because of fate or destiny, but because she could not let this happen.

R'vor would not understand.

Needless to say, Cat could not leave immediately. She knew only part of the route, and she also knew she had to leave alone.

They would think her a traitor, and she could not bring herself to lie and say her route led west. She would not see Losana again.

When the cult found out she did not intend to join them, she fully expected they would kill her. Probably far more painfully than if she had done it herself or asked R'vor. The feeling of impending doom, however, strengthened her instead of the reverse. She was not afraid. Not now.

However, there was much she had to prepare. First, she returned to the academy. She would have to say something to Kevan, she supposed. He had seen the distress with which she had left.

She was surprised he had let her go. In his place, she would have slain her before she could leave. It had seemed the obvious solution.

Perhaps he was not capable of violence. Many men were not, and his specialty certainly did not require it.

A different student, a girl, let her in. "Where is the library?"

The girl smiled. "Follow." She led her through the corridors.

Cat thought that she would get lost here, there was almost no decoration, the place all looked the same. The library, though, was oddly familiar. After a moment, she realized the stacks had been laid out in the same manner as the one in Losana. "I can manage from here. Thank you."

She knew she would have to be quick. Word of what had happened would spread, inevitably, and then her life would be forfeit if anyone caught her. Debt or no debt, there was no way any mage would not jump to the obvious solution to the problem. No way they would take her on alone. They would surround her, they would take her down, and they would kill her.

She found the book she needed quickly, she copied the page in personal shorthand, glancing around. Perhaps she was paranoid, but that did not mean they were not out to get her to some degree. There were footsteps. She ducked out a second entrance, the precious sheet in one hand, and then out into the daylight.

She headed for the market, knowing that they would try nothing in a crowded space. Perhaps they were right, but the desire to live was strong in her again. For now. She could not let it get too strong, not with what she carried.

It was what had to be done, but their way was premature. Be yourself. She would not go gently, and she would achieve something before she departed the stage. That was what Neir wanted, but it was also what Cat wanted. The two moved in step.

It was to Neir's temple that she went, changing her appearance as she wove through the crowd. If anyone noticed, they gave no sign.

She would be safe in the temple, even if she had to slip out the back door. Besides, she owed Kera a goodbye.

She found the healer in a back room. "I am leaving."

Kera studied her for a moment. "I see a woman with a death wish."

"Maybe." Cat breathed in, let it out in a long sigh. "I am going to try and stop something very bad from happening. I doubt I'll survive." She was not being entirely honest, but she really did not want to tell the entire story to the priestess.

"You should..."

"There's no need to risk anyone else. I have a plan, and I know what I'm doing." She sounded confident, but Kera still seemed skeptical.

"Everyone needs somebody to watch their back."

"If I go alone, there is no risk to anyone else and I have a far greater chance of getting where I need to go."

"Arok-Kor. What do you plan on doing to the cult?"

Cat's eyes closed for a moment. "Nothing. I hope."

"Will you betray those who saved you?" Kera's tone was soft.

"I hope not. The truth is, that there are things in motion that have to be stopped, and if the only way to stop them..." Cat tailed off. "Let's just say that if this isn't stopped, everyone dies."

Kera paled a little. "Arok..."

"It's not Arok." Cat had not meant to tell her. "Not this time. It's Solus."

Kera turned white. "I..." For a moment, she looked about to bolt. Then, softly, "I will ask Neir for guidance."

"She's been talkative lately." Except that Neir had given her no sign or signal that she was doing the right thing.

"I...noticed. Perhaps this is what it has all been about. Perhaps not."

"I could be lying through my teeth, after all."

Kera studied her for a moment. "I don't think so. You never struck me as dishonest or evil."

"I am not sure that we are not all evil, and all good, at different times."

"You may well be right." Kera looked at her, then she turned, heading into the sanctuary.

21

Cat did not expect to make it back to her tavern room. When she tried, she sensed three mages staking the place out. Two were obviously low powered, but she had no need to tangle with them.

She did not plan on taking the caba. She did not plan on taking anything she did not absolutely need. This time, it would be her wings that carried her north. She purchased water and supplies, and made sure she had lightweight goods she could trade with the nomads.

The merchants did not bat an eyelid, she had changed her semblance into that of a lean, hard swordswoman...she had thought of a male guise, but that had felt like too much dishonesty.

Be yourself. Once she had what she needed, with the sun already fading, she headed for the west gate, slipping out of it. The guards paid no attention. They were concerned with who was coming into Merico, not leaving.

How far should she go? She settled for walking until she could no longer see the walls of the city. The temperature was already beginning to plummet, but this was a better time to start out than the heat of the day. Even for her. The dry air was against her skin.

The rains! She had not even thought about the rains. Two weeks, and the desert would be a quagmire and experience its brief green season. Could she get to Arok-Kor in two weeks?

Yes, she decided, and she did not have to worry about what might happen afterwards. Or if she did, she would probably have no problems waiting out the rains.

It was of no concern. She could not wait until spring, in any case.

She did not have that much time. Ice flowed through her vision, and it caused her to rush into action.

She leapt skywards, angling her flight north, dropping her glamor as she did so. If anyone was using magical tracking, hopefully, they would not be able to distinguish her from a pureblood.

The wind was cool under her wings, but she paced herself. This would be a long flight with few rests. She felt up to it, however. She felt magic flow through her.

They had trained her to restrict her power, not to unleash it. What was she capable of if she did? Not taking on a god, and would what she did trigger a godwar? Could a godwar be worse than what they had already seen?

Would she cause it in her attempt to prevent it? Her body was occupied, her mind got to wander. She let her wings carry her and tried to focus her thoughts.

Would she? It was possible, anything was possible, but perhaps her intent would be read by the gods. Perhaps she would be forgiven if she screwed up...by them. Never, though, by the person who mattered most.

She would never forgive herself.

The desert was featureless. It would be easy, Cat thought, to become lost up here. The stars told her the direction of north and she knew Arok-Kor was 'almost due north' of Merico.

It would have to do. She flew high, high enough to be out of the range of casual arrows...she could not risk being shot at. Somebody might get lucky. Even the thought of that made the wing that had been injured ache a little. Psychological, she knew...she was more than fully recovered. Nobody wanted to be shot, though. Especially not out of the sky, especially not when it meant to fall.

She could die pointlessly yet. Perhaps it was all pointless. Two weeks on the wing, and she knew she had to find an oasis at some point. She could not carry enough water aloft.

Still, she had a confidence...she told herself that feeling as if the gods were on her side was stupid. She told herself it was the dumbest thing she had ever done or considered.

That did not help. She was buoyed up by the wind. It simply felt so good to fly that she could not imagine failure.

Addict, she told herself, wryly. Addicted to flight as some were to mead. Then, it was at least a healthy addiction. She just hoped she could hold out. Her wings already ached a little.

No. She was up to this. She had to be. If she was not, then she would die. Or end up in the hands of the nomads, who might well bring her to Arok-Kor in chains. It would depend on who offered the highest bounty...them or the mages.

She still did not know that the mages sought her life, she only knew what she would do in their place.

So, north. The desert below her was the sand sea, now, dunes seeming to march across it with the direction of the prevailing wind. A cross wind, she noticed with a frown.

She frowned. A strong wind could mean a sandstorm, and she would lose time avoiding one. Flying into one of those was not quite her worst nightmare, but it came dangerously close. She had never experienced one, but T'la had warned her once, that if she ever came to the desert...

Don't fly into the clouds. They'll blind you. The wind picked up at the thought, then eased again. She leaned into it, determined not to let it blow her off course.

From the ground, people would see a speck that might be a bird relatively low or a demon at altitude. An odd sort of wistfulness came through her. Could they ever have a world where the reaction to a demon was not to hide the valuables and the children? Where the two races acknowledged one another as equals? It had been heading that way, but the gods seemed determined to prevent it.

Except Neir. Or was Neir working on a different agenda, one Cat did not know.

She glided down towards the ground. She needed to land, to rest her wings, and she saw a change in the sand that might indicate water.

It did, although it was a little brackish. She had to filter it through part of her robe to render it drinkable. Still, it was water, and she drank sufficient before glancing around.

It would be easy to imagine, she thought, being the last living thing alive here. Yet, even as she had that thought, a lizard slithered out of the sand, lapping at the water. It showed no fear of her.

She probably could not catch it anyway. "Hey. Guess I'm not alone after all." Of course, the animal ignored her. It was not an angel and did not understand her words. It just lapped at the water, then vanished back into the sand. It had very small legs, she noticed, as if halfway to becoming a snake.

That reminded her that there were rumored to be great serpents...sandrakes...in the sea of sand. She should probably not stay groundbound long or risk becoming supper to one of them. They were probably big enough to see her as prey. "Well..."

No answer, but then she had not expected one. She would probably get no further guidance from the gods.

She stepped away from the spring, looking around again. If there was anything larger than a lizard, she could not see it. Good. She did not want to run into the nomads at this point. Or anyone sent out from the city.

A shadow passed overhead. She glanced up. Demon. Whoever it was circled.

Company after all, it seemed. She did not wave, but watched as it descended.

Oh hell. "R'vor. How the heck did you find me?"

He opened his hand. Within it was the communication stone she had given Tava.

"Tava sent you."

"You went off half-cocked on your own. What did you expect?"

"You know where I'm going." He did not know, of course, what she had taken from the library. "If you come with me..."

He cut her off. "You need me. Kera told me everything. You did not cause it." He lifted a taloned hand. "You are not to be blamed for the circumstances of your birth."

"That doesn't matter. It doesn't matter what the cost is to stop it...but I won't have you pay it. You've been through enough." Her eyes flicked to his wings, still spread.

He folded them. "You will die."

"If that's what it takes. I'm not suicidal now, R'vor. I don't want to die any more than you do. But if I have any power to stop it."

You are not capable of taking on a god.

Well, she did not intend to.

"And if you start a godwar?"

"If you saw what was shown to me, you'd understand why a godwar might be preferable." She shivered. "I'd rather have neither. Hell, R'vor. I want *peace*."

"But I don't think you alone can create that."

"Nobody can do it alone."

"And if freeing Arok is the only way to stop Solus, there will likely be a war."

"I plan on *talking* to Arok." It was the first time she had admitted any part of her plan to anyone, even R'vor.

"Don't talk to Arok...at least not first. Hasn't it occurred to you that there's a far simpler conduit?" His wings closed, close around himself. "Cat. Don't talk to Arok. Talk to Birrur."

It was so simple put in those terms. And she had talked to Neir. What was Birrur? A crippled goddess, bound to subservience under Neir for her crimes. And Arok's wife. No doubt she could reach him. No doubt she could speak with him.

Cat's wings lowered.

"We all miss the obvious. Why don't we try that, now, before haring off to Arok-Kor."

"I don't know how to get her attention."

"I do. But not here. There's enough water here to attract a sandrake."

Cat nodded. "I was just thinking that." She spread her wings and leapt skywards, R'vor following her.

Birrur. The mystery of why Birrur had such a small sphere had been explained to her. Yet, what had she been before then...and could be again? "R'vor," she said as they landed a few hundred yards away. "Who is Birrur, really?"

"Isn't that obvious? What was the plague?"

"An act of..." Cat tailed off. It was obvious, it was as if something had kept her from thinking of it. "Birrur is War."

"Indeed."

Cat dropped to the sand, lifting her wings. "War." It was so obvious. But now Birrur was bound under Neir, and there had not been a war since the time of Arok. "If she were unbound, then..."

"You can't have peace without war, I don't think, or vice versa."

She shook her head. "If there's a godwar, that itself *would* unbind her. If there was a major war, then Neir would lose control of her." Was that what Neir was worried about?

No. She was suddenly sure of that. "Well, then. I know how to get her attention." Cat stood again, as if restless, but it was to draw one of her blades.

R'vor simply nodded. "Don't overdo it."

Cat smiled. "Trust me." Then she drew the blade across her wrist, releasing a few drops of hot blood. It touched the sands and almost seemed to sizzle in contact.

Silence. For a long moment, there was silence. Then a snake poked its head out of the dunes.

A moment later, there was hot wind, and the air shimmered. Cat glanced at the snake, then at the form that was neither quite here nor not here. Myrk, keeping an eye on...

Birrur appeared as a demoness. But not an ordinary one. Her coloring was rich, deep gold, not the greens shading to red that were more common. Almost like the demon equivalent of a firehead, Cat could not help but think.

Almost like... She dropped into a curtsey, hardly daring to look. The snake seemed closer to her, as if he'd sneakily moved towards her while she was focused elsewhere. "Lady."

"So, you're the one." The voice was incredibly feminine, rich and deep.

"I suppose I am. I..." Cat tailed off.

"Why would you think I would want anything other than bloody war?"

"If Solus continues, there will be nobody left. The world will be wiped clean, not just of demons."

"Ah. You do see to the heart of it. But the question remains. You do not seek war. So, why come to me?"

Cat knew that Birrur was enough here to destroy her. Perhaps that was why Myrk was there. Birrur might be restricted and limited, but she could still kill one uppity mortal. "Because it's smarter than going to your husband."

Birrur laughed. A demon laugh, a sharp hissing sound. "I seek my freedom and his."

"And what would you do with it?" That came from Myrk, who was now coiled next to Cathren.

There was, for a long moment, no answer. Perhaps the goddess was not sure what she would do with her freedom. Cathren kept her head down. R'vor was...she glanced around. R'vor was hiding behind the corner of a sand dune, never mind that this had been his idea. He had probably not expected it to work.

She almost wanted to do the same thing. "What I want," Cat began softly, "is peace, yes. I know that there will never be complete peace. It's not in our natures. I want an understanding between human and demon."

"You want to no longer be caught between two worlds." Birrur stepped closer. The sand did not move under her feet.

"It's not about me."

"Of course it is. No matter what you might do for others, some of it is going to be about you. It's in your nature."

"I don't expect to survive the next few weeks. So..."

"Stand." Birrur's voice was soft.

With a glance at Myrk, Cat obeyed, rising to her feet. Her wings spread outwards a little for balance.

The goddess met her gaze. Held it. "Perhaps yes...you have strength, and you have the training of a warrior."

"I will do anything to ensure that both humans and demons survive."

"And you will not settle for one or the other."

"There are parts of the world more comfortable for demons and parts for humans. There is no reason we can't share Yirath, there's no reason why we can't all live."

"There will always be war. And this will be a war."

Cat glanced at Myrk. "Your mistress?"

"The war is inevitable. Its ending is not, yet."

"Then there will be death."

"Yes." Myrk abruptly moved, gliding across the sand towards Birrur. "Your freedom is likely to come. The question is whether you can act like an adult this time."

That was clearly Neir speaking. And the tone was so much like Liesa that Cat was finding it very hard not to laugh. Laughing would be a bad idea.

"Am I supposed to cut a deal with *her*?" Birrur indicated Cat with a taloned hand, but her eyes were now on the serpent.

"You are supposed to act your age." Myrk's voice had definitely become more female. "As for her..."

Cat remained standing, not sure she should even be hearing this. And Myrk changed to some language she did not know. Not demon tongue...she was quite fluent in that. Was that the language of the gods?

It must have been. Birrur answered with a rather short response, then switched back to normal, human speech. "Very well. I will talk to my husband. But I still see little use for humans."

Cat shook her head. "Some of us see use for them." She knew she should not speak, that she was only going to anger the goddess. "I might be half human, but I've found that humans and demons have more in common than most would admit. But I'll tell you the use of humans. They create things. They *build* things. Demons make beauty, but it's transient. It's song and the dance of the air. The world is enriched by both."

Birrur had fixed her gaze on her again. Cat felt every layer of her soul laid to bare, but she held her ground.

"It might not have been what was intended, but it works. If people could just grow up, it would work even better."

There was silence. Then the goddess nodded to her. Yes, nodded. Then...she vanished, leaving heat haze for a moment.

Cat swayed on her feet. It could not be loss of blood...the cut had already healed. Perhaps it was emotional strain, but she felt the ground rush up towards her, and then nothing.

It was dawn when she came around. R'vor was crouched over her, offering a waterskin. "Drink."

"I have a headache."

"I'm surprised you don't have more than that."

"How much did you hear?"

"Cat...you weren't even there for about fifteen minutes. I didn't hear anything."

"Oh hell." R'vor had not vanished behind a dune after all. Birrur had not come *here,* she had drawn Cat *there.* "I...okay. I think I made some progress. Watch out for snakes."

R'vor laughed. "There was one hanging around, but it's gone now."

"You know. I want my alchemist's shop. My...normality." Maybe Cat should have been more careful what she wished for.

You are not capable of taking on a god. Yet, in a way, she had. Maybe Myrk had meant in combat, in battle or duel of spells. She had held her own in conversation. But then, Birrur had, indeed, seemed more like a petulant child. She laughed weakly, drank a bit more water, and struggled to her feet.

"What's so funny?"

"Neir telling Birrur to act her age and sounding *just* like my foster mother."

R'vor shook his head. "Cat..."

"I know. But...I heard it. I might not have been meant to, but I did." And she wasn't mocking the gods, the laughter felt like easy laughter, as if with a friend.

She was going to damn herself with her effrontery. She was going to be destroyed by them if this continued, yet, she could not seem to hold herself back. "Dammit, R'vor. I can't keep acting like this."

He answered her only with silence.

"R'vor..." She turned away, stepped away. He probably did not want to be close to her. She would contaminate him.

You are not capable of taking on a god. Myrk was trying to restrain her. He was not succeeding. Not right now, not in this moment.

She hated herself. But instead of saying anything more, she lifted off into the air. R'vor did not immediately follow.

Had she permanently damaged their friendship? But he had been fine...until she had laughed. You didn't laugh at the gods. Even if you felt certain the gods were laughing with you, you still did not... She was breaking every rule there was, and she had to stop if she planned to stay alive. If she planned to continue to exist.

They would...yet, they had not touched her. Why not? Because Neir still needed her. That was the only explanation. The wind carried her higher. She looked towards the mountains, and remembered the vision of the snow spreading down their slopes, growing away from them, covering everything. Killing everything.

She would face even total destruction to stop that. Be yourself. Neir had told her to be herself. Did that mean she had a license to say what she thought? She had said what she thought to Birrur, and only got a nod. A cold one.

The goddess did not *like* her. It almost seemed like it might be personal, which was crazy. Taking a dislike to a mortal? Why bother? Solus was mad with her for a reason. She had never, herself, done anything to Birrur's followers...few and pitiful as they were.

The goddess, of course, wanted her freedom and would get it. Once she had it, would she destroy Cat? Or...no. There was respect, somehow, mingled with the dislike.

Gods are not supposed to respect mortals. She circled, riding a thermal, trying to catch her thoughts.

She was a unique entity, created by magic, the fusion of Yirath's two sentient species. Therefore, perhaps, she was being given license that would not have been to most. And there was one obvious reason why Birrur might dislike her. She might not forgive her for being female, and thus an inappropriate vessel for Arok's spirit. Neir had seen to that, or so Tava had always insisted. She wondered if Tava had spoken to Neir...or, perhaps more likely, to Myrk.

A dragon circled above the desert, drifting out from the mountains. It had clearly seen something. Dead cabas, perhaps. Dead humans, quite likely.

Cat angled her flight, speeding up towards it, but she realized after a moment that it was an illusion of perspective. It was at least two days' flight away, and by that time, whoever was in trouble would be out of it, one way or another. She banked back, returning to her circle. Perhaps other scavengers would wonder what she had seen, in the desert below. Perhaps not. Likely, they knew not to bother following demons a lot of the time.

What, she wondered, did the dragon make of her? Something odd, something unnatural. Something it would not and could not trust, for sure. Her rapid flight, though, had taken her out of earshot of R'vor.

She felt the arrow hit, before she could hear any sound. It struck her in the breast, not hitting anything vital, but it lodged in the muscles that supported her wings.

She was being forced down, and the pain that flowed through her was hideous. She tried, tried to fly back towards where she had left R'vor, but all she could manage was a downward spiral.

Her swords were pulled from their sheaths in a moment, and she tried to manage the concentration for demonfire. She could manage only a few licks of flame, and the arrow did not catch.

It was best left in there anyway. She knew that, and she hit the ground harder than she intended, blades drawn.

Would they approach her, or would they shoot her again? She hoped that it was nomads who still thought there was a bounty on demon wings. Such might listen to her. Or might back down when they realized what a rare bird they had caught.

It was nomads alright. They rose up from the sand, their robes smeared with it for camouflage.

She crossed her blades in front of her, a gesture that meant she would not attack unless assaulted further.

They regarded her with expressions she could not read behind their veils. "The mages want her dead."

The blades snapped outwards as she heard that. "You have not taken me yet."

It was bravado. She could not fly. R'vor might or might not have heard her. And several had bows. All they had to do was fill her with arrows. So, it was over.

Calm came over her, and with it the demonfire, forming around her into a wall of flame. A chance. They would find it hard to shoot through it. They tried nonetheless, but the shafts caught alight.

"Take her. You can't even bring down a winged demon?"

She would have to hurt them to stop them. She knew that, as much as she did not wish to. She released enough of the demonflame to reduce the aura as they approached, focusing it onto her blades. One was less bold than the others. He fled, to the curses of his leader.

"Do I have to do everything myself?"

"How about we do just that?" Her right arm was impeded by the arrow that was still in her flesh, but her left was free. She had never been strongly right handed, and he had no magic. She might, even in this state, be able to take him. There was a heat in her blood. She tried to regain that unnatural calm, but she knew she was in grave danger of losing it to battle fever and pain.

That, in this situation, would get her killed. "I'm not stupid."

They were closing on her. Either she burned them or she died here and now. Or... She leapt, letting fire explode around her. She could barely get aloft, her right wing was not properly responding to her demands. She might cripple herself, flying with this injury. She might...

She had work to do still, and it was not better that she died here, dammit. She could expect no help from the gods. No, there could be no divine intervention this day. That happened only in stories.

Then again, so did angels chatting with her. And she felt, abruptly, as if there was a presence here.

Not Neir. Birrur...breaking through her bonds, Cat could feel it. Neir could not hold her. Or intended to let her go.

War. The war had started. This might even be, itself, the first skirmish. She leapt higher. Kill him, some instinct told her.

No. She did not have to kill him, and she would not burn them. She would not... She was not that kind of a person. Except perhaps she did have to kill him. She could not fly fast enough to escape. She swooped, her blades extending in front of her.

One of them pierced the leader's chest, even as something hit her leg, an arrow perhaps, grazing it despite the aura.

He went down. She knew he was dead...and so did his men. They scattered.

She collapsed to the sand no more than fifty yards away. Had any of them had their courage, she would have been dead or maimed for sure.

22

It was in that state that R'vor found her.

Cat sat by the fire. Her shoulder was bandaged. "You should not fly," R'vor was telling her.

"We are a little far from anywhere to get there any other way and the cabas are gone. We cannot go to an oasis."

"You could use your glamor."

Cat closed her eyes. "I can try. But if I slip in my concentration, then we are even more doomed."

"If we stay here, we both die."

"You go. Go to one of the oases, buy water, come back. I will be fine."

R'vor seemed to consider that. "You are the one being hunted like an animal."

"It's a big desert. I would have to be unlucky...or them using magic, and if they are using magic, I certainly don't need my wings to fight them." It was the only way, and she had to convince him of that. She could not let him stay here until they both died of thirst, after all.

After a moment, reluctant, wings drooping, he left.

She settled back against the sand. He would not be long, and her shoulder would heal. She hoped. Well, if she was crippled, she could hang on until...

She shook her head. She would not make it any distance if she could not fly. She could not go back to Merico, she could not trust the nomads. If she could not fly, she was dead anyway. There was, too, only one place she could go to have a chance to live.

She had no choice, after all, but to go to Arok-Kor. She closed her eyes. Well, no. She could try and go west, try and get across the mountains. It was possible the academy in Losana would protect her. It was also possible they would not. Not if they got the same information. The same... She shook her head.

She was lost, and she knew it. There was no chance of survival for her except in the arms of those who had always been her enemies. "You know, you told me to be myself."

She got no answer, but then, she had not truly expected one. Myrk was not, after all, following her around. At least, she would hope he was not. Or maybe she was supposed to answer this one herself.

How could she be herself when her course of action was narrowed down to one path? When her choices were go to Arok-Kor or die?

Her shoulder felt warmer. Perhaps that was an answer in itself. If she went to Arok-Kor, what would they do? Try to use her to free Arok, in some means. The war had already started, and she had, after all, been part of it.

No, she realized. The war had started when the Solusians had thrown the healers out of Merico. That at least was not her fault. Yet, if Solus was moving now...

...he might have anyway. Ice falling from the sky, ice and fire, and the world covered in white. A fresh start for the gods? Well, she was not going to let it happen. Except she lacked the power to stop it, even with the spell she carried with her.

If she was to use that, then where? Had the Solusians sought to capture her alive, she could have used it to at least slow them down, but they wanted her head. Literally. She was sure they would settle for no lesser evidence of her death.

After all, she could fake it easily enough without that. Even with, with the right help, she might be able to. Then she would have to live under a fake name, without showing any magic but glamor...and even that would be risky. She could not disguise herself by any mundane means.

No. It was not a solution. She opened her eyes. The sky was darkening rapidly. Night did not so much fall in the desert as crash. It would be cold soon, but she could handle that. Her shoulder still felt warm, and the pain had flowed out of it. She watched as the stars came out one by one.

That was when she saw it. A star moving, across her field of vision. A falling star...except that it did not vanish, but continued going until it vanished below the horizon.

She frowned. The cold suddenly flowed into her, and she was not sure it had any physical source.

It was cold, and it was a cold that struck to the heart of her. It was about to start, and she did not have as much time as she thought.

No time to come up with an alternative plan. And there, flying towards her, was R'vor.

The demon descended towards her. She stood, extended her wings. No stiffness, no pain.

"I'm guessing Neir is still with us."

"It's about to start. I have to go now." Cat stepped towards her friend.

"Not without me."

"Are you willing to risk getting killed in Arok-Kor?"

"If I must. I am not letting you go alone."

She could see the determination within him, could almost feel it. "Then let's go." And she was airborne...yes. The damage had been fully healed. She did not thank Neir out loud, she did not feel she had to. She did not feel...and she was streaking north, as fast a pace as she could sustain.

"What triggered this?"

"A falling star that did not fall." They could barely hear each other over the sound of their own wings, she had to raise her voice, and it came hard. Her breath was mostly being used to fly.

"What do you plan, Cat?"

"I am not sure. I know it has to be done there."

"Well, the only thing Arok-Kor has that nowhere else does is an active shrine to Arok."

"I know. It may be that stopping Solus will take all of the Gods...including Arok and Birrur." That was what grew within her.

All of the gods...and perhaps then some.

"So, after it all, the prophecy will come true after all."

Would Cat let herself be used as Arok's vessel? Yet, she had summoned Birrur with only a few drops of blood. What was she? Well, she knew, but she had an uncertainty within her. "Yes, but under my terms. Not Arok's."

"You can't bargain with the..." He tailed off.

"What choice do we have?" She knew they had none. And if she failed...then Neir and Seliene had contained Arok before, they could do it again. She felt the wind under her wings, felt it lift her higher into the air.

She appreciated it. This might be the last truly free, truly joyful moment of her life. There was nothing to be done but let herself enjoy the flight. Let demon instincts, for once, take over. Flow through her. The stars were bright above. Could she use magic to remove her own fatigue?

She knew what would happen if she did. It would all catch up with her at the most inopportune time.

No, she would have to pace herself, rest when she had to. For now, though, she felt good, streaking through the night. She and R'vor would be shadows against the stars.

They landed an hour or so after dawn.

"I'll take first watch," R'vor offered.

"You've flown more." Cat was going to insist on this, and besides, she was not sure she could sleep. She was not sure she wanted to sleep. She worried about what might lie behind her eyelids if she closed her eyes.

In the end, though, she had to. She woke from troubled dreams.

The sea of sand extended around them. Even from the air, they saw nothing but mirages...and Cat had learned rapidly to identify them. She would not be fooled. R'vor would certainly not be. He flew a little behind her, even if he was normally the faster. She was not stupid. The demon was covering her back.

She wondered if the best guise now was that of a demon, rather than the human woman she preferred to appear as. Once she got close enough, of course, she would prefer to be seen as herself. "I am wondering if the best way to get in is not to let myself get captured."

"Given they want to recruit you...that might not be a bad idea."

"But there's you."

"I honor all gods, remember. I'm willing to say a couple of prayers to Arok if that's what it takes."

She smiled, even though demons did not, generally, smile. "Just be careful. I don't want anything to happen to you...anything more, that is."

Neir might have fixed R'vor's body, but she was sure there was still darkness in his mind.

"I think I am in more danger from the Solusians than the Arokians, the same as you. They would probably love to convert me."

He was probably right. The desert extended around them. The feeling of not having much time was still present, but it had eased a little. She felt she could relax.

Or perhaps, now she was on the journey...but had it been Neir nagging at her or something within herself?

For all she knew, this close to the center of his church, it was Arok pulling at her. Drawing her. The prophecy had said she would be the vehicle of his return.

Laran and Tava had always taken that literally. What if it was not? If that was the case, she might survive...but in eternal exile. She could not return to human society having done it, that was for sure. She could live amongst demons.

She could...she knew...she would always have the option of remaining within Arok's church. Of serving the god of fire and summer. Oddly, that might be the best course of action...she could perhaps be a voice of moderation.

Yet, she still had the spell, and if that was what it took...then she would not be worrying about it. She had some reason to hope.

Or did she? She was not even sure, as she flew north, that she wanted to survive this.

The oasis was unoccupied when they landed. R'vor filled their canteens, Cat moving halfway up a nearby dune to get a better look. She was not about to take off again anytime soon. They would need to sleep again, but watch on watch. This was clearly a place nomads...demon, human, or both...came. For once in her life, she hoped if anyone arrived they were demons.

The demons who had asked her to join them or die came to mind. They had been half-hearted about it...they had made threats, but lacked the strength to carry them out. Well, they would like as not show up again before the end. She thought they were Arokian cultists.

They might not attack her when they saw her route. Or they might. Or they might come and offer her and R'vor an 'escort'.

If she came into Arok-Kor a prisoner, it would not be ill suited to her goals, as long as they did not find the parchment. As long as they did not guess at all of her plan.

She stood there, the sand under her feet. Some of it had got inside her boots, perhaps inevitably. The sand got everywhere, and she would be glad to be on more solid ground. "The sand..."

"Before we get to Arok-Kor, it turns back to rock. The city is on a river, there is some agricultural land."

"You've been here." Not an accusation.

"A couple of times, trading." R'vor shrugged. "The people here are just people, center of Arok's cult or not. If you avoid the priests themselves, they seem quite normal."

"Mostly demon..."

"Mostly human. You know about demons and cities. Technically, they're all under Arok's patronage, but not all take it seriously."

Cat nodded. "I think it would be best if I either enter as myself or as a demon."

"Definitely. A demon male and a human female traveling together would be the talk of the city. It depends...do you want them to know you're there right away, or shall we scout out first?"

Cat moved back down the dune to join him, drinking from the spring itself, not answering for a long moment. "Scout first if we can," she said, finally. "We might learn something."

"Most of the demons in this area tend towards a reddish coloration."

Cat nodded...thinking for a moment of Birrur's golden hue. No doubt the goddess manifested like that to stand out. She had never seen a demon quite that shade. "Got it. The swords won't stand out."

"It might be best if we told them you were my wife. Or you could mimic me and be my sister."

"Wife is probably best. I don't want to get courted by half a dozen young demons and I don't feel like being ugly." She flickered a teasing grin at him.

"You could never be ugly."

"Flirt." Not that R'vor was... She frowned for a moment. "R'vor, why have you never married?"

"Because the one female I really loved chose somebody else. It took me a little while to recover, and I've never found one to match her." He studied Cat for a moment. "There have been times when..."

"Well, I'm not. It wouldn't work, and..."

"You still don't expect to survive this."

"No. I don't. I hope mostly to ensure that you do." That was, indeed, her primary concern. R'vor's survival mattered far more than her own. "And besides. I'm not interested in males."

"More's the pity."

"Perhaps I should be your sister after all."

She turned away from him for a moment, looking for something else to say, dredging the recesses of her own mind. She found no answers before she heard something.

Whoever it was had seen her unglamored self...but...no, that was no person.

The sand itself was moving.

"Sandrake!" R'vor hissed. "Get aloft. Now."

Cat did as she was told, her wings protesting with every beat, the burn deepening through her muscles into her heart. R'vor was a mere length behind her.

"Damn. That thing's huge." It was a giant serpent...no. It was clearly kin to dragons, having the vestiges of legs and wings, but they were small and held close to its body. It was as if it was on its way to turning into a snake.

"That's a small one."

Cat squeaked, "Small?" She flew higher. "But it can't fly, right?"

"No. And we have full canteens. We'll just have to continue a little further." R'vor sounded as if that appealed to him about as much as it appealed to her.

"Wait."

There was another figure near the sandrake, the serpent was diving towards it. A red-brown demon, blending in to the red sand.

"We..."

"If we don't help her, what do we become?" Cat swooped downwards. Why was the demoness not flying? It was a female from the size.

Then she saw her wings. The left one had been slashed a couple of times, perhaps by the sandrake, perhaps in some other fight. It was not damage that would not heal, but it was enough.

She could not carry her in this state. Instead, she murmured the one spell she used the least...a flight spell, lifting the injured demoness upwards.

The sandrake dove for them. Missed, barely, as Cat towed the stranger higher into the sky.

"Now you've pissed it off," R'vor quipped.

"Good." The demoness...definitely a female...said nothing as Cat twisted to look at her.

They did not make it much further before all three collapsed to the sand...but they had flown far enough to avoid the sandrake's nose.

That was really all that mattered, as far as Cat was concerned. They were clear.

Exhausted as she was, she moved to examine the damaged wing. "What is your name?"

The demoness still did not speak. "R'vor, I think she's in shock."

R'vor was rummaging in his pack. "I can stitch the wing. Do you have anything we can give her?"

Cat frowned. "I only brought a first aid kit."

Still, the demoness remained silent. She did not cringe away from them, but neither did she reach out.

"Almost like..."

Cat blinked. "Can you hear us?" She moved so she could study the demoness' face. Not a twitch of reaction. "I don't think she can.

The demoness looked between both of them.

Cat pointed to her ears, then pointed to her.

Demons don't nod. The gesture is more like a shrug through the wings.

"Deaf. Good catch." R'vor began to make quick hand gestures, some form of sign language.

Now the demoness responded. "Give her what painkillers you can. I'll fix the wing."

23

An hour or so later she was patched up. The reminder that demons could have weaknesses, even handicaps, sobered Cat a little. She did not know the sign language, although it seemed a variation on the somatic gestures some mages used to cast their spells.

A variation, but not the same thing. No magic associated with it. It was something that, surely, humans could learn, if they were willing to listen.

Another reminder. However, their new companion could not fly straight away. Nor could they leave her here. Cat felt time draining away. They could not afford this, but what kind of person would she be if she left anyone, human or demon, to die in the desert.

"We have to take her with us," R'vor voiced.

"We can't wait for her to heal. Can we carry her?"

"I think we may have to. Short of Neir intervening again...which she shows no sign of doing."

Neir could not intervene every time, Cat thought. Even a goddess...had her priorities. Or, perhaps, she was testing them. Seeing what Cat would do.

For all they knew, the deaf-mute demoness was herself a test of some kind. For all they knew she had been sent. Cat assumed nothing at this point. Nothing. She was also keeping her eye open for snakes at any time. Even when in the air.

"I think she expects us to solve *some* problems for ourselves." She had fixed Cat's shoulder, but the mute one...of course, the mute one might be sworn to Arok deeply. "Is she Arokian?"

R'vor nodded. "Yes."

"Then we take her to Arok-Kor. Probably the best place."

The next evening they were off again, supporting the injured female between them. Her name was V'ra...that she had written in the sand for them.

It sounded almost like a human name, Cat thought. Veira was considered pretty common. Perhaps her parents had heard it and thought it was pretty, perhaps it was simple coincidence. Who knew where her egg had been laid.

For that matter, who had raised her? Some demons would not bother raising a deformed or handicapped hatchling. Human Arokians might well have been her foster parents.

She was heavy, she slowed Cat down, and part of her did want to simply leave her behind. That part, though, she silenced.

Eventually, though, they flew above a camp. The mute demoness, unable to shout, gestured frantically and tried to pull them down.

After a moment, they spiraled down into the middle of the desert.

Cat had not managed to put up any kind of a glamor. It was as herself that she touched down in the demon camp.

Presumably, these were V'ra's people. Two males moved to greet them. They dismissed R'vor, focusing all of their attention on her.

"Of all the things...people...we expected to see," one of them said, stepping towards her.

She held her hands out flat, palms up, in demon greeting. "We found your friend being harassed by a sandrake."

"Thank you. We offer you our hospitality. But I know only your nature, not your name."

"Cathren Black." It felt like a moment for formality. "My companion is R'vor."

The male turned towards R'vor for a moment, studying him. "The hospitality is, of course, for both of you."

It seemed, though, that he was far more willing to welcome Cathren than...some random demon. That had to be what R'vor was to them, all he was. They did not know him. Their behavior was actually reasonable and to be expected...as annoying as it was.

Cat glanced around the camp. "We will not impinge. We only came to bring V'ra home."

"To where are you heading?"

A stupid question. Where else would they be going, in the Sea of Sands? "Arok-Kor."

"So, you join us after all."

"I have not yet made such a decision," Cat admitted. "But I need truth, and the truth can only be found by listening to both sides."

The demon regarded her. "And one who has always listened to both sides...which I suspect you have."

He saw, she realized, a half-demon in human garb and accompanied by a demon. What better way to illustrate being bound by both sides?

"I have seldom had the luxury of not paying attention to both. I'm hoping that the war can still be avoided."

"I doubt it can. Are hunters from Merico still being paid a bounty for demon hide?"

"No," Cat said, simply. "Although the message might not have got to all of the nomads yet. I'd give it a bit before approaching the city."

He moved to the campfire, dropping into a squat comfortable for demons. It was less so for Cat, who had no tail and who's legs were configured in a human manner. She dropped to a sitting position instead, lifting her wings. "Thank you. Do you have any other news?"

"Watch out for Solusians. They got chased out of Merico, but they're probably going to be stirring trouble elsewhere." Cat rested her hands on the sandy ground. "And there will be war. I still hope it can be prevented, but at this point, it's a very slim chance."

"And thus, you go to Arok-Kor. Do you go to learn?"

"I hope so." A pause. "Perhaps you can help me." She rested her hands on her knees, not knowing what to do with them. "I have never been told Arok's side of the story."

The demon studied her. "But I am sure you would not wish your human kin destroyed."

"Nor my demon kin. I wish a world in which the two races can dwell in relative peace. Total peace is impossible, I know that."

"And that is indeed what Arok and Birrur sought. He felt that the humans did not belong. That they were too different."

"The question is whether he still seeks that." She elected not to mention that she had spoken with Birrur. Likely, she would not be believed.

"And that question is one we ask and have not received an answer to." A pause. "Perhaps we have asked in the wrong way."

"Perhaps I could try asking." Cat made a wry face. "But what is about to happen might only be stopped by releasing him." She frowned.

"As you are, indeed, prophesied to do. I remain surprised the humans let you live."

"Neir intervened. Personally."

"Perhaps, then, Neir wishes his return."

"Solus is about to do something stupid. Neir is just trying to stop him." And Neir, Cat reminded herself, was neither good nor evil, and only on the side of maintaining the cycle of life. She would care if humanity was destroyed, but for her it would be the lesser evil than the destruction of all life on Yirath.

Should she tell this demon that Birrur was free? For now, she elected to hold that card close to her chest. Not that this was a game, not by any stretch of the imagination. She saw ice falling.

"Then it is true. The ice fall will happen."

"It might yet be stopped." Arok, perhaps, had tried to warn his priests. "But I cannot pay its cost in the lives of others."

She could pay her own, but what was one person's blood? The parchment tucked inside her shirt became a presence of which she was greatly aware. Even with it...

"You are not what I expected. I expected...I have to admit...somebody more human."

He did not mean it as a compliment. "There are good humans and bad ones, good demons and bad ones. And we're different enough to share."

"And which side will you choose to live on?"

Cat laughed. "I don't know. Maybe I'll spend part of the year in Losana and part traveling the trade routes. Divide my time."

If she survived. "Except that right now I can't go back."

"Because they know you intend to fulfill the prophecy."

That was not quite the truth. She elected not to correct him. "Perhaps. I don't know whether I do or not yet."

Telling this demon that she was going to try and cut a deal with Arok did not seem particularly intelligent...even if she felt she could discuss the actions of the gods. Even their motivations. As if they were people she knew, not the powers that governed the world. She shook her head.

She was nobody...or was she? She was mortal, but she was also unique and, it seemed, significant. She wished she had been born some ordinary child...except she could not decide which race she would have preferred to be.

"You do not know what your best course of action is."

"Who does?" She looked up at him. "You're being very reasonable. I would have thought you would try to talk me into it."

"Believe it or not, I want peace too. And some reason to certain matters. V'ra is my daughter."

"And somebody tried to talk you into letting her die." She was not stupid, she could read between the lines of what he was saying. "That would have been somewhat foolish."

"Had she been born with no arms or no wings, I might have considered it. But she manages very well."

No wings. Cat felt her own twitch at the thought, she remembered what had been done to R'vor. Then undone, at Neir's hand. Some might argue she owed the goddess, but she was fairly sure that debt had been paid.

"Ah. Even for you, the thought of not having wings is painful."

Cat laughed sharply. "I have never been able to help feeling that way." And Laran had never understood. She sometimes wondered why Laran had not...maybe because he had understood more than he let on.

Maybe because he knew it meant nothing to who and what she was.

"I'm surprised your human friends did not clip them."

It was so close to her own thoughts that she flinched. "They were not stupid. Not that they knew what to do with me, but..."

"Perhaps they thought you would be useful to them intact. And it would have made no difference other than the level of your anger."

That was, perhaps, it. Laran had wanted her happy in her gilded cage. Had she grown up unable to fly and knowing, through deep instinct, she should, then she would have fled at, oh, twelve. She would have fulfilled the prophecy, quite willingly, as a teenager. "Humans aren't stupid."

"I have never thought that. Foolish, maybe. Blind, at times. But anyone who thinks an enemy is stupid is likely to end up dead."

"We don't have to be enemies."

Oddly...he let her have the last word.

They broke camp the next morning. By tacit agreement, V'ra's father would escort her and R'vor to Arok-Kor. Traveling in a group was safer, even if it did make her a little wary and nervous.

Still, he had shown her nothing but respect. She liked him. He reminded her of Kera...he reminded her of other priests she had met.

He also admitted that mistakes had been made. She respected him, she would have done so even if they had been, truly, enemies.

As it was, he was a potential ally. He would stand with her against the extremists, because of his daughter. The thought of using V'ra's handicap that way made her stomach turn a little at her own actions. Yet...the cult might well be taking certain things too far, as were the extremes of demon society.

There was a middle road. R'vor, taking down one of the lightweight tents, folding it into a flight pack, represented an aspect of it. Kera, who had not hesitated to treat him, was another.

If the two races could work together, could prove themselves to be worthy allies, then they were halfway to peace between the gods.

She had thought of it as working the other way around, but now she was not so sure. If they could show Solus evidence that demons did not have to be a threat to humans, perhaps he would back down.

It made sense to her, even if it made no sense to anyone else. She took a share of the load as they moved aloft. Two of the others...hirelings, was the impression she got...were helping V'ra. Her wing would not return to full strength for probably a week.

Demons healed fast, fortunately. The sea of sand extended beyond them, she altered her flight so she was next to R'vor.

"What do you think?"

"He is almost too reasonable."

"Well, he'd like to convert me, and he knows better how to do so than most who attempt it." That was the obvious, clear truth. "At the same time, he gives me some hope. You can work with people like him."

"You can. Now we need a Solusian we can work with."

Cat frowned for a moment. "There was at least one reasonable one in Merico. We'll manage." She shifted position so the wind funneled her words more towards R'vor than away.

He had, however, fallen silent. Their flight was swift and northerly. She thought on the far horizon she saw a city. It could have been a mirage, but it was in the right place and direction to be Arok-Kor.

The right place. She suspected it would be a lot like Merico, in truth, white walls to keep out the heat. Too much white. Well, she could get used to that. She already was getting used to the off-white of the sand.

Fortunately, she had sun goggles, or she might have been dazzled by it. Her eyes were shielded behind them. Her wings felt stronger, though, almost as if the closer she got to Arok's shrine...

Had her magic become stronger? It was possible, although if so, she doubted it was proximity to the shrine so much as distance from

Losana. She was beginning to grasp how much they had bound and weakened her power.

She could not even blame them for doing so. Yet...yes. She could feel it, the place of her birth calling her. Drawing her towards it.

She could not help but shudder a little. She had been raised to believe this to be an evil place. An evil city. A place from which she had been rescued.

Then, though, she had been a helpless infant. Now she was an adult, and a trained mage. And she approached on her own terms.

She wondered if the rumors about women being property here were true. She hoped not. Or perhaps, it was something she could change.

She shook her head. It was something she would like to change, but none of it would matter if the icefall happened. She had to have that one, absolute, priority. Unbending, unchanging. She could not step aside from her path. Even if it was the wrong one, she was trying with all of her being. That had to count for something.

The sea of sand was starting to give way to rocky ground, there were even plants. She felt safer once she had left it. The sandrakes could not fly, but they could not stay aloft forever. If she never ran into another one, it would be too soon.

Eh. She was thinking in clichés now. A sign that she was tired. They spiraled downwards.

"You keep up well, halfbreed," the demon priest growled, but there was something in his eyes that indicated he was teasing.

"There's nothing wrong with my wings," she quipped back. Fortunately. Of course, she'd managed to damage them twice on this journey. A third time was entirely likely to happen. They were the biggest part of her, the easiest target.

"It was your level of fitness I was worried about. Living in a human city..."

"I've been working out." He had a point. When she was a teenager, she could not have made such a flight, for sure. She simply had not spent enough time aloft. She had improved since then. She wondered how much her appearance had changed. For the better or the worse? The only scar she had was a slight one on one wing membrane. Somehow. How had she escaped being marked? Sheer luck, or Neir's hand? Or the fact that demons did tend to heal a little quicker than humans?

"Good. We are two days from the city, and V'ra is slowing us down enough." He glanced at his daughter. "Not that I hold it against her...except that she flew too close to a sandrake."

"I think she's been punished enough for that."

"Sandrakes tend to inflict their own consequences, yes."

Cat glanced to the north. "Two days."

"And what will you do when you get there?"

"I'm not sure yet. Hopefully I can avoid being hauled straight to the central temple and ordered to summon Arok right there."

He laughed. "I'd suggest a disguise, but..."

Cat activated a glamor, forming the seeming of a green-brown demoness around her. "It would not fool the priests."

"No, but that is very, very good."

"I'm good at illusions." She did not mention how often she had used one to hide her wings, to look like a human woman. He could probably guess, but it was not something to brag about. Not here.

"What else are you skilled in?"

"Alchemy," she admitted. "And, of course, fire magic."

"Your magic is more demon than human...and something else. I do not know. Perhaps a side effect of..." He tailed off.

"Given magic was used to conceive me and given I've had a lot of training, it's not surprising..." She met his eyes for a moment.

He gazed into her, then shook his head. "You are probably right. Also, somebody has attempted to hold you back."

"Do you blame them?"

"No." He moved away, to start making camp, so they could rest through the hottest part of the day.

Cat watched him go. "That is an honorable demon."

"Indeed. If there were more like him...on both sides." R'vor had come up behind her.

"Of course, he is trying to recruit me, which is probably making him nicer."

"I'm not so sure."

For once, she let R'vor have the last word.

24

The south gates of Arok-Kor were pink, Cat noticed with some amusement. Definitely, distinctly, pink. The wall was built of some kind of sandstone, and had been left its natural, somewhat effeminate hue.

They were high, but then, this city had been besieged before. Likely, it would be again, the way things were going. If there were human armies approaching, though, they were far enough behind the group of travelers not to be seen or heard.

She had taken on the demoness guise...and, after thought, had matched herself to R'vor. T'la might be offended if she ever found out, although Cat took care to select slightly different coloring. Still...she was saying she was T'la's sister as much as R'vor's.

Of course, that would make her an eligible female, but she had handled human flirting. Demon flirting was even easier to deal with. As a rule, they were more likely to take no for an answer.

The gate guards were both demons, carrying spears, but they let the party right in. Presumably, they recognized M'kor, V'ra's father. One of them leered at V'ra, but paid no attention to Cat. She wondered if she had made herself ugly. Or if V'ra, despite her handicap, was simply considered something of a catch. More so than some stranger who was clearly of another tribe, anyway.

She stayed close to R'vor. Once inside, though, she saw mostly humans. They wore the same white robes as those in Merico, and both sexes seemed to veil their faces when outside. She thought she saw as many women as men on the street, but it was hard to tell under the shapeless garments. Only the largest of breasts would affect their folds significantly.

There was a more subdued quality to the crowd than in Merico, however. A tension in the air that Cat wondered about. Could it be that they feared a war here? Or could it be something else?

She wondered how...serious...most of these humans were about the patronage under which they lived. It was possible, even probable, that some of them would just as soon Arok remained in exile.

"I need to find a tavern," she mumbled to M'kor.

"My home is on Sekan Street. Anyone can give you directions."

"You live in the city?" she was surprised.

"I keep a residence here. It is useful. I am not here that much."

Useful for dealing and trading with humans, she supposed. It made a certain amount of sense. "Alright."

She and R'vor separated from the group, moving through the streets. Nobody seemed to be paying much attention to them, or to the demon child she noticed weaving through the crowd.

She reached down to put a hand on her money pouch, almost certain she had seen his hand dip into somebody's pocket. She was not here to feed juvenile thieves. He looked a little on the thin side.

It was...on the face of it, not her problem, although if he asked her for money, she would buy him food. The tavern was obvious...it had a colorful sign of a blue canik hanging above the door, jutting out into the street.

The only other color was demon hide, contrasting vividly with the white preferred by the humans. Most were the reddish hues she had seen as dominant amongst the eastern tribes. In the tavern itself, she saw only one other demon, and he seemed to be in the full process of drinking himself into a coma. She wondered what over.

What did they drink here? She realized it was likely to be raksha, and steeled herself. At the counter, "Do you have mead?"

"It's very expensive, lady." The barkeep was human, an older, grizzled man with only one eye.

She sighed. "Raksha, then."

He glanced past her at R'vor, who nodded. Two glasses of raksha were poured and slid across the counter.

"Will the two of you be wanting stew?"

No doubt the stew would be heavy on meat...she wondered if he made two bowls...one almost pure meat for the demons, one heavy on vegetables for the humans...or just one and served vegetables as an extra.

A mixed society would have its challenges. Yet, these people seemed to be making it work. Nobody was even staring at her.

Well, the drunk demon was now, and she recognized that stare. He was too drunk to be any kind of problem. Besides, R'vor had turned and was now staring him down.

"Oh, ignore him. He's in here every night. It's amazing how much one of your kind can put away if determined to get drunk."

Cat laughed. "He was admiring the view. Will I have to...dissuade him?"

"Probably not. I think he's already too drunk to move."

She wondered, inwardly, what had reduced him to such a state. However, she was in demon guise, and disgust for his weakness was the only emotion she could reasonably permit herself to show. Anything else would make *her* look weak. She only had a certain amount of time before the priests sensed her presence and 'invited' her to the temple.

Not that she intended to resist. Or tell them anything but the truth of the matter.

"So. What do you think of the rumors out of Merico?"

"Not all of them are rumors," Cat informed the barkeep softly. "We barely got out of there. I hear that the cult got tossed out on their butts, though."

"Good. Mericans are bad enough as it is without somebody whipping them into righteous fervor."

She said nothing about his prejudice...for that might blow their cover. "Everyone goes nuts if somebody does that."

The man paused, glanced around, "I'm worried it's about to happen here. Most people just want to live their lives, but the priests are convinced we're about to be besieged by the south again. And spouting their stupid prophecy about Arok coming back."

"What if he does?" She kept her tone even. She neither wanted to come over as dismissive of the god or as a fanatic herself.

"I think most people are happy with their lives the way they are."

"Most people always are. It's the few who aren't who mess everything up." She would have been...no, she would not have been entirely happy in her alchemist's shop, but...

"That's the truth of it. You're from the other side of the mountains?"

"Yes. We are traveling...exploring."

"And looking for a mate, I'd suspect. That male you're with..."

"My brother."

"Thought as much. Be careful. You don't want to catch the eye of one of the fanatics. Wouldn't end well, I don't think."

She flickered a grin. "I can hold my own. And nobody's going to be breaking my heart in a hurry." Demons were every bit as vulnerable to that as humans.

"Good. I don't want to see you back in here ordering a *pitcher* of raksha."

She could not envision herself drinking any amount of raksha, although she thought she could stomach the small glass, and doing so would make her blend in. "I won't. How about that stew?"

R'vor had claimed a table not far from the drunk. She moved over, setting the shot down in front of him.

He made a face. "Guessing no mead."

"Not at any kind of reasonable price. Next time, we should bring a few casks...we could sell it at a huge profit."

"Good idea. I hadn't thought about it being expensive here."

"Probably hard to raise the bees. Or something. Or it really is that most people prefer raksha." She drank part of hers and made a face. They were obviously outsiders, so she didn't bother to hide her disgust. "I don't think raksha is good for anything but getting drunk quickly."

"I'm pretty sure that's what it's made for. You could try watering it down."

"Not sure that wouldn't make it worse." Then she lowered her voice. "Our barkeep isn't too fond of the cult."

"Good. It's good to know not everyone here is a blind follower."

"I didn't think they could be. Although they do not seem as happy as in Merico."

"No. They are preparing for war, and you do not have to be a blind follower to fear that consequence."

Cat had to agree. She downed the rest of her raksha in one swallow, rather than having to taste the stuff. A wench came over with their stew, setting it down and departing rapidly.

After all, there was no point flirting with demons. Cat did watch her go, but surreptitiously. She was worth watching, but in her current guise... Showing interest in a human would betray her. How much she cared about that remained unclear and uncertain.

They would find her sooner or later. It was just a matter of getting as much information as possible. The stew was actually good...a little more spiced than she preferred, but not so much so as to have her wishing for water. She could not quite identify the meat, but as long as it was not human or demon, she did not care.

It was probably caba meat. She had not seen much else in the way of livestock. The thought that it might be canik meat hit her, but she thought that would be rather tougher.

"So, what do you plan next?"

"Next, I plan on getting some sleep." She was glad to rest her wings, glad she did not have to fly today. But she definitely needed sleep. Her mind was a little fuzzy.

Part of her could not believe, too, that she was here, in the heart of the enemy...and being treated well. They were just people, here.

Arok's priests might be another matter. She knew even some of the human ones thought that humanity was a scourge on the face of Yirath. Because they did not belong.

They did not belong. Rationally, Cat knew that was even true. Humans were so different from the other creatures that walked the world, that it was obvious to anyone that the gods had brought them from elsewhere. Nothing else was remotely like them. Demons...belonged to an extent, but even they were designed differently, with the hand of intelligence visible. She wondered if that was what it took to make intelligent beings with souls...or if such could arise from the descendants of beasts.

Well, she would never know. The gods had done what the gods had done, and undoing it would be genocide.

A demon youth came running into the tavern. His wings were held tight behind him.

"There's an army moving through the desert!"

Great. Well, kids will blurt, of either species. Cat did not move, but glanced at R'vor. "I am going to get some sleep."

"And afterwards?"

"It might be best to go to the temple."

She did not know how far away the army was. Had they come looking for her? Or was it the cult of Solus, recruiting everyone they could?

The latter seemed more likely. One did not send an army after one woman, one sent carefully chosen assassins. It was a knife in the back she had to worry about.

But she needed more information. Refreshed, and still disguised, she slipped out without R'vor, leaving a contact stone by his bedside.

He could call her, thus, if he needed her, and although he was no mage, he was demon, with enough magical ability to do a simple scry.

The streets were even more subdued. Few people were out, and even fewer of them women. She saw no children whatsoever.

She moved towards the gate. There, she might find somebody willing to tell an armed demoness what was going on. Worst case scenario, they would ask her to fight.

Which she would not do. Not in this war, not in the war she was determined to end, if possible, before it began.

A couple of people moved out of her way, eyeing her blades.

This time, the gate guards were human. One turned to her. "Mercenary?"

"Sometimes," she admitted. "What's going on?"

He regarded her. "About two hundred humans, armed, approaching from the south."

"Ah, so not much of an army, then."

"No, not really."

She relaxed, and did not mind him seeing that. "They are probably followers of an extremist cult of Solus...the one that's been causing all of the trouble around Merico."

The guard studied her. "I'd ask you how you knew..."

"I was part of throwing them *out* of Merico. Apparently they've decided to attack even without support from the city."

She doubted two hundred humans, even with magic, could do any real damage to this city. Kill a few wall guards, maybe.

"Idiots."

"The water supply is properly secured, right?" If she had a small force against a city...

"Nasty mind."

She shrugged. "Not really. Mercenary, like you said."

The blades proved it, and she was, of course, not wearing her academy ring. She might not put it on again, thinking about it. Then again, it meant something to her. It did mean years of hard work, it did mean that she had proven herself to the humans.

It no longer meant her identity. She was who she was without a piece of jewelry.

"Your help would be appreciated."

"I'm here on a different mission..." She held up a hand. "Not hostile to Arok-Kor, I assure you, but it would sort of wreck my plans to get killed fighting Solusians."

He laughed. "Yes, it would. I'm guessing your mission probably involves handsome men."

She laughed demon laughter. "It might at that."

Well, if she had everyone thinking she was on the hunt...then she really would be fighting them off. Or maybe he had just made a lucky guess.

"Good luck with that."

She nodded and turned away. Should she go to the temple? Without R'vor, that seemed somewhat unfair. It might appear that she was deserting him. Instead, she wandered over to a marketplace. Spices and meat were for sale, and fruit brought from the coast. She was not sure how they preserved it...if there was a spell for such, she did not know it. Might be a good thing to learn, if there was. A pen full of canik pups raised a cacophony as she passed, competing for the attention of potential buyers.

Had she not been in the situation she was in...as it was, she looked ahead resolutely, ignoring the young creatures.

Instead, she purchased some kind of kebab from one of the traders, gnawing on it as she wandered. It all seemed very normal. One of the storekeepers yelled 'Stop Thief', grabbing the collar of a young girl who had a bitten fruit in her hand.

Well, hopefully her parents would deal with her. At least she did not see evidence of the rumored sexism. Was that only in the cult? The priesthood?

Then she saw R'vor. He was making his way through the crowd towards her, lifting a taloned hand to draw attention to himself.

She changed course.

What she saw on his face bordered on anger. "They might not," he said softly, "treat women as second class citizens, but they don't seem to care about wife beating."

Cat frowned. But even in Losana, there were some who thought a man could do with his woman as he wished. They usually had their lesson taught to them, gently, by the female warriors and mages. Actual wife beating, though, was punished...logically. A man who took a belt to his wife would find a whip taken to him. Children were another matter.

Liesa had never taken a belt to her. She had never needed to. "That's not important right now."

"I taught a few the error of their ways."

"I think we should..." she tailed off. "Let's go find some lunch." She was not hungry, but distracting R'vor seemed desirable right now. Before he went off on some righteous crusade that would not be appreciated.

She did watch how couples were to each other, and saw perhaps a little more deference in wives than she would have in Losana. But nothing that would indicate that women were property in this society.

An exaggeration. Or a way of making the enemy seem less human, less moral, so people would be more willing to fight them.

"The cultists are," R'vor added, "about half a day away. Short of teleportation, I don't see them getting into the city."

"Of course, they could be a distraction. I suggested they secure the water supply."

"Good thought."

Cat had not managed to get the distance, but then, she was unclear on how long it would take to walk through the desert. Or ride...she rather assumed they had cabas, even if they did not have trained cavalry. Nobody in their right mind would walk through that. The nomads were dependent on their beasts of burden.

She remembered Teola, wondered if she would see her again. Wondered which side she was truly on.

An odd thought to have right at that moment, and her head snapped around.

She was there, albeit her face and head covered, Cat recognized her movement and form.

Softly, "We've grown a tail."

R'vor nodded. "Then how about we go where the tail would least expect."

Cat flickered a grin at him. "It's a human tail, we *could* just go right to the demon neighborhood. Or..."

She glanced at Teola again. The woman nodded.

"She knows she's made. Let's just ignore her."

Maybe Teola had not intended to be a tail, but the very fact that she was there was enough to bother Cat...a little.

Where she was, the sorceror was not likely to be far away. Was she here to make sure Cat stuck to the script?

Cat planned on doing a fair amount of improvisation. For now, she turned north, inward towards the citadel. But it was not Arok's temple to which she set her course.

* * *

Birrur's temple in Arok-Kor reflected her original and true aspect. Friezes of fight scenes lined the walls, all well executed. Cat felt an odd sensation as she walked in.

An uncertainty, a tension. Had Neir finally released her sister goddess from her bonds, or was what she felt the edge of it? The possibility?

No priest or priestess stood within the temple at present. R'vor went towards the altar.

He honored all gods, she remembered. Perhaps he had always known who Birrur really was, and simply never told Cat.

Why would he have told her? She had not asked. Or, perhaps, Laran had forbidden it. R'vor had listened to Laran...enough to satisfy the man that he was not seducing her.

Seducing. That word reminded her for a moment of how long she had been celibate. Well. She had endured longer before.

The air above the altar shimmered, and R'vor stepped back. Cat shook her head, moving forward, moving between him and it. If Birrur was going to be angry, then she should at least pick the right target.

"You must go to the Citadel," the air said.

"I intend to. I simply wanted to know what was happening here first."

"You have to get there before he does."

And the presence was gone. Birrur, begging her for help? It made no sense unless the goddess was desperate. Desperate enough to overcome the aura of dislike that had accompanied their previous conversation.

Cat turned and ran from the temple. Fortunately, although it was not built onto the Citadel as Arok's was, the distance was not far. There were no other temples. She suspected those here who served other patrons kept their own shrines, quietly. Or not. Perhaps it was forbidden.

She shook her head a little, her wings half spread as she ran for the Citadel. She did not drop her glamor, not yet.

And then, she was inside Arok's temple. A feeling flowed through her that she could not describe. She should not be here. She knew that, what she felt mingled fear and welcome. As if the god, as much as he could touch this place, did not know what she would do.

She did not know what she was going to do. R'vor was suddenly behind her, his own wings spread, glancing around. "Cat..."

"The sorceror is here. I don't know what he plans, but it's not good."

There had been other entrances she could have used. Why had she chosen this one?

Because it was closest, because it was most convenient, but it also slowed her down. She inclined her head to the altar, then headed for the priests' entrance.

Which was blocked by a demon guard. Rather than words or deeds, Cat simply dropped her glamor.

She had never seen demon eyes widen so swiftly. It was clear he did not know what to make of her presence, and he was young. An acolyte, perhaps.

Gently, "Please let me past. I need to speak with the high priest." Not that she was sure what she would say.

"You..."

"I am."

The boy looked, for a moment, like he would block her path in any case. Perhaps he suspected this was the glamor not her prior appearance. A not unreasonable thought or suspicion, given the circumstances.

She might have wondered the same thing were their situations reversed. Then he glanced at R'vor.

Then a woman...a human woman...stepped out into the corridor. She murmured something, and Cat felt the tingle of a standard dispell run over her.

Somebody else suspicious. She had nothing active except the link-stones, which should not be affected. So, rather than show tension, she showed her hands. The fact that her swords were fully sheathed.

"So. It is you in truth."

Cat shook her head. "I don't have time. There is somebody coming who..." She tailed off.

"Somebody who might be a danger? I do not think two hundred troops can breach our walls."

"A highly competent mage." She wondered who this woman was. Of course, she could, in theory, *be* the high priest. Or his consort. Or his deputy. Or one of the ranking priests of Birrur. She could be anyone. Cat kept her tone even. "One with an agenda of his own. He attempted to escort me here by force, but..."

"But you do not think he is one of us. Come...and your companion also." Her eyes flicked over R'vor. "Why do you warn those you were raised to fear?"

"I'm not fond of war."

"You carry the tools of it."

"And on occasion, yes, I have had to use them. That doesn't mean I want a war." Cat shook her head. "Does any sane person?"

"Some enjoy the challenge. Can you honestly say you do not gain a certain pleasure from a fight?"

Cat considered that. "On occasion. But I gain none from death." Which in this place?

"Sometimes, death is necessary."

"Sometimes it is." Cat could not disagree with that. "Sometimes even war is. That does not mean I'm going to take joy in it."

"She doesn't like you."

Cat did not need to ask who she was. "I noticed." Was it because she was not about to turn into one of Birrur's worshippers? Or was there something else, something Cat neither knew nor understood?

"I am not sure whether I do or not."

"I don't ask to be liked." She thought she knew, now, who this woman was. "But you really do need to watch out for this individual. He is good at layered illusions."

"Tricky." The woman seemed to relax a little. "I doubt you're in league with him."

"I am not sure. He has claimed to follow Solus and Arok both. I don't know which story is true."

"Come."

Cat stepped through the corridor. The Citadel was richly appointed...almost too much so. The tapestries were too busy...and most showed scenes she did not care for. Scenes of war and chaos and fire. They were dominated by demons.

She shook her head, she wanted out of here. Was she a traitor? Was she even a traitor to herself?

Neir had told her to be herself. She sought the answer of her own heart...and remembered the icefall. Which was worse? There was only one answer to that question.

If she lived, though, would she be trapped here? There was more than one way in which one could sacrifice one's life. There was death, and then there was the sacrifice of hopes and choices.

Yet, she had no hopes or choices. Very softly, "Did you kill my friends?" She meant the generic you, the collective you.

"I did not."

"You know what I mean."

"You think that we are some kind of united force. We are not. They were slain to bring you here, but not everyone agreed with that course of action."

Oddly, Cat could accept that...although she was not sure she would let the one behind it live, should she find out who it was. She did not voice that. She simply followed. She could feel R'vor behind her, a shadow. Was he as uncomfortable as her? She did not look back towards him, not because she did not care, but because she dared not show weakness in this place.

She would not be their servant. And then she was in an inner courtyard.

She let out an involuntary sound. It was beautiful. Water flowed through it, a valuable resource here. It irrigated a garden of trees. They were dormant now, but she was sure that when the rains came they would bloom...she could already see the buds, waiting. Trailing flowers flowed along the artificial stream. The path was tiled in red and blue, in abstract patterns.

"You admire our garden."

"Quite impressive. Better yet in a couple of weeks."

"Indeed. We can divert enough water to ensure the trees survive, but not to cause them to bloom."

"It would be bad for them, anyway." Producing fruit and flowers out of season did not seem to help the long term health of any plant. Cat was no gardener, but she knew that much.

"Wait here. Please." And the woman moved away.

"A priestess of Birrur."

"Yes." Cat turned to R'vor, who had finally spoken. "You do not have to stay, my friend."

"I will not leave you in this place."

"And if I must die here?"

"I will not leave even your dead body to them."

Cat thought that excessive. "R'vor...what's the worst thing they could do? Burn it?"

He closed his eyes. "You..."

"I am sworn to no God. Remember that." She did not care what happened to her body once she had no more need of it. She did not believe funeral rites or their lack could harm her soul. Neir would protect her. "It's okay, R'vor. If they did end up with my dead body, they would just toss it on a pyre, demon style, right?"

He took a deep breath. "You're right. I just..."

"You want me to be safe. You want me to be your little sister again.

I'm not. I'm a grown woman. One who loves you, but one who must do this."

25

The doors opened. Two children came from the far side...both boys, one human, one demon. They seemed quite relaxed together. The human one was holding the door open...

...and in walked an ancient man, supported in part by a carved cane.

"The child who was taken returns as a woman," he said, finally.

"On my own terms. I will not serve you."

"I could ensure that."

He was old, and he was not a mage, but she knew who he was. He was one of Arok's highest priests...and he was human.

"You could, but would it not be better to hear me out, priest?"

"Ah. You know who I am."

"Your species surprises me. Do you seek the end of your own kind?"

He moved to sit on a white bench, by the flowing water. "Sit." His eyes flicked to R'vor. "You bring a bodyguard?"

"I bring a friend." She moved to sit on the other end of the bench. "Not that he would not protect me if needed, but he's not my servant."

"And the answer is...no. Arok has never wanted the *destruction* of humanity. But I no longer know as clearly what Arok wants. He was...not pleased with me."

"Because they got away with me. Of course, from what I hear..."

"He was even more not pleased with Neir's intervention. You were supposed to be male. You were also not supposed to have a soul. There were wards supposed to stop that."

"Then how?"

"I am not clear on the how myself. None of the invaders were killed, so your soul did not get in that way."

Maybe, Cat thought, she would have to ask Neir. Or maybe... "Maybe Myrk sneaked in with it."

"That was my personal theory. That snake should not have been able to get in here, but..."

"He was probably hiding in somebody's pouch." Cat made a great show of checking her own.

For some reason, that got a laugh from the priest. "But Arok has not spoken to me since. Of course, it takes great effort for him to do so."

"Perhaps he will talk to me."

"Perhaps indeed. It would certainly seem to be worth the attempt. Yet, he might, gender or no gender..."

"I know the risk."

"I would offer to protect you, but in truth, I doubt he will listen to me."

"Tell me one thing. My mother?"

There was a flicker of something in his eyes. "She volunteered, knowing it would be her death. I tried to talk her out of it. I would rather it had been any other woman in the city."

Cat felt a stillness, and for a long moment she could not speak. "Your daughter." When they came, the words were a whisper.

This man...had condemned his own daughter to death, had condemned his grandson to being a mere vessel for a God. And she could not hate him, could not judge him. Was what he showed remorse for those deeds, or only regret that he had failed? Somehow, it did not matter.

Yet, she could not quite forgive him either. Could not quite let go. The tension flowed between them, she wondered if R'vor had been close enough to hear. "I don't think I can quite call you grandfather."

"I did..." And he tailed off, the excuse he would have spoken dying on his lips as he regarded her.

"I do not care what Arok wanted then. I care what he wants now." The truth flowed out of her. "I care about ensuring the survival of the world."

"And you came here?"

"Solus is the one who is the threat right now, a threat to all of us. And this mage may or may not work for him."

"The mage is being watched for. Anyone using magic who enters the Citadel will be stopped...we have demon guards quite capable of that. And if he kills them, the alarm will be raised even if they did not have time to do so themselves."

It made sense. And Cat knew enough to know such a deadman alarm was possible. Perhaps it was something that should be used more often, but most did not want to admit that people might die. At least there was honesty here.

"I must..."

The two children had, at some point, left. Now one of them came back, the demon.

"The city is breached! The Solusians are within the walls!"

Cat was on her feet. Her hands went to her blades, but no. They were not what she needed right now.

"How?" the priest asked.

"We're not...sure. They seem to have infiltrated the fall caravans."

"Perfect." He sounded almost respectful. "Lady..."

"I think I can handle them if they get this far. But it is the sorcerer we must worry about."

"No doubt he is with them. How else would they be disguised?"

"To get into this city? I would be tempted to use mundane disguise...if possible. Of course..."

He laughed, cutting her off. "We knew you were here."

Her wings actually drooped. "That proves my point. This man is good, but he is not so good that he can hide the magic itself."

"Unless, of course, they chose a location where magic would be expected."

Cat let out a breath. "The sorcerer is coming here. I do not know what he will try, but I can be sure of that."

"I will deal with him."

She shook her head, put one hand on the old man's arm, looked down at him. "No. I will."

A foolish decision on the face of it. But the man would come to the temple. Why had somebody who served Solus wanted to bring her here?

Or would he have led her instead in circles in the desert? Then there was the question of Teola.

Cat stood in the gates of the temple of Arok, ready to defend those who had been her sworn enemies. Of course, the only reason was that evil fought evil. Or was it?

Was anyone truly evil? Certainly nobody was truly good. It was not the sorcerer who approached, though.

It was Teola. She threw back her hood. "Are you going to kill me?"

Cat shook her head. "I haven't decided yet."

"Of course. It is my lover you seek."

If Teola was here, then her mate was no doubt seeking another entrance. "I seek somebody who can give me a challenge."

Teola drew a sword. "You might be surprised there."

It was a light blade, a fencing blade. Something suited to the strength of a woman who had not spent years in training. Yet, Cat did not dismiss her. "I would truly rather not do this."

"Because you would rather be in my bed?" The woman circled.

"No, because I know full well that you are a distraction." Cat drew her blades. "Tell me, is he going to try and enter through the servants' door?"

She would obviously get no answer, but it was Teola's face and stance she was watching. She could have used some help here.

She did not twitch.

"The kennels, perhaps?"

At that, Teola lunged forward. She was faster than Cat had expected, but Cat was ready for whatever might come, her blades sweeping together to knock the single one aside. No. She was not good enough to do more than stall her.

The sorcerer was sacrificing his lover in a distraction. If she had needed any convincing that he was not a good man...or woman. She was still not sure which he was. But for now, she had to get rid of Teola.

She began to swing her blade for a killing blow. Then she laughed, turning it aside. "You almost had me."

She could see the magic around her now. The sacrifice that was being made here was visible. A standard dispell was not going to budge it. So, instead, Cat leapt upwards, wings sweeping down, getting herself out of range of the other woman's blade.

She had been meant to kill her and trigger the trap spell. She had been meant to... Well, she would not. The kennel entrance. Except, wait. She pulled out the link stone. "R'vor. I need you."

"Need me to do what?"

"Get out here and keep Teola busy, but whatever you do don't kill her."

"Deadman on her?"

"Nasty one." She could hear R'vor's wings almost immediately, but then she dropped to the kennel entrance.

The caniks were upset. He was already here, and they strained against their tethers, hissing and chirping at her.

"Easy. Easy." Not that she had ever been good at handling caniks. She wove through them and to the inner door.

Was he heading for the temple or the living quarters? Teola, no doubt, had instructions of her own, should she survive the fight. Cat felt sweat bead on her brow, her heartbeat was up, but otherwise she felt quite calm.

The temple. He had left the door open...or had he? She was no fool...she tossed a pebble through before entering.

It exploded into light. If he was using magic inside the temple, then that was rude at the very least. She murmured a dispell, releasing the trap before stepping inside.

He stood by the altar. "Fireproofed, of course."

He meant to desecrate the temple. He meant to weaken Arok.

"We meet again."

He turned. "You."

"How long did you plan on leading me in circles in the desert?"

"As long as necessary."

"You could have just killed me." She still had her blades out...and she prayed, for a moment. To Neir...and to Birrur.

"That would be foolish. But soon you will be destroyed, as if you had never been."

Foolish to kill her? Or did he simply not wish to kill a mage? It was a legitimate concern...she could have a nasty trap spell set on herself. Some did, as insurance against attack. "I will not allow you to desecrate the temple."

"No. You switched sides. Unfortunate, but expected. Although, given they killed your foster father."

She shook her head. "I grieve. But there are more important things at stake. Like the plan that would wipe Yirath clean of life."

"Only demon life."

"You truly believe that."

"I am going to deal with you now." He began to murmur a binding spell.

Cat threw one of her swords. It did not quite fly true, not striking the mage himself, but tearing through his robes and imbedding itself in the altar. She had hoped it would kill him. Breaking his concentration was a good second choice.

He tugged it out. "Good demon steel."

She could tell from the way he held it, though, that he knew nothing of how to use it. Good. He would not...could not...attack her that way. But he was starting the spell again.

And R'vor burst into the room, thrusting Teola ahead of him. "I found this wandering in the courtyard. It seems to think it can fight.

She seemed more defiant, Cat noted, than afraid. R'vor dropped her to the ground. There was no sign of the sword she had been carrying.

"You are of no matter, demon."

But he had been interrupted again. "I was hoping I would not have to kill you." He had a trap spell on him, but it might be worth it. Might be.

"Kill me and I will win."

"You've already lost. I would like my sword back now." She twisted her blade to knock it out of the sorcerer's hand. "R'vor. I think we need to gag this piece of trash." She could not allow him to cast any more spells.

R'vor moved, however, and thrust his elbow into the sorcerer's midsection, then his fist into the man's jaw.

He doubled up and went down.

"Now he can't cast *anything*," R'vor said, grimly.

"Too easy."

"He wasn't anticipating a physical attack."

"No. Still too easy. It's not him." She frowned. "If he can fool me with a fake aura, though, he could be anywhere."

The man's face changed, shifted. An older man, a grey beard. He had some magic, but not as much as their target.

"I can't deal with an illusionist who can fool mage sight."

"We have to." Cat's tone was grim. "He has to be dealt with, and he has to be dealt with now."

"Then where is he?"

"The priests' quarters, maybe?" Cat started to go that way, but found herself hitting a magical barrier. "Damn him."

She was trapped, for a moment, in Arok's temple. And how could she be sure who the unconscious man was?

How could she be sure who anyone was? There was no god of deceit, but if there was, she felt as if she was up against him now. Maybe there should be. Maybe...

She took a deep breath. R'vor was trying the other exits. "He's directly affecting a temple. That..."

"I know. The protections on this place must be weakened by Arok's exile." The god, in no position to protect his own. She forced another deep breath.

Then she reached within herself. *Cat,* Laran's voice seemed to echo in her mind. *You should not...*

You're the one who tried to cripple me, she told the memory. "R'vor. Stand back." And she formed an orb of demonfire, throwing it at the field blocking the door.

The field shattered into brilliant golden pieces. "Even Solus has no right to desecrate the temple of another."

"Cat..."

"No. I'm tired of this. I'm going to find him and I'm going to throw him out of the city." She paused. "I'd kill him, but..."

"He'd probably take you with him."

"It might be worth it." She was already halfway down the corridor towards the priest's quarters. "That guy won't wake up any time soon, right?"

"He'll be sleeping for a little while. Of course..."

"Somebody will come across him, and they'll either wake him up or kill him. We can't stop." Which way should she go?

"Up," a voice whispered in her mind. She thought it might be Birrur's voice.

There were stairs. She pounded up them, wings half spread. It felt as if she would be climbing for a long time, then she was in an upper corridor.

Another set of stairs. Spiral, but wide...this place had been built for demons, there was no cramping here. And no compromises. The thought that she might stay here forever hit her again. That what people in the south would perceive as her 'treason'...

And then she was in a tower room. This time, she thought she had found the real thing...but he was ready for her.

R'vor thrust her out of the way even as the spell went off, crackling across the room.

She gasped. "R'vor!"

There was no response. Her friend had been transformed into grey stone.

Cat scrambled to her feet, her blades drawn. "I should have killed your friend."

"Not a friend. But useful." There was anger in his tone, though.

Perhaps R'vor had taken the one shot he had at that spell...the spell which would have taken her out of the game without killing her. Now R'vor was trapped forever within the rock...and the anger rose. She could not kill this man. If she killed him, he would trap her...she knew that now.

He did not want her dead. Then, perhaps... "We seem to have met something of an impasse," she informed him, her voice dangerously soft.

"Indeed we do."

Neither of them was willing to kill the other. If she knew...no. She would not use that spell. She could almost hear R'vor screaming.

Maybe if she smashed the statue...but she also knew that she could not waste his sacrifice. Could not waste his act of love.

But. It was an impasse. Of course, if she could render the sorcerer unconscious. She tried one of the simplest spells of all, one which induced sleep.

It bounced off his wards. "Nice idea."

She strengthened her own protections, in case he decided to try the same thing. She could sense him building energies. He planned on trying the petrify again, but he needed time.

There was a vase on one of the plinths. She threw it at him with her left hand, a sword ready in her right. He dodged to the side.

You will have no more need of them. Neir's voice, in memory. Neir.

No more need of them. She felt something flow through her...and then she drew both blades and set them down.

"So, you will not fight me?"

"I will not let you turn me into stone. However...I can see the traps you have set. You do not wish my death, but my imprisonment."

"Of course."

"Because even if you kill me, I can still free him."

"If you do, then you doom humanity."

"If I do not, then I doom Yirath."

"Ah, so your loyalties are, after all, to demonkind."

She could not let him complete that spell. "The icefall would destroy everything."

"Solus will protect his own."

"To inherit what? A world with no crops, no light, no beasts of burden?" Keep talking. Keep talking, keep...no, he was going to cast it. She had only one chance...a spell she had never successfully cast.

As the blast came towards her, she spoke the words...and a mirror appeared between the two. He scrambled to the side to avoid his own spell, returned.

"You are getting better. Perhaps we should end this. Solus!"

Was he calling on the god himself? A voice in her ear said, "Don't worry."

Myrk's voice, and she could not help but smile. She could not respond.

"You do not fear even the god?"

"I can't take on a god. Why fear?" Why fear, indeed, what she could not prevent. She had...not lost.

Myrk was here. Which meant, for all intents and purposes, Neir was here. He had used her as a conduit, somehow, or perhaps simply as a beacon.

And he was death and healing. She was going to die. She accepted it, embraced it.

The god came. It was brilliance and light. And a soft voice, "So, you cannot bind her yourself?"

Cat did not bow. She did not feel in that moment that Solus deserved it. "Perhaps we can sort this out without anyone else having to be hurt."

"You speak to me like that?"

Myrk's voice in her ear. "You anger him."

"Good," she whispered.

The god was in human form, light skin and hair to represent the sun. "Whom do you..." And then his eyes narrowed. "Myrk. Stay out of this."

The snake shifted on her shoulder. "No."

"She does not belong to your mistress."

"And if you do what you seek, then nobody will."

"It's a good time to start over."

The sorcerer turned towards Solus. "Start over?"

"It is time."

"You promised to protect your own."

"Your soul is in no danger."

"You promised me my life." There was something more like sorrow than rage in the man's voice.

"The icefall will destroy all life," Cat said, softly. "You even admit it. What makes you better than Arok?"

"Both humans and demons were mistakes."

The sorcerer chose that moment to do something truly foolish. He threw a fireball at Solus.

With a gesture like swatting a fly, the god sent it back at its target. The man screamed, the flames consuming his flesh.

Myrk hissed. "Touch his soul and my mistress will come here *herself.*"

"He is mine."

"I am definitely starting to think Arok would be preferable."

"Without me no life is possible."

"That doesn't give you the right to end it. That's Neir's place. You're overstepping." She knew she was about to be erased from existence. She did not care. Perhaps Myrk could protect her soul, perhaps not. But here, facing the god, she felt a strength within her. He could destroy her utterly. He could turn her into a statue with only a thought.

Death would be an escape from this. Was that why Myrk was here?

"As are you. You have no right to speak to me like this."

"I will stop this, or die in the attempt." Solus could no more kill her than his servant could. Whatever trap Neir had set on her...and she was now sure that was what it was. Why Laran would not kill her. Why Tava had spoken for her life.

Neir had set a trap spell on her life. But Solus could get around that. He could so easily ensure that she never died.

"Neir has set this up nicely, but I do not have to kill you to be rid of you."

"Then why the hesitation?" He was hesitating. It was an odd realization. He did not want to harm her. Why? Because he feared Neir's anger?

Could a god die? Was Neir, after all, the true supreme god, the most powerful of them? But if Solus died, the sun would go cold.

He too had his own trap spell. Or was it a trap spell? Was it, perhaps, something else?

She felt a sudden weight on her shoulders, weighing down her wings. She felt the sense that everything had come down to this moment. She needed to know. She needed to know for sure what would happen if she died.

Power was growing within her, but it was not enough. Not enough to take on a god. Enough to take on any mortal mage.

Enough to call Arok. "Without war," she said, softly, "the oppressed remain oppressed. Without chaos, the world remains stagnant."

"With too much chaos," Solus countered, "the world dissolves."

"Isn't it your job to stop that from happening?" She was snapping at a god, but the energy flowing within her was growing. Growing, but not enough. It was not, quite, enough for the spell that she had carried with her, that now burned in her mind.

To summon a god, it would take a circle of six mages. At least. To do this, it might take half an academy and leave them all exhausted. The power within her beat against a barrier, an obstacle. It threatened to consume her.

And Solus took one, small, step backwards. Not out of fear, but the expression on the god's human-seeming face was one of absolute startlement.

"I'm sorry, Cat," Myrk said softly.

She was pulling the knife out of her belt. "It's okay. I knew before I even left Losana."

26

Cat could not move. Solus had paralyzed her. She could perceive, she could breathe, but she could not move. The power within her had built to its limits. In a moment, she thought, her flesh would catch fire...and if it did, she would almost welcome it. Had she been turned to stone.

"I can't let you do that."

She found she could still speak. "I can't let you destroy the world." Yet, she knew she had lost. She had lost the moment she had come into the presence of the god. Even Myrk had not been able to help her.

If she could speak, she could cast. She could attempt the spell anyway, but without her life's blood, she did not have the power. She knew it. And she could not use magic.

The air became clear. Clear and certain, and then there was another demon in the room. One that leapt into Solus, physically barreling him to the ground.

Birrur. Nobody had called her. Or had they? Time had not stopped outside this room, surely, but R'vor was imprisoned.

Her grandfather? She still could not move a muscle. Solus thrust Birrur off of him. "Stay out of this. Neir does not have the right to free you."

"Neir did not," Birrur snarled. "You did."

Even a god could not predict the results of his actions, perhaps, not always. But Birrur stood, moving away from Solus, circling so she did not turn her back on him. "There will always be war. Binding me was a mistake."

"I will destroy you."

"You don't have that power. You know what would happen if one of us were to face the final death."

Cat tried to move again. With Solus' concentration dented, perhaps...and she managed to move her hand about an inch towards the knife.

Solus snarled. "Then I will cast you so far into the abyss between the stars that it will take you the world's life to return!" He lifted his hand, apparently to do just that.

Birrur laughed. "But I would return. Bind me again, and I will break free."

War was needed. Cat wished, oh, how she wished, that it was not. But she knew she was right. "Birrur..." She could still speak.

Solus turned a little, as if he had forgotten she was there. "How about this as a deal, Birrur. I give you her...for all eternity...and you step out of my way."

Birrur laughed again. "Oh, you know how to play a girl."

"You hate her. You hate what she represents. You hate what your husband had to do."

Cat could almost feel the bonds dissolving, but she did not move. Nor did she ask. What was growing within her was not fire...as much as it threatened to consume her. It was ice. It was as if *she* was the ice fall.

"So, you give her to me...on the condition, of course, that I do not kill her."

Solus smiled.

Birrur's laugh was a little nasty this time. "A fair deal. An entirely reasonable deal."

Anger flared within Cat, exploding within her, turning into ice and fire. She would not let even the gods determine her destiny.

And the field around her shattered. "I am not sworn to any god. You cannot touch my soul without my consent."

Was that really the rule?

"No, but we can touch your body." Birrur stepped closer to her. "I could, for example, cut off your wings."

Cat flinched.

"Ah, perhaps you are demon after all."

She had the knife out now, although she could taste and smell her own fear. She did not want to die. Was there no other way? "Why do you hate me?" she asked, the weapon in her hand.

Solus seemed to be watching with amusement. Had he released Cat so Birrur could play with her? To stall the goddess, perhaps.

Birrur smiled. "Things are not that simple, Cathren."

Cat knew this moment was her chance to end it...or perhaps, after all, she could have done so...

No. She had to be in the temple. Or, at least, the Citadel. This place was as good as before the altar.

And the knife flew from her hand, stinging from the bolt Solus had thrown at it. "Oh no. You don't get to do that."

Cat had no claws. No weapon. No means of doing what she had intended to do. "Myrk."

He could do it. But his response entwined with her thoughts, she knew the snake had not spoken out loud. "I can...it is your choice. But..."

"But what?" She formed the words in her mind, stopped them before they reached her lips.

"Birrur."

Cat's stomach clenched. The goddess hated her. She would...

"Yes. That is the choice."

Myrk was asking her to let Birrur kill her. Why? "I trust you, but..."

"But you are afraid. Of course."

Birrur had turned, and it looked as if she was about to leap at Solus again. He had his hand lifted, forming a barrier, a shield.

"They're going to duel..."

"Exactly."

And Cat understood. If she drew Birrur's rage onto her, then there would be no more direct combat between the gods...and the direct combat would destroy Arok-Kor. "Birrur," she said, clearly. "You don't hate me. You're just jealous."

She hissed, starting to turn.

"Jealous of my freedom. Jealous of the fact that your mother likes me better than you."

Neir was Birrur's mother. That had not been in the legends, as if Neir's followers sought to deny the connection. Yet it was now so obvious.

Solus seemed to realize what was happening. "Birrur. Don't be..."

But the demon-formed goddess was already leaping towards Cat. She had no weapons. All of her instincts screamed at her to dodge. With all the willpower in her, she stood her ground. The sword tip caught into her flesh just above her left hip and tore up and across her body. It left in its wake unimaginable pain.

Oh gods. Was it even enough? Or would she linger in this agony for hours? She dropped to one knee, looking up at Birrur. The demon form was fading, the goddess seeming to glow more and more brilliantly. Was she changing, or was it a side effect of what was happening to her?

Birrur dropped to one knee, grasped Cat's shoulder, looked into her eyes. She was an ancient entity. She was not stupid. She knew Cat's intent in provoking her had been her own death. There was hatred in those eyes, but also something else. And an almost gentle note in her voice, "It's done."

The energy within Cat seemed to be breaking free of her. She was still breathing, but each breath came harder, and with each breath she felt more and more magic at her command. "Thank...you..."

It hurt. It hurt more than she had ever imagined. She had always thought her spirit would just leave her body, but Birrur had...had gutted her, had done fatal damage, yes. But not swiftly fatal. She felt slightly sick...but then she remembered. Remembered what she had to do.

It was hard to talk, it was hard to say the words of the spell that would call Arok here, the spell that would take at least six trained mages. Or one, dying, pouring her own life force into the spell. Birrur released her, turned, was defending her from Solus as she died.

Not just hatred in those eyes. An odd form of love. An odd form of love that had made her make it hurt, because it had to. Because otherwise she would not have had time.

She spoke the words haltingly, each one a struggle, a battle. Her body was racked by the pain, her spirit was trying...she wanted to just die already, but she had to finish this. The last word came from her in the barest of whispers, and the power surged through her.

She had thought the pain before unimaginable. Now it built to a crescendo. The power of it set her body alight...but it did not matter, she felt the flames for only a moment before...everything in the room shifted. Changed.

Birrur was gold and red, the red the shade of blood, she was light that only threatened or promised demon form. Solus was pure white, although he shimmered at his edges in the color of the rainbow.

And Arok. Arok was red and the deepest of blues, and he transcended everything that was demon. He had made them not in his own image, but in a form he loved. A form he considered absolute beauty. And he turned towards Solus. "Get out of my temple, Brother."

No attack. Anger, yes, but it was under control. As if the god had more important things to worry about.

"I already started it."

"Then we will stop it." He turned towards Birrur.

Cat looked...down. What she saw was smoldering ashes, all that was left of her. Yet, she did not feel as she would have imagined a ghost would. She felt entirely alive, entirely real. And powerful. What she had used to summon Arok had been but a small measure of the power she now held. The power that had slept within her. No wonder Laran had locked her down.

She had heard rumors that sometimes, very rarely, a magic user could remain for a while after physical death. "Is there anything I can do to help?"

Arok and Birrur, turning towards her. And then Solus, moving...no blasts, this time, but he seemed determined to physically tackle her. She was in their world now. If he killed her...a second time...she would experience the final death and be gone.

She leapt to the side, but...Solus fell to the ground. After a moment she realized why...the brilliant form of Myrk, coiled around his legs.

The serpent had tripped him up. Or perhaps that was how her mind understood it. Were these forms real?

Was the blue and red hand that reached for hers a hand or merely a flow of energy? It did not matter. She touched Arok's hand, closed her fingers around it. Birrur was looking at her almost quizzically. No more hatred in the goddess' gaze. Arok's other hand was taking that of his wife.

She saw. A falling star, plunging towards Yirath, yet it was almost the size of the moon. It was cold and ice, and it would brush the world, dropping pieces of itself. It would drown the world.

It was not a metaphor, it was real. "Push it," Arok murmured, in demon tongue.

Cat's hand could not, surely, be large enough to perform such a task, and yet it was. Her hand on one side, Birrur's on the other. And Solus...pushing back.

She could see or sense his face, everything seemed real and yet uncertain. It was all energy, and it was all...magic. Not the star, but everything they did. No, it was beyond magic. It was raw power, and it flowed through her. It had always been there, locked away, now...

And Solus went flying. The falling star flew off, pieces of it falling towards Yirath, pieces she knew would cause only a light show.

The sun god was picking himself up. Anger on his face fading to resignation. What would the other gods do?

Cat did not know. The power flowing through her had dropped to a dim roar. Arok released her hand.

"Maybe," Cat said softly, "We can have peace now."

"Peace with him?" Arok turned towards her.

Solus was actually edging away. Taking on Arok and Birrur, perhaps, was beyond him...and Myrk was still there.

"I'm not above kicking his butt. If I could. He does deserve it. But..."

Arok stepped towards her. "I know what you want. You want to protect the humans."

"And the demons." Her eyes met his. She could feel the power that burned from the god of chaos. She could feel Birrur. Both at full power, despite the task they had just performed. And she a mere shade. "I did everything I did for peace and balance."

The tower had faded out around them. She was not sure when. They were nowhere and everywhere. They were in a place lit by the stars. What place did she have here? She could still feel that power, though. She was not afraid of Arok. She knew, now, that he would not harm her. That Birrur....had already harmed her enough.

"Which is all very well," Birrur said, "But I am war."

"And war is going to happen. The only way to prevent that is to do what Solus planned and wipe Yirath clean. It's a matter of making sure that war does what it is meant to do...brings strength, brings honor...without..."

An image flowed into her mind for a moment. An image of men on some other world, fighting through the mud, fighting over mere feet or inches of ground. "...simply bringing nothing but meaningless death."

"And you," Myrk hissed, "were willing to give your life to achieve that."

"I just wanted to stop Solus and stop the humans and demons from destroying each other. When even the gods start taking sides...somebody has to..." Cat tailed off. "I know. I am not...exactly important here."

The serpent hissed. "Not important?"

"I am..." Cat tailed off.

"You place yourself between the sides, you stand in balance between human and demon, male and female...you accept that war and chaos are as needed as justice and order."

Solus had stood up. He watched now.

"And you speak for somebody who was about to get everyone killed. You speak in a place where all reason tells you speaking out of line would get you destroyed." That was not Myrk's voice. It was Neir's. As she approached, the snake shrank down, then leapt to form a necklace around his goddess' neck. "Solus. You...are on probation. One more attempt to set yourself up as the only god, and I will replace you."

Cat understood. Solus was only the king. He had no power, no true power, in the face of Neir. Who was death. She could cause him to die. To cease being a god.

Neir continued, with a glance at Cat, "Arok. You will not harm the humans...or I will replace *you*."

Arok merely nodded. "I reserve the right to deal with those individuals who deserve it."

"Of course. Birrur. You are free....but understand that you must remain within your place."

Birrur still held Arok's hand. She said nothing, but her eyes flicked to Cathren.

"It is alright," Cat found herself saying. "It needed to be done..." And had it got Birrur's odd dislike for Cathren out of her system? Perhaps. The realization, though, flowed through her. She would never again taste Liesa's stew. She would never fly above the desert. She most certainly, now, had no need of her blades. R'vor...perhaps she could beg for his release. She would never again know the touch of another woman.

Neir stepped towards her. But Arok shook his head. "One moment. Please."

Years of exile had done nothing to lower his power...yet, Cat felt less and less overwhelmed by it with each passing moment. Less and less concerned. "Arok."

"You are not, and never were, a half-demon. You were formed from my essence, to be a vehicle to return to the world. Neir...had other ideas. You are my daughter."

"Oh no..." Everything flowing together, into a knowing that she did not need to be told. "Wait a minute..."

"You cannot be anything but what you always were. The only question that remained was what path you would choose. I did not ask you to choose balance and peace. You found that for yourself." Neir stepped towards her. "And we need you. We need you to keep this from happening again."

For a moment, she wished Neir was wrong. For a moment, she longed for innocence again... Then she laughed...a laugh that was, in itself, part of the energy that now flowed into her, accepted. "I know."

Yet, the first act of the Goddess of Balance was not to discipline those who had harmed her...but to free a certain demon from the spell that imprisoned him.

After all...every goddess needed a high priest.

Epilogue

Yva looked at the woman she had spent the night with. "That's...the most detailed telling of the ascension of Balance I've ever heard."

She shivered a little. For some reason, she was disturbed by it.

The woman laughed. "Maybe the gods are tired of all the incorrect versions."

"You mean the one where Cathren was married to R'vor? Or the one where her foster parents..."

"People will tell stories the way they tell them." The woman mused, looking towards the dying embers of the fire. It would be dawn soon, early on this side of the Great Mountains.

Yva nodded. "I like the snake best."

The woman laughed. "Ah, our old friend Myrk." There seemed to be affection and humor in her voice.

"Who are you, really?" Yva finally asked, quietly. "I owe you so much."

"Because I showed you who you are, who you want to be?"

"Yes." She let out a breath. "Or rather you helped me show myself." And it had been a good night, under the stars, learning the way her body could take pleasure from another woman.

"There's always one. Every year, there's always one who needs that...whether it's this or a life path that should not have been chosen." The woman smiled. "Balance is about being yourself."

Then she stood.

"Wait," Yva said.

"I can't."

And then she was gone, and a moment after there was a sound as of the beating of wings.

Yva knew better than to follow. "Cathren," she murmured.

Every year the gods came to Yirath for three days to remind them what it was to live as a mortal. To feel, to enjoy a bowl of stew, to see the wind, but also to see the poverty, the imbalances of the world.

Or, Yva thought wryly, to get laid.

But what the goddess had given her was twofold. The realization of what she wanted.

And the story, the story in all its beautiful wonder, that had surely taken more than three days to tell.

She knew what was being asked of her, and she laughed. She picked up her bedroll, loaded her bemused-looking caba, and rode down out of the mountains.

To the Goddess' temple.

Author's Note

This book started in an online RPG, although this Cat shares essentially only two things with that version: She has wings, and she's a lesbian.

Yirath is a world that is meant to stretch a little beyond traditional high fantasy. It has dragons, but they play only a small role. There are no elves, no dwarves, and the continent of Yirath, or at least the human-inhabited part of it is in the southern hemisphere.

Yirath holds two sentient species; humans, who were clearly imported or transplanted from somewhere else (I left this ambiguous, but one can assume Yirath's original humans did indeed come from Earth), and demons, who were magically enhanced/bred by the gods from the local saurians, with their closest natural relative being the dragonlets Cat sees at one point. There are no mammals on Yirath other than humans, and the reptiles are/should be seen as more like dinosaurs. Some are domesticated.

Yirtah is a hotter world than Earth, which means that light skin is a disadvantage; Yirathian humans thus tend towards medium shades of brown. There's no intended politics in this decision, it just made sense for the world building. There is only one continent known to humans, but as humans have never crossed the tropics the rest of the world remains, for now, a mystery. Demons might know more, but they aren't talking.

The interaction between good and evil, peace and war, and law and chaos in this book is intentionally complex; this is not a grimdark book but it is certainly not a noblebright one either (I have my own issues with the noblebright movement). Blame the fact that I have been playing D&D without alignment for twenty odd years. Even the gods aren't "good" or "evil," they rather...are. They're people, with their own complexities. Which all leads to a story where the expected bad guy may well not be.

Right now, I plan on this being a standalone novel. Will I revisit Yirath in the future? Possibly, but I make no promises.

Acknowledgments

As usual, full acknowledgements to my husband, Gregory. To my editor, Jennifer Melzer (everything that is good is her responsibility, all remaining mistakes are mine) and my cover artist Starla Huchton.

To the various people, long lost to time, who helped me come up with the original Cathren Black.

Other Books

Other Books by Jennifer R. Povey

The Silent Years (Mother, Crone, Maiden)

The Ky Federation novels
Transpecial
Araña

The Lost Guardians Series:
Falling Dusk
Fallen Dark
Rising Dawn
Risen Day

Daughter of Fire

The Lay of Lady Percival

www.ingramcontent.com/pod-product-compliance
Lightning Source LLC
Chambersburg PA
CBHW022136240626
47153CB00007B/2383